BIG DATA
A STARTUP THRILLER NOVEL

Lucas Carlson

CRAFTSMAN FOUNDER
CARLSBAD, CALIFORNIA

Lucas Carlson
lucas@carlson.net
www.lucascarlson.net

Publisher's Note: This is a work of fiction. Names, characters, places, and incidents are a product of the author's imagination. Locales and public names are sometimes used for atmospheric purposes. Any resemblance to actual people, living or dead, or to businesses, companies, events, institutions, or locales is completely coincidental.

Book Layout © 2013 BookDesignTemplates.com

Ordering Information:
Quantity sales. Special discounts are available on quantity purchases by corporations, associations, and others. For details, contact the Special Sales Department at the address above.

Big Data/ Lucas Carlson. -- 1st ed.
ISBN 978-0-9960452-6-1 (Paperback)

A C E 0 2 4 6 8 B D F 1 3 5 7 9

For Valentina

The real problem is not whether machines think, but whether men do.

—B. F. Skinner

Prologue

SAN FRANCISCO, Calif. /PRNewswire/ — Local man crushed by machinery — The San Francisco County Sheriff's Office responded to reports that a man's body was discovered near Pier 80, east of the Mission District. The man's body appears to have been crushed by a shipping container. At this time, the body has not been positively identified, and an exact cause of death is still pending. The California State Medical Examiner's Office will conduct an autopsy, and the San Francisco County sheriff's detectives are investigating the circumstances surrounding the man's death. The San Francisco County Sheriff's Office is currently working with the owners of Pier 80 to establish the man's identity and to determine how the incident occurred. More information will be released as it becomes available.

Detective Sergeant; Thomas Layton

Chapter 1

I was at the New York Stock Exchange to ring the opening bell when I saw the gunman. Henry grabbed my shoulder and when I turned, he was moving his lips. But I couldn't make out the words in all the chaos.

I met Henry that morning. I'd been instructed to come to the stock exchange's side entrance, a nondescript door in an alleyway.

"I'm your liaison," Henry said, grinning wide. He pulled out a business card. "Been here before?"

I shook my head and brushed my hair off my face. I took the card, handing him one of my own. For ten years, I'd been handing out the same cards. But this would be one of the last that still read "CEO."

"Well, I guess everyone sees the trading floor. I'll give you a real behind-the-scenes tour."

I said, "It's every entrepreneur's dream to do this once in their career."

Henry let out a high-pitched laugh. "I have a good feeling you'll be doing this more than once."

Henry held the door open for me, and I stepped into a small concrete room with a security guard in one corner and an old timecard machine on the wall.

The guard checked my ID, patted me down, and waved me through. Henry guided me through the cement corridors. The doors were all red, the same shade of a barn and unmarked. It felt like a maze.

"I have to admit, I'm pretty nervous."

"Oh, don't be. Tons of people ring the bell. Opening and closing. Twice a day, every day. I mean, you're still a big deal, don't get me wrong. It's not every day we get a high-powered Latina CEO walking through these doors. Yesterday, it was the Sugar Plum Fairy from the Met, believe it or not. But all you have to do is press the green button."

I wasn't nervous about pressing a button. I was nervous because ringing the bell was my last official duty as CEO of Ancien. It was my last day. The board of directors had already hired the new guy, and he'd been shadowing me in meetings. Getting to know the staff. Working on smaller projects here and there. In just a few more hours, the sun would rise on the West Coast, and Thor Massino would officially take my place.

"Is Thor here?" I asked.

"He got here an hour ago. He's waiting in the coffee room. Didn't want the tour, just the Wi-Fi password. Can I introduce you to our head of IT?"

Thor probably wanted a head start on his new position. No doubt he was writing a barrage of important emails to important people. After all, that's what I should have been doing.

"No."

Henry scrunched his nose and looked awkwardly down at his watch. "Oh, well. I didn't realize how late it was. Need the restroom?"

"That'd be great."

Poor guy. Taking life so seriously. Rules. Schedules. Why didn't more people realize how silly it all was? Impossible bosses. Impossible family members. Impossible strangers. Everyone trying to please everyone else. It wasn't until I stopped playing by other people's rules and started making my own that I got anywhere in life.

The only thing that differentiated the bathroom door from all the others was that its red color was broken up by a small white-stenciled woman.

"If you can, make it fast. I needed to get you to hair and makeup five minutes ago," Henry said as I walked in.

I stood in front of the mirror in a cold sweat. Maybe there was still time to back out. What if I just didn't show up? Maybe they wouldn't ring the bell, and the IPO wouldn't go through. My company would stay mine. Then I realized how crazy I sounded, and I splashed some cold water on my face. I had to get it together. This was going to happen—the train had already left the station. There was no turning back. This was merely a formality. If I didn't ring the bell, Thor would take my company public, and he would take all the credit. Grab all the glory from the decade of hard work I'd poured into this company. Ten years and this was how the board thanked me? By replacing me? Of course, they didn't call it that. But that's what it was.

There was a knock on the door. "Miss Valencia, you okay in there?"

"Coming."

"Luna, happy to see you," Thor said.

I forced a smile but said nothing. The place was buzzing. We stood on a raised platform overlooking the trading floor. It smelled like sweat and money. The air conditioner blasted behind my neck, which usually would have bothered me, but today, the cold air felt fresh under the spotlights.

"Okay, you two," said Henry. "The cameras are over there." He pointed toward the center of the trading floor's ceiling. I could barely make them out, nestled between the blue-screened monitors hanging every-where. It was like standing in a Buffalo Wild Wings made for money geeks. "You don't need to say anything. Just smile, wave, and push the button."

Thor waved at men on the floor. The perfect politi-co. A sea of suits were casually talking to each other. In a few minutes, when the bell rang, it would be chaos. But in that moment, there was nothing to do but hang out. A few of them even waved back.

"It's easy. There are three buttons. At nine thirty, press the green button and the bell goes off. If the green button doesn't work, push the red button."

"What's the third button for?" I asked.

Henry cocked his head and squinted.

"You two will be great. Just remember to relax and smile. Two minutes to show time," he said. "I'll be wait-ing behind this curtain."

I was not ready. This was not right. Such a stupid event. This was not how it was supposed to happen. Why was I doing this? Just rolling over and giving up my company without a fight. A company I had worked so hard to build from nothing. I'd been warned—been told to be careful about who I let on to the board of di-rectors. But every time we raised money, it was a deal-breaker if the investor wasn't given a seat. And now I had to lie in the bed of my making.

"Everything okay? You look nervous."

I didn't respond.

Thor had a warm and gentle demeanor, but I had spent enough time with him to see it was all a facade. He was a rat. No, a super rat. Everyone else had bought the act, but not me. He didn't like other people any more than I did—he just knew how to hide it better. Sure, it was easy to like him. He was so damn good at being phony. But deep inside, I knew this guy was rotten.

"You know, you've done an amazing job building this company. I have to admit, I've always been jealous of people like you. Founders who can create something as powerful and amazing as Ancien. You built something to be proud of. I promise I will do everything I can to take good care of it. But today is all about you, Luna. Enjoy your moment."

As Thor spoke, vomit inched up my throat. And not just because of the platitudes. The light on the dashboard turned green: this was it. It was time to press the button. The crowd below me began to yell. I reached my hand toward the button and froze. That was when I saw the gunman.

Chapter 2

I stood there in shock, watching the mob of men on the trading floor yelling and pushing against each other, trying to get away. I saw a small man with a long nose fall flat on the floor one moment, and the next he was trampled by a stampede of suits. Those on the outside of the crowd didn't seem to know what to do. For the most part, they stood still, blocking the exits of the people near the gunman.

But in the center of the crowd, space cleared as if it were Moses, parting the Red Sea. Alone in the middle of the mass of people, stood a tall black man holding a gun in one hand and something I couldn't make out in the other. Around his torso, he'd strapped a bomb. I could only guess that the object he held was a dead man's switch. If someone killed him, the bomb would go off instantly. But the man looked just as terrified as those trying to flee. He wasn't moving. Just holding his hands high in the air and screaming. I couldn't understand what he was saying; the room was filled with so much noise.

"Thor, let's go. Let's get out of here," I cried. But Thor was no longer at my side.

Henry grabbed my shoulder. But I couldn't make out his words in the sea of sound. I shouted into his ear.

"Where's Thor?"

Henry shook his head.

"Come on," I said. "We need to leave."

A group of makeup artists and cameramen peered around the curtain at the mayhem.

"Come on, people," I yelled. They seemed mesmerized.

I heard a loud pop. Then two more in quick succession. My feet started moving before my brain processed what was happening. The screams became frantic. Even after the shots had been fired, most people still weren't running. They were just watching the events unfold as if this were some reality TV show.

I ran for the exit and made my way into an empty concrete corridor. There I found Thor. He was on the phone, but I couldn't hear what he was saying. I tried to get him to come with me, but he refused, looking angry and turning away. Somewhere along the way I had lost Henry. For a moment, I considered going back for him.

But my instincts told me I needed to get out of there as quickly as possible.

I dashed past two men in suits running in the opposite direction. I wondered if they were running toward the action or away from it. I tried to ask them which way I needed to go in order to get out, but they didn't stop and soon disappeared around a corner.

The thick concrete walls blocked all but the most immediate of sounds. I heard only my own footsteps. I imagined people still screaming on the trading floor. I imagined more gunshots. Or did I actually hear them? I couldn't tell. I thought I knew where I was going, but the corridors all looked the same. I stopped and turned around.

Then I heard footsteps.

"Henry?"

No reply. The footsteps got louder.

"Henry, is that you?"

A man came around the corner, breathing heavily. He walked with a pronounced limp, and there was blood on his leg. He was young. Maybe nineteen or twenty. Just a kid.

"Luna?" he said. I recognized him. It was the shooter.

The kid was tall and lean. I didn't see a gun, but I tried to scream anyway. Nothing came out. I told my feet to run, but they wouldn't. I was paralyzed. My mind froze. All I could do was watch in terror as this young man approached me. He looked like he wanted something. He wanted me.

My legs sprung into action, and I was off. I whirled around and sprinted down the hallway. With his limp, I had a good chance of living if I could only keep these hallways straight. This maze of concrete would literally be the death of me.

I turned another corner and stopped to catch my breath. To listen. For a moment, I thought I was safe. Then I heard limping thuds. He was running faster than when I first heard him. I looked around. I was in a short corridor with a dead end on one side, and a long hallway on the other. I couldn't see what was at the end of the corridor.

I turned into the dead-end and ducked into the last doorway I could find. I tried the door. It was locked. I thought about running for the next one over, but before I could, there he was. Why was he following me? Why wasn't he trying to escape? How did he know my name? I held my breath and made myself as small as possible against the door. I heard no footsteps. He must have stopped.

"Luna, I need to talk to you."

His voice was thick with terror.

"This is not what it looks like."

I squeezed my eyes shut so hard they hurt. I kept telling myself I was invisible. I wasn't there. This wasn't happening. He would move on.

At last, he started running again. I didn't dare take a breath yet, but I thanked God and promised Him that I would go right back to church the moment this was over.

Then, my phone rang. The ringtone echoed through the empty hall. Immediately I started fumbling to turn it off. It was Thor. Fucking Thor. Of course. I managed to shut it off. But the gunman heard. He was coming back. Quickly.

Chapter 3

"Please. Let me explain."

In the last few seconds before the gunman arrived, I reached into my pockets. My dad always insisted that I should carry mace everywhere. It was on my to-do list, but I had never gotten around to buying it. My fingers wrapped around my keys. Maybe I could jab them into his eyes. But he was much taller than me, so reach would be a problem. Before I could come to any decisions, he was in front of me.

"Stop or I'll mace you."

I held up the only other thing in my pocket, a tube of red Yves Saint Laurent lipstick. I glared at him with the angriest expression I could muster.

"I'm not going to hurt you," he said. "I'm not armed. I just want to talk."

For the first time, I actually looked at this kid. He was on the brink of tears. He looked and spoke more like a Harvard student than a crazed lunatic.

"I swear, move and I'll spray."

"I'm sorry, I know this isn't ideal, but it was the only way I could think of to get your attention. I've been trying to contact you for months. I tried getting in touch with anyone at Ancien, but nobody would listen. I tried talking to the police, but they laughed me out of the room. I'm a nobody. You're the only one who'll understand. You've got to believe me—I'm desperate. I knew you'd be here for the IPO, but I couldn't figure out any other way to get your attention."

"Shooting people?"

"I didn't shoot anyone."

"I heard the shots."

"Someone shot me. That's why I'm bleeding. All I had was a BB gun and spray-painted toilet paper rolls."

He pulled back his overcoat to show the bomb. Up close, it was clearly not a bomb. I lowered my lipstick. Slightly.

"What could possibly be so important that you had to talk to me like this?" I asked.

But then a thundering roar interrupted us. "Freeze. Put your hands in the air."

A SWAT team filled the small corridor. They looked like a group of aliens to me. Every inch of their bodies was covered, and they wore strange masks over their faces. Sounds of boots on concrete filled the air. More urgent shouting.

"On the floor. Hands behind your head."

The kid lifted his hands slowly, looking resigned.

"Luna, please. You have to help me. It's a matter of life and death."

"Shut up," yelled the leader of the SWAT team. He kicked the back of the kid's legs, knocking him to the ground. "Hands behind your head."

They pushed the boy to the ground and handcuffed him. As they hauled him from the corridor, he yelled back: "Find me in the Woods."

Chapter 4

Like every other former New York cop that morning, Alex Sonne had already heard plenty about the case on the news. The crazy kid carrying a fake gun and toilet paper rolls. He knew about the unknown shooter who'd almost killed the stupid kid. The NRA was on TV calling him a national hero. The press had already decided it must have been one of the floor traders with a concealed weapon. But Alex knew guns were not allowed in the stock exchange. No, this had to have been something different.

"The guy's gone off the deep end," said the Captain. "I mean this is New York. I've seen more than my share of crazies, but this one's a real piece of work. Keeps talking about conspiracies. How tons of people will die if he doesn't talk to Luna Valencia."

"Where's his lawyer?" asked Alex.

"Didn't want one. We've been talking to him for four hours straight. Won't eat or drink. Won't tell us his name or anything about himself. No ID. Fingerprints didn't match anything in the database. So we need an Alex touch here. We're getting nowhere."

"Where's Luna Valencia?" Alex asked.

"Dunno."

"What do you mean?"

"We didn't exactly know a Looney Tune was going to be asking for her nonstop. She left Wall Street at noon when she and everyone else were cleared. Hasn't shown up at her hotel since. We'll find her."

"And the real shooter?"

"Hasn't been found yet either. He was seen leaving the building. Various eyewitnesses corroborated the sighting, and the surveillance footage confirmed it."

"Let me see him."

"Just get me a name. That's all we need."

Alex let out a guttural snort and went into the room. Here were two young cops he knew. Real firecrackers. Jack and Anna. From their body language, Alex could see they were playing a knockoff version of good cop, bad cop. He could also see that it wasn't working. Whoever this kid was, he wasn't in a state of mind where regular interrogation tactics would work.

The cops looked at him. He nodded, and they left. The kid was mumbling incessantly. He wasn't paying attention to anyone or anything. In his own world.

Alex sat there quietly for five minutes or so, watching the kid. He couldn't pick out any individual words, just the general sound of muttering. The teen rocked slowly back and forth, and his eyes held a thousand-yard stare.

Slowly and quietly, Alex asked the kid a question.

"Wanna see Miss Valencia?"

Now the kid made eye contact. Alex had hooked the fish; now it was time to reel it in.

"I can bring you Luna, but I'll need something from you first."

This was a trick Alex had learned raising his son. His son's inability to articulate what he wanted used to make him exceedingly frustrated when he didn't then get it. Although, "frustrated" was a nice euphemism for what actually used to happen—flying off the rocker was more apt. Screaming, flailing, throwing things. Alex's ex-wife hadn't been able to handle those fits. She used to start screaming as manically as the child.

Alex had learned to do the opposite. He would keep calm, and in a quiet voice, simply ask his son if he wanted a strawberry. His boy would stop crying instantly. He had been understood. Alex knew that people would cooperate much more freely when they felt appreciated. Worked at any age.

The kid was still staring at Alex.

"I'm Alex Sonne. I need you to explain what happened this morning. Do that and I will find Luna. Deal?"

"No."

Progress. Got him talking. Alex left the room.

The Captain put a hand on Alex's arm. "Looks like you're losing your edge."

Alex didn't reply. He went to the other side of the one-way mirror and sat and watched the kid. He was no longer mumbling. No longer rocking back and forth. Now he was just sitting motionless.

Jack and Anna were sitting at a small table in the back, drinking coffee out of paper cups.

"Nice one, Alex. Smooth work, Sherlock," said Jack. "Why'd we even call you in, old man?"

Alex didn't take his eyes off the kid in the room.

"Do your goddamn job, and I'll do mine," said Alex. "Go make yourselves useful and find Luna Valencia."

Jack walked right up to Alex's face.

"Come on, let's get some more coffee," said Anna. She grabbed his arm and pulled him from the room. Alex remained motionless, staring at the kid.

After a few more minutes, the kid came up to the window.

"Fine, I'll tell you what you want to know. But I'm only going to talk to you. And you better have Luna back there ready to talk to me when I'm finished."

Chapter 5

Thor Massino tried to make his voice as authoritative as possible. At the request of the police, he was still in New York, while everyone else was in the Palo Alto office, which meant holding the meeting over telepresence. Thor was in a special room at his hotel, designed specifically for high-powered executives to hold meetings like this. There was a big oak desk in front of Thor in the frame, but it was empty.

He said, "I'd like to call this emergency board meeting for Ancien to order."

The room on the other end of the screen was bustling. This was never supposed to happen. Half the people in the conference weren't expecting to even still *be* board members.

"Please, everybody, sit down. Let's come to order," he said. "Thank you all for coming together on such short notice. I know what an inconvenience it was setting this up. I'm told we have two board members on the phone. Are you there? Can you hear me?"

There was a momentary pause.

"Yes, I'm here. This is Doug Kensington in Seattle."

Another board member from Los Angeles came on.

"Good. I think that's a quorum," Thor said. "As you all know, this morning there was an attack on the New York Stock Exchange, interrupting our IPO. The stock market has been shut down for the rest of the day, at least. This means we are still a private company, and you all are still Ancien board members. For the time being."

"Where's Luna?" asked Phillip Jones, a portly man in a gray suit sitting at the head of the Palo Alto table. Thor had planned to let him go in the first round of cuts. Nice guy, but he was in out of his depth.

"That's one of the reasons we called this meeting. Nobody knows. She disappeared after the attack and hasn't returned to the hotel. She hasn't been in contact with anybody that we know of."

"Did you go into her hotel room?" asked Phillip.

"No. But the hotel staff did, and she's definitely not there."

Phillip scoffed.

"Anyhow, as I was saying, Luna's missing. My hope is that she is just recovering from the shock, but there's a possibility that her disappearance has something to do with today's events. If so, we need to prepare for the worst. There is legal paperwork that she needs to sign immediately after the IPO is completed. Or more accurately, that the CEO of Ancien needs to sign. Therefore, as the first order of business, I'd like to propose to make myself acting chief executive officer."

"Pending Luna's return, of course," said Phillip.

"Of course. Whichever comes first."

There was a long silence.

"I'll second that," said Doug Kensington on the phone.

"All those in favor?" said the man sitting next to Phillip. "Let the record show the proposal of Thor taking over as interim CEO has passed unanimously."

Thor smiled broadly.

"Not unanimously," said Phillip. "I don't see any need for this. Once the company does finish the IPO process, you'll be CEO anyway. It's redundant."

"Corrected. The proposal passed nine to one."

Thor wanted to fire Phillip right then and there. He was CEO now. He could do it. But all in good time. Right now, he had more pressing concerns.

Chapter 6

Alex strode into the dark interrogation room and sat down at the metal table. He pressed record on the beat-up tape recorder.

"What's that?" asked the kid.

"I don't trust digital files," Alex replied.

"Good instincts."

"Name?"

The kid sat quietly again, probably thinking through his decision to talk to Alex. Then he opened his mouth.

"Taye Flanagan."

Alex knew the trick was to get them talking. Once they said the first word, whatever it was, the rest would come out quickly.

"All right, Taye, let's start with this morning. What were you doing at the New York Stock Exchange?"

"No."

Alex studied Taye's body language. His arms were crossed, and he wasn't making eye contact, instead staring down at the floor. Clearly, Taye had something to get off his chest. But Alex had to be careful. If he was too aggressive, the kid would shut down again, and they'd be right back where they started.

"Okay, what do you want to talk about?"

"Get me Luna or I won't talk. I've already tried talking to the police. Got me nowhere."

"You haven't tried talking to me."

Alex was a big man. Not just tall but wide, too. He would be an imposing figure next to almost anybody. He squatted down as low as he could to be at eye level with Taye. It hurt his knees, so he grabbed onto the table for support.

It worked. Taye uncrossed his arms.

"People are dying."

"What people? Where?"

"Everybody. Everywhere."

Alex tried hard not to roll his eyes. He didn't want to suffer through another lunatic's philosophical antics. But something told him Taye wasn't just another deranged weirdo.

"Can you be a little bit more specific? We're all dying. Everyone's dying."

"No, no, no. That's not what I mean. I'm a data scientist. I study large amounts of information to come up with trends and predictions. In any given year, about fifty or sixty million people die worldwide. That sounds like a big number, but it's less than 1 percent of the seven billion people on earth."

"So?"

"So the number's going up. Fast."

Alex thought for a moment, letting this sink in.

"Genocide?"

Taye leaned forward in his seat.

"That's what I thought at first, too. But no, I dug into the demographics. People are dying faster all over—in every region of the world—at a higher rate. This year there were five million more deaths than last year."

Alex thought for another moment.

"Sounds like it's within the realm for error," he said.

"No. Statistically, it's way outside the norm," said Taye.

"Some kind of disease?"

"That's what I thought next." Taye's eyes sparkled. "So I researched the causes of death. This is where things get weird. No single cause of death has increased statistically any more than any other."

"I'm an investigator, not a mathematician."

"People are dying from every possible cause faster than we used to. Slips in the shower. Cancer. Heart failure. Car crashes. Every cause of death has gone up dramatically in the last year."

Taye sat back in his chair, and Alex started to pace.

"So how does Luna Valencia fit into all this?"

"Her company, Ancien. It's the largest big data company out there. They have the best platform for analyzing big data using machine learning on the planet."

Alex gave a confused look.

"Like artificial intelligence. Anyhow, they have a robust ecosystem. They opened their platform to allow developers and researchers to build their own stuff on it. Ancien was critical in helping me figure all this out. Ancien's linear regression analysis is second to none. But when I reached out to Ancien about my findings, I kept hitting brick walls. Nobody would take my research seriously."

"I can see why. It's a pretty incredible claim."

"I figured if nobody else understood, Luna would. But getting ahold of her is damn near impossible."

The door swung open, and Jack and Anna sauntered in.

"That's more than enough, Alex. We can take it from here," said Jack.

"I'll only talk to Officer Sonne," Taye said. Then he turned to Alex. "And you—you promised I could talk to Luna."

"You'll talk to whoever we say, when we say it," said Jack. "Alex. Out. Now."

Alex pulled the cassette from the tape recorder and slipped it into his back pocket. the Captain was waiting for him outside, his arms crossed.

"Good work, Sonne."

Alex grunted.

"I told you all we needed was a little of your verbal grease. Now we've got a name, you can head home. We'll take it from here."

"This is the kind of bullshit that made me quit this godforsaken shit show. Everybody shoving each other to claim the high-profile cases. It makes me sick."

"The tape, please."

Reluctantly, Alex pulled it from his pocket and handed it over.

"Go home. And don't forget to send me an invoice this time."

Chapter 7

I knew what the kid meant when he told me to find him in. "The Woods" was the nickname for Ancien's developer ecosystem. He was on the platform. All I had to do was find him, which wasn't going to be easy. There were over a hundred thousand developers working in the Woods, so it would be like finding a needle in a haystack.

The first thing I needed to do was get to a computer. If I went back to my hotel room, someone would almost assuredly try to bother me, and I needed some time to focus. A kid had risked his life and ruined his reputation to get my attention, and I needed to find out why. It wasn't like Ancien needed me anymore anyway.

So as soon as I was cleared by the police from Wall Street, I wandered the city aimlessly until I stumbled upon an Apple Store. It was big enough and busy enough to hang out for a while without being noticed.

Ancien was a platform for analyzing big data using every method of machine learning available. Linear regression, analysis of covariation, gradient descents, neural networks, and support vector machines. All built into a cloud operating system that had instant access to digital representations of much of the world's information, both historical and real-time.

Put simply, Ancien was the smartest supercomputer in the world, and anyone could build an application on it.

And this kid desperately wanted me to see his app.

So, I logged into the web portal and started searching. Since the IPO was interrupted, I was still technically CEO. This meant my account was still privileged, and I could browse freely. Of the hundred thousand developers in the Woods, the majority of them would still be kicking the tires. Most of them hadn't even deployed their first live application yet. So that narrowed down the list to about twenty thousand accounts.

I was guessing this guy wasn't acting as part of a company, so when I took out corporate accounts, I was able to narrow down the list to ten thousand. Still unmanageable. Maybe if I had my laptop, I could build a program to search for me. But not here.

I opened another browser and loaded CNN. Maybe the news would tell me the kid's name. No such luck. *The police are not releasing any information at this time.*

Then my computer pinged. When you logged into the Woods, you could chat with other developers. Evidently, someone wanted to speak with me.

Phillip: Hey, where are you?

Luna: Hiding out at an Apple Store

Phillip: You ok?

Luna: Yeah. Scared but ok

Phillip: Thor's taken over

Luna: What do you mean?

Phillip: Just held an emergency board meeting, named himself acting CEO

Luna: Douche

Phillip: He wants me to revoke all your privileges

Luna: Why?

Phillip: He says it's for corporate security

Luna: Can you stall them?

Phillip: You know what, I think I am coming down with something. Maybe I better see the doctor before I do any more work for the day

Luna: You're the best, Phillip

Phillip: Be safe

Luna: You too

I had to act quickly. Phillip was my chief operating officer and second in command. We went way back. He was my twelfth hire, and one of my best. He was my friend and coach—not just an employee. I didn't want to get him in trouble.

What else did I know? Okay, the kid was young. I could use that. When we implemented the chat functionality, we had to start collecting years of birth to comply with the Children's Online Privacy Protection Act. If I had to guess, I would say he was somewhere between seventeen and twenty-five.

That limited my search to one thousand. Then, I tried people between eighteen and twenty. Three hundred. It was incredible to me that there were three hundred college students around the world with production applications deployed on Ancien.

I could search through three hundred apps in a reasonable amount of time. Hopefully, I'd find an account that stood out to me in some way. Since the kid had told me to find him in the Woods, he had to have left me some kind of trail. Some digital equivalent of breadcrumbs. It would take a little time, but nobody was going to be interrupting me here.

Chapter 8

On his ride home, Alex mused that the best chance they had of closing the stock exchange case was to find Luna Valencia, and quickly. He also knew that Jack and Anna weren't going to realize this until it was too late. Those young cops had graduated the academy so recently their hair was still wet. The Captain ought to have known better, but he was more interested in planning retirement trips than working cases these days. That and he loved watching fresh meat squirm—one of the few pleasures of the job left to him after so many years.

It got dark early and was beginning to rain heavily. Alex pulled the cassette from his pocket and shoved it into the car's tape deck, turning up the volume. He'd switched it with a blank tape back at the station. Not like anyone was going to check it soon anyway. It might cost him this paycheck, but he figured it was worth it. He wanted to hear the kid's story again. He pressed rewind, then play, and heard the kid's voice.

"People are dying."

"What people? Where?"

"Everybody. Everywhere."

The idea gave him the creeps. If this kid was right, what could be causing these millions of deaths? How hadn't more people noticed this anomaly? Weren't there government agencies tracking this? The World Health Organization? Someone? How was this not on the news?

Jack and Anna were in way over their heads. These questions only raised more questions. But the biggest one was: why did he care so much? This wasn't his case. Hell, he wasn't even a cop anymore. He'd been forced into early retirement last year. Now he picked up odd jobs as a part-time private investigator or as a part-time consultant for the police department.

He hadn't heard much from his old squad recently. In fact, he'd been pretty surprised to hear from his former Captain that morning. He wondered now why he had even been called. Probably because the kid was black. Maybe he thought a black cop would be able to bond with the kid better or some shit like that.

Then he thought of Simon, his sweet little boy. He couldn't help but wonder if whatever Taye was studying was responsible for Simon's death. Millions of untimely deaths. Had his little boy been one of them? There was only one way to find out, but if he left it up to Jack and Anna, he would never get an answer.

He had to find Luna Valencia. Shouldn't be too hard. People were never too difficult to locate, especially after a traumatic experience. As Alex sat in traffic, he gazed up at the Empire State Building and tried to put himself in her shoes.

Something big had just happened to her, so she would want to go somewhere familiar. He wondered why she hadn't gone straight to her hotel. He mentally recalled the notes that he'd glimpsed before going to the interrogation room. The police had seen Luna near Taye when they caught him. So Taye must have said something to her. Must have told her something.

It dawned on Alex that Luna was probably sitting at a computer. There were only a few places in New York that a person could sit at a computer for a long time without being noticed. The library was far away from the stock exchange, but she could have caught the subway. No. There was somewhere easier and much more accessible. He made an illegal U-turn and stepped on the gas.

Chapter 9

I found him. Taye Flanagan. He'd been trying to contact me in the Woods for months. I just hadn't whitelisted him, so none of his messages got through.

His app was good. Actually, it was exceptional. He called it Gaia. The kid had an extraordinary gift with computers. I'd thought I was advanced when I was his age, but there was no way I would have been able to grasp the concepts he was working with here.

"Ma'am, can I help you?"

"No, just checking out the new iMac. The screen's pretty amazing."

The salesman agreed and tried to tell me more, but I brushed him off as politely as I could. He gave me a snarky look and walked away.

Now I had to figure out what Taye was trying to tell me. To an end user, an app is just the utility you get from it. Like sharing a picture with a friend. Looking at the code behind the app is like pulling back the face of a watch.

Most watches have digital quartz movements that look like cheap circuit boards printed in China. Most apps are the same. Their code is a mess of open-source libraries patched together by some spaghetti and meatballs.

But every so often, you can pull back the face of a watch to find a secret work of art, full of perfectly placed precious metals and gems. It's breathtaking. That's how I felt about Taye's code. This kid was a true craftsman. It wasn't just readable code; it was a joy to read. It was like looking at the Mona Lisa of code.

Just then, I noticed the sales guy looking over my shoulder.

"Can I help you?" This time, I was asking him.

"What programming language is that?" he asked with such interest that I decided to answer fully.

"Conifer. It's a dynamically typed Lisp without parenthesis tuned for machine learning."

"Like PHP?"

I shouldn't have even tried.

"Yes, like PHP."

He walked away. I had no idea if he caught the sarcasm.

I needed to get back to work. What had Taye done here? The code was beautiful. Most people, when building an app in the Woods, would take a generic template or example code and repurpose it to their liking. Even large and popular apps on Ancien used the templates as almost a de-facto standard.

But Taye had started from scratch. I could see straight away that he was using a neural network, which mimicked the way scientists thought neurons communicated. But figuring out what a neural network was trained to do wasn't necessarily straightforward; most of the magic of neural networks was hidden in layers of data that even the programmers who built them couldn't understand.

The code wasn't documented, but it was beautiful. I wrote the initial version of Ancien myself. Most of the tutorials were based on my first templates. This code was much better.

As I navigated through the maze of code, I finally figured out why I was having so much trouble understanding what it did.

If Taye's code actually worked the way I thought it did, he had made a major breakthrough in machine learning. His application was trained to understand computer code itself.

He had taken Ancien—the world's most powerful supercomputer—and unleashed all its intelligence on learning the fundamental language of computers themselves.

This was brilliant. Machine learning experts tended to research specific classes of problems: photos, videos, self-driving cars, handwriting recognition, speech recognition, financial transactions, even Internet search results. And at this point, the majority of the commercial applications of this research ran in Ancien's cloud platform.

But Taye was exploring a new class of problem: having computers fundamentally understand themselves. I gasped as realization flushed over me.

Taye hadn't written Gaia.

Maybe he'd written the first version of it, sure. But since then, Ancien itself had been refining it and improving it on its own. My own baby was responsible for this code.

This was the most significant development in machine learning in fifty years. Code understanding code. Without human assistance, interpretation, or intervention. This could solve so many other problems in the world of artificial intelligence. This was the holy grail.

Chapter 10

I was just getting ready to leave the Apple Store when someone tapped my shoulder.

"Luna Valencia."

The man's voice was deep and guttural. He said my name with as much authority as my father used to, whenever I got in trouble as a young girl.

"Who are you?" I asked.

"Alex Sonne. I'm with the police. We need to talk."

His hair was white and short. He was tall and demanding, and his eyes pierced me with a look that wanted the truth.

"How the hell did you find me here?"

"I've been doing this a long time. Look, we need to talk. It's important. Can I buy you a cup of coffee?"

I logged out of the Woods, and he led me to a café across the street.

"Tall bold," said Alex.

"We don't brew bold after eleven," explained the barista. "But we can make you one in a pour over. It will only take a few minutes."

"That's okay, just a house coffee. And whatever she wants."

I ordered a chai latte. We sat down, and Alex told me that Taye was demanding to talk to me.

"So why are you here instead of the police?"

"Just got here first, I suppose. Look, I think the kid has issues, but he's not dangerous. Just desperate."

"Isn't that the same thing?"

"Only in people with a weak conscience."

"So he's got a strong conscience?"

"He says people are dying, and he's apparently trying to stop it. I mean put yourself in his shoes. Who's going to take some black kid's conspiracy theory seriously these days? You have to give him credit. It took balls to do what he did to get your attention."

I sipped my latte. The kid's story was pretty vague, but it made sense. If it was true.

"You believe him?"

"I don't know what to think just yet. But I don't believe we'll get to the bottom of this until you hear him out."

"What else do you know about him?"

"Not much. The police probably have a full dossier on him by now, but I'm not the police. I'm just Alex."

"I thought you said you were the police?"

"I said I was with them, not one of them."

"And if you bring me in, you'll get brownie points?"

Alex shrugged and said, "I've got my reasons. Let's leave it at that."

I decided not to push it—yet. He was clearly hiding something, but he didn't seem dangerous. He didn't ask me about the Woods or Gaia, so I assumed Taye hadn't told him. I wasn't going to tell him yet, either. No matter what he demanded from me. As far as I was concerned, at this point, nobody needed to know about Gaia but me. Not until all the consequences could be thought through.

"So will you come with me?"

Every muscle in my body wanted to run right then and there to the police station, where they were keeping Taye. I needed to know more about Gaia. About what Gaia was capable of.

"Sure."

When we arrived, the police station was in chaos. Cops were interviewing witnesses and taking statements—and there were a lot of witnesses.

Alex seemed to know where he was going. He pulled me into a crowded area where I rubbed against many of the same suits I'd been standing above earlier.

It was the first time I'd been in a real police station. I was expecting to see something like the set of *Law & Order*, dark and dirty and brooding. But it looked more like *The Office*. Bright fluorescent lights made the space far less dramatic.

We arrived at a small desk in the back corner near a water jug. A bald guy was filling out paperwork.

"Captain, this is Luna Valencia."

The guy turned around and looked me up and down.

"Pleased to meet you." But before I could say anything he said to Alex, "Why'd you bring her here?"

"What do you mean why'd I bring her here? She's the only person the kid wants to talk to. She's here to talk to him."

"Too late for that."

"What do you mean?"

"I mean you're too late. The kid's been stitched up and shipped off. He wouldn't talk anymore after you left, so we decided a night in the pen would loosen his lips."

"Jesus Christ, Captain, you guys really have a way, you know. Where'd you send him? Tryon?"

"Yep," he laughed.

"He'll be lucky to last the night."

"He'll be fine. It'll be late by the time he gets there. He'll be sent straight to his cell."

"Yeah, and what about in the morning? This kid isn't made for that. He's soft."

"He'll be fine."

"For all our sakes, he'd better be."

Chapter 11

During the bus ride to the juvenile detention facility, Taye went over the plan in his head. He still thought it was a good one, though things weren't going exactly how he had hoped. He hadn't expected to get out completely unscathed, but he had hoped to talk to Luna more. To explain himself. But this was still well within the working parameters. Nevertheless, he was kicking himself for failing to give Luna more clues when he was being hauled away by SWAT. But at least he had mentioned the Woods. Ideally, Luna would have found Gaia by now.

The bus stopped, and the guard jumped out, coming to the back door. There was only one other person on the bus with Taye, and he hadn't spoken a word. He was skinny and pimply and stared silently at the floor, which suited Taye just fine.

"Get out," the guard shouted.

The other kid waited for Taye to get up first. Taye shuffled to the back and hopped out the open door with his hands still cuffed together.

"Taye Flanagan," the guard said.

"That's me," said Taye.

The guard looked Taye up and down.

"That's me, *sir*," said the guard. He waited expectantly.

"Sorry. That's me, sir."

"We gonna have trouble with you, boy?"

"No, sir."

"Better not."

"Caleb Frankel," said the guard.

The other kid didn't say anything. Just kept looking at the floor.

"Hey, boy, you speak when spoken to," the guard yelled. He kicked Caleb in the shin.

"Yes, sir."

"That's better," said the guard. "You better learn quick. This place don't tolerate wiseasses."

Caleb didn't respond. The guard went on, "You two will be roommates."

Taye looked over at Caleb. This was going to be interesting. Taye continued to silently review his master plan as they ushered them into the central facility. The kids were brought one by one into a room with three guards. One of the guards patted Taye down while the other two watched.

Then he and Caleb were escorted into the prison. Taye had never been in trouble before. Never even so much as grounded or sent to detention. He imagined what prison was going to be like. He had done his research. Amazon's recommendation engine had suggested *Orange Is the New Black*, *What Really Happens in Prison*, and *You Are Going to Prison*. Taye had laughed at the simplistic approach those algorithms had used to come up with the books, but he read them anyway. He assumed that juvenile detention would be different than adult prisons, but probably not by much. So far, everything was going as smoothly as could be expected.

The inside of the prison reminded him of his high school. The walls were white, and there were yellow lines painted on the floor. He was told to follow them. Taye looked up at Caleb and saw the kid shivering. Taye had assumed Caleb was a stone-cold delinquent who had been here so many times that it was practically a revolving door for him. But now he realized that this was probably Caleb's first time, too. And he looked more scared than Taye felt.

The cell was completely enclosed. No bars to look out into the hallway. It smelled like putrid sweat. The guards pushed them both inside and told them that lights were going out in five minutes. Taye asked what time it was. The guard said eight fifty-five. It had been a long day, and he was ready to sleep.

"Top or bottom?" Those were the first words Caleb said to him. He took it as a good sign that Caleb was letting him pick.

"Bottom."

Caleb climbed into the top bunk without another word. Taye threw himself on the bottom one. He checked his leg. It was only a flesh wound, but it still hurt. Then, once more, he thought through his plan and all its contingencies from the beginning. Checking for any rough spots or sharp corners.

Chapter 12

Alex dropped me back off at the Four Seasons. By the time I got to my room, I was exhausted. I looked at the clock. I wouldn't need any sleeping pills tonight.

Before he left, Alex asked if he could come pick me up first thing in the morning so we could go see Taye in prison. I'd been intending to try to visit Taye as it was, so I said yes.

I lay on the bed, enjoying the plush sheets and the smell of clean linen. Then I debated grabbing my laptop and playing around with Gaia some more. Chances were good that Phillip wouldn't be able to let me keep my root privileges much longer, so if I wanted to learn more about Gaia, now was probably the only chance I was going to get.

It took some effort, but I rolled off the sheets and picked up my laptop. Then there was a knock at the door. I hadn't ordered room service, so I ignored it and logged into my laptop. Then I heard the door open.

"Hello? I don't need turndown service. Thank you anyway," I yelled.

An old Latina woman appeared at my bedroom door.

"Housekeeping?" she said.

"No gracias querida, no esta noche."

She smiled and said, "Buenas noches" as she left.

I knew that Gaia was Ancien's own supercomputer system applying every bit of processor power to improving the writing of code itself, but I still didn't know what Gaia's intentions were.

After all, every computer program—even ones as complicated as Gaia—was built with some sort of purpose in mind.

For the first time, I booted Gaia up on my terminal. Earlier at the Apple store, I was just looking at the code. I never actually tried running it. It didn't exactly come with a manual.

Gaia's possibilities were endless. A neural network that understood the underlying structure of code was itself an amazing discovery. The most advanced neural networks that processed images could identify the gender and ages of everybody in a photograph. And when you hooked them up with Ancien's enormous big data stores of structured data, they could even more accurately describe what was happening in an image.

For example, it could take a picture and tell you, "Three Pomeranians running around a park with a llama," or "A fifty-one-year-old woman crying of happiness while holding a baby."

These modern breakthroughs in image processing were breathtaking, but if a computer could understand code in the same way it can recognize images, it would enable a new generation of technology. If code could finally understand itself, technological breakthroughs would be able to start happening faster and faster. If a computer could intuitively know what any piece of code was trying to do and how to make it better, the possibilities would be endless. Faster Internet connections, better medical technology, smoother robots, smarter phones, software with fewer bugs, banks with less fraud—the list could go on and on.

I wasn't feeling sleepy anymore. But then, I was filled with dread. It occurred to me that the converse was true as well. Gaia could just as easily be tuned to find bugs in software in order to exploit security problems and break into online banks. My heart sank. I needed to know not only what Gaia was supposed to do, but what had already been done with it.

I heard the front door open again.

"Hola? Olvidaste algo?" I yelled.

Nobody responded.

"Hello?"

The lights went out.

A few moments later, I felt a cold damp cloth covering my mouth, and I smelled something foul, like a strange disinfectant. I tried to scream and heard someone shushing me. The man told me to calm down, that everything would be just fine. That I should take a deep breath and relax. As if I needed to be told to take a deep breath. My body reflexively gasped. I tried to kick, but the man's grip was firm.

I woke up in my hotel room. My head was throbbing. I looked around. I was still clothed. Nothing seemed particularly out of place, other than the bed linens, which were scattered on the ground.

Then I saw my attacker on the floor. I screamed. He was tied up with plastic zip ties like a hog for the slaughter. But he wasn't struggling, or even moving. He was passed out.

"Hey, calm down, calm down," came a voice from behind me. I was still screaming. It felt like I couldn't stop. I turned around and saw Alex standing there with his hand to his mouth, urging me to be quiet. If only I could.

Then he slapped me in the face, and I stopped.

"You okay?" he asked.

"What happened?"

"I saw we had a tail when we left the police station."

"And you didn't think to tell me?"

"I needed to know what he wanted."

I shook my head and said, "I guess he wanted me."

"Yeah, any idea why?"

I thought about Gaia. I wondered if this was the right time to tell him. I also wondered if this attack could be related to Gaia. I'd assumed Taye was the only one who knew about the app, but what if he wasn't? What if Taye had created Gaia, but now someone else was using it?

"No."

"You sure?" I knew he could tell I was holding back. Sure, he had just saved my life and all, but I still didn't know him. We'd only just met a few hours ago. And he seemed weird. Confident, but contumacious.

"Look, I told you I don't know. Maybe Taye does. We need to go talk to him."

"The prison opens in a couple of hours. Get cleaned up. We'll grab breakfast on the way."

"What about him?"

"He'll be okay. I'll move him to the room with the ice machines. Someone will find him, and he sure as hell won't be in a hurry to explain how he got like this."

"Don't you want to know who sent him?"

"He already told me."

I must have been out for a while.

Chapter 13

Taye woke up after a restless sleep. He didn't have any way to tell the time, but he could see the faint morning light coming through the sliver of a window.

He looked up at Caleb. Still asleep.

Ideally, Taye hoped the police would come early to bring him back to the station for another all-day interrogation. He would keep asking for Luna. Eventually they would give in. They had to. They only had two days before they either had to let him go or charge him, and there was no way they were going to let him go. As long as he didn't ask for a lawyer, they would get increasingly more likely to give in to his demands.

Maybe they would even send Officer Sonne back in. Out of all the officers he'd encountered, Taye liked him the best. He seemed to understand. Or, at least, he pretended to. Maybe if Taye could sit at a computer for a few minutes, he could use Gaia to hack into the police department's systems, and then he could see the cops' notes about him. But he doubted they would let him use a computer. This was probably going to be one of the hardest parts of life in prison.

The lights flicked on. It must have just turned six. Caleb made a noise, and the cell door opened automatically. Taye decided he would stay sitting on his bed for as long as possible—the less interaction with others, the better.

"Who's the new blood?" came a throaty voice from outside.

An enormous young man came through the door. He was wearing an orange jumpsuit that didn't fit him.

"Looks like two short-timers," he said.

Caleb turned around and faced the wall. The fat kid stood on his tiptoes, staring at Caleb.

"What's your problem, cracker? Cat got your tongue?"

Caleb curled into the fetal position.

"Leave him alone," said Taye.

The kid turned his attention to Taye.

"Oh, looks like we got ourselves a hero. I'll make this easy on you. Because I'm nice, you see. And I like food. You give me your food every day for the next week, and we'll be good friends. Understand?"

Taye nodded.

"Good. I knew I liked you. Your cracker roommate not so much. But you're okay."

He hit Caleb's bed frame and left the cell.

"Thanks," whispered Caleb.

Taye got up to stretch. He wasn't going to be there for a week. And he'd fasted for two days once, just to see what it was like. Uncomfortable, but not bad. The bullet wound on his leg hurt worse than any hunger would.

"Don't mention it," said Taye. "First time here?"

Caleb turned to look at Taye. His eyes were puffy and red. He nodded.

"Don't worry," said Taye. "Mine too. Let's just stick together, and we'll be fine, okay?"

Caleb nodded again.

"What are you in here for?" Taye asked.

"Drinking," said Caleb.

"I didn't realize that was a criminal offense."

"It is when you drive."

Taye raised his eyebrows and nodded.

"You?"

"Disturbing the peace."

Caleb jumped down from the bunk.

"Wait, you're not the kid from the news, are you? That's sick. That's you, isn't it? I'm in prison with someone famous? Were those real bombs? Why'd you do it?"

Taye didn't want to talk about it. He decided to get some air and look around. As soon as he walked out of the cell, he heard his name.

"Taye. Taye Flanagan."

He turned around. It was a guard. Not one of the ones that had locked him up last night. A new one.

He nodded.

"Come with me. You've got a visitor."

Taye was glad the cops wanted to get started early. Especially now that the other inmates had figured out who he was. The guard took Taye by the arm and started leading him out.

"Hey," he heard Caleb's voice behind him. Taye looked back, but Caleb wasn't talking to him. He was talking to another kid in an orange jumpsuit. "Do you know who I'm bunked with? It's the crazy kid from the stock exchange."

Taye rolled his eyes.

"Come on, keep walking. Just act normal."

The guard pulled Taye past the door labeled visitors. Taye paused.

"Come on, kid. Today's your lucky day. Don't ruin this for either of us."

The guard led him into an office at the end of the hall, then closed the blinds and turned off the lights. Taye wondered if the cops were going to just keep interviewing him in prison. But when the guard unlocked the back door of the office, Taye's heart started beating faster.

"Come on, come on. Don't fuck this up." The guard gestured rapidly, pointing to the open door. Taye walked through it, into a corridor that looked like it was used for maintenance. There were no lines painted on the floor. Prisoners were not supposed to be here.

"I can only open this door for five seconds before it sets off an alarm, so you better be ready to run, kid. Outside there's a cleaning van with the back door open. Just jump in and close the van door."

Taye froze. This was not his plan.

The guard took out another set of keys and unlocked the door.

"Ready?"

Taye didn't respond.

"Are you fucking ready?"

No.

"Jesus Christ, kid." The guard swung open the door, reached over, and pushed Taye out the door, slamming it shut behind him.

Taye stood still. It was cold outside. Sunny but freezing. He could see his breath in the air. Just like the guard had said, there was a cleaning van sitting in front of him with the back door wide open, blocking the view so nobody would be able to see him just standing there.

"Hey," he heard a voice. "What are you doing there?"

Taye wanted to explain that he wasn't trying to escape. But nothing came out of his mouth.

"Get in, get in," the voice urged. A young man with long greasy hair wearing denim overalls came up behind Taye and pushed him into the back of the van. Taye landed uncomfortably and winced in pain. "Sorry, dude, but we gotta go."

Chapter 14

When Alex and I arrived at the juvenile detention center, police cars were everywhere, their sirens blaring.

"This isn't good," I said.

"Wait here," said Alex. He parked and went to talk the officer closest to the entrance. He pulled out his private investigator badge and the officer examined it closely. They talked for a few minutes, then Alex pointed at me, and the cop covered his eyes to get a look. He spoke into his walkie-talkie for a minute. They shook hands, and Alex came back to his Camaro.

"What happened?" I asked.

"Taye escaped."

"What?"

"You heard me."

He turned on the engine and put his hand on the clutch. I put my hand on it to keep him from shifting into reverse.

"What are you doing?" I asked.

"Leaving. What do you think I'm doing?"

"Can't we get in and try to find out where he's going?"

Alex laughed a deep belly laugh as though this was the funniest thing he'd heard in years.

"I'll drop you off at your hotel and maybe the police will want to talk to you. Or maybe they won't. Maybe you fly back to wherever you're from, or maybe you stay. Our little Hardy Boys expedition is over."

"We can't give up now. I'm sure they'll catch the kid soon, and we'll be able to talk to him then."

"Look, lady, we're done. The kid's just escalated an already precarious situation. Whatever you and I think of him, there's no way any truth comes out now. Innocent people don't run. That's what the cops think, anyway. And once they make up their mind about something, they'll do just about anything to prove their case. I've seen this play out a thousand times."

I sat there and took this in. It made sense. But Alex didn't have all the information yet. He wasn't making an informed decision. I still didn't trust him, but then again, I didn't trust anyone anymore, so why should I hold that against him?

"I haven't told you everything yet," I said.

Alex paused.

"Then I guess we're even."

This time, I was the one to hesitate.

"What do you mean?" I asked.

"You first," he said.

This was going nowhere, and I wasn't keen to keep going around in circles.

"Taye created a computer program that can understand—and I think even write—computer code. It's an application running on the system I created, Ancien—the biggest supercomputer on earth."

Alex looked at me expectantly.

"And?"

"What do you mean 'and'? This changes everything."

His blank stare pissed me off.

"You're going to have to dumb it down to a two-bit nail for me."

"Look, computer programmers have been writing code that then writes more code since the beginning. One of the first computer programming languages was Lisp. Lisp was created in the fifties and even then the line between code and data was blurred."

"You're losing me."

"The problem is, when humans write code that writes more code—also called meta-programming—it can only write as much code as a human can imagine. It's more of a shortcut for a lazy programmer than a more intelligent piece of code. It's not like the computer actually knows what the human intended."

Alex nodded slowly.

"Taye's application allows the computer itself to understand the intention behind any piece of code. If the programmer were trying to write code that would log you into your email, Taye's program would know what the programmer was trying to do and suggest an even better implementation."

Alex smiled. It looked like he was finally getting it.

"So, it's like the computer is starting to understand itself?"

"Yes. Which is incredible. If a computer could improve its own code, it would be able to make technological breakthroughs at incredible speeds. Even a crappy programmer with an idea for an app could just start describing the idea, and the computer would build the application itself. There would even be medical breakthroughs. This could speed up cancer research by decades. The possibilities are endless."

"But how is this all connected to the increase in the death rate?" asked Alex.

"I have no idea."

"That's why he did what he did at the stock exchange?"

"Yes, exactly."

"How many people are dying?"

"Five million."

I gasped, choking on saliva.

"That can't be right," I said.

"He says that it's not just any single cause of death, either. Every cause of death has increased proportionally."

"That makes no sense."

Just then, someone knocked on the passenger-side window. I turned to see a cop. My mouth went dry, and I felt like I'd just been pulled over. The cop mimed for me to get out of the car.

I asked Alex, "What do I do?"

He shrugged. "Roll down the window."

I did so.

"Hello, officer," I said cautiously. "Is there a problem?"

"Are you Luna Valencia?"

"Yes."

"Get out of the vehicle, ma'am."

I hated being called ma'am.

"What's the problem?"

"Get out of the car. Now." The urgency in his voice worried me. I looked over at Alex, who shrugged again.

"Ma'am, I need you to step out of the vehicle." He hit the top of the car.

I opened the door, and immediately he grabbed my arm and pushed me against the cold metal door. Searing pain soared up my arm.

"You have the right to remain silent." He continued Mirandizing me, but Alex burst out of the door and demanded, "What the hell is going on here?"

"Sir, please remain in the vehicle."

"Just tell me what she's being accused of, will ya?"

"Obstruction of justice and aiding and abetting a fugitive."

Chapter 15

"Any news on Luna?" asked Doug Kensington.

"No," said Thor. "Does it matter any-more?"

"Everything matters."

"I'm sure she'll pop up soon," Thor said.

Both men had flown into the Bay Area that morning. Thor from New York and Doug from Seattle. They had Ancien's boardroom to themselves. It had been built to Luna's taste, which Doug had always despised. He thought it was too stylish, with details like crown molding in the corners and dark woods mixed with white marble. He preferred a clean and modern design—something more Swedish.

When Luna started Ancien ten years ago, nobody imagined it would grow this big. The first offices had been in a sketchy part of Cupertino, but after raising half a billion dollars in venture capital, they built a beautiful campus in Palo Alto. This came with the added benefit of being able to hire PhDs in machine learning right out of Stanford—usually before they even graduated. In fact, it became so hard to scale the talent, not only for Ancien, but for their competitors like Google, Tesla, Apple, and Amazon, that they were now hiring these undergraduates as soon as the ink was dry on their major declaration forms.

"And Taye?" asked Doug.

"I've made a call."

Doug strode toward the window and stared blankly out. This place still felt strange to him. Too much sun. Having come from Seattle, he was used to seeing 80 percent of his life covered by rain. Now it was reversed, and everything felt backward.

"I hope you called someone who can do the job this time," said Doug.

"They are very good."

"And Gaia?"

"Our team is still having trouble understanding how Gaia works without someone with more experience around to explain it. Just when we believe we have it all under control, it keeps changing on us. Like it's evolving."

Doug thought about this for a while.

"We need Taye and Luna here," said Doug. "If we can't keep things under control once and for all, my plan will fall apart at the seams. I didn't come this far just to give up. Remember that I made you CEO, and I can un-make you just as quickly."

"Calm down, Doug, calm down. Even if we don't get those two, my team is working on the problem. One way or another, we'll stay on track. Look, I've got other pressing matters to attend to now."

Thor left the room.

"If you want something done right," Doug muttered to himself.

Chapter 16

Taye was brought directly to the Ithaca Tompkins Regional Airport. The driver of the van escorted him onto a private jet, which would take him across the country.

This was so far outside of Taye's original plan that he had no clue how he was ever going to get back on track. Once, when the van had stopped for gas, he'd thought about making a run for it. But what could he say? How would he ever explain? He realized just how bad it looked to have broken out of prison. Even if he hadn't meant to.

At this point, he knew strategically what his next step was. But it felt so wrong. So counterintuitive.

Taye had been the best chess player at his high school for three years straight. The first year, though, he was among the worst in the club. But it wasn't for lack of studying. Taye knew all the common openings and was well versed in the middle and end games. The trouble came whenever he wasn't sure what move to play next. He would burst headfirst into some fancy, half-baked maneuver that would inevitably end up falling apart and costing him the game.

Taye became the school champion because of a simple remark from his chess coach. She said, "When you aren't sure what move to play next, just go along with your opponent. Let them feel comfortable. Wait patiently for them to make the fancy half-baked move. Then tear them apart."

So Taye boarded the jet without a struggle. At least, without an outward struggle. He wanted to kick and shout. He wanted to do anything. But he knew he had to let things play out and wait for his opportunity to get the upper hand.

How much worse could things get for him anyway? He went into one of the country's most well-known landmarks with a fake gun in his hand and a fake bomb strapped to his chest. Getting into more trouble would be difficult. In for a penny, in for a million, it seemed.

He thought about all the times he'd tried to get people's attention. Once, he'd waited in the District Attorney's office for ten hours. They wouldn't even give him an appointment. Eventually, they called in security to drag him away.

After all, who was going to take a young black man seriously? Up until he staged a terrorist attack, nobody believed him. He had to conform to the stereotypes America expected to even get noticed. A computer genius who discovered one of the most disturbing conspiracy theories in history? Too far from the norm to be plausible. A terrorist? That they could buy.

So after failing to get the attention of the press, authorities, or anyone else who could help, he did what he knew would get their attention. He grabbed a fake gun, strapped on a fake bomb, and snuck into the New York Stock Exchange. It was risky, but he was desperate. His big gamble was hoping that the police and guards would take the duct-taped toilet paper roll for a dead man's switch and wouldn't kill him.

As the jet took off, Taye watched the cars and buildings below getting smaller. Then it came to him. How this new turn of events could fit into his master plan. This didn't need to be a setback—this could be a blessing. As soon as he was out of New York, his crime would be expanded from the state level to the federal. His case would now get significantly more attention—if not in the press, then at least in the caliber of cops and agents who'd be trying to talk to him.

He could explain how Thor had discovered him writing apps for Ancien. That he'd been hired to solve one of machine learning's most interesting unsolved mysteries.

Originally he'd been told it was a secret research project, and that was why he wasn't allowed to interact with the rest of the company. Which worked fine for Taye—he preferred to keep to himself. But when someone else started making changes to his project—seemingly to use it in ways he hadn't intended—he'd gone down the rabbit hole. Taye needed to make sure the police knew just how deep this whole thing went.

Assuming he could survive long enough to explain at all.

Six hours into the flight, Taye spotted the Golden Gate Bridge, and shortly after that, they landed in San José. A driver picked him up at the airport and took him directly to Ancien headquarters. Taye had hoped they would have to stop for gas like in New York. This time, he would have made a run for it. But no such luck.

Thor was waiting for him in the Ancien parking lot.

"You're a very brilliant young man," said Thor.

"I guess that's why you paid me the big bucks," said Taye.

They quietly walked into Ancien and up to Thor's office.

"You know, I have to hand it to you. You've got more guts than I thought you did. I didn't give you enough credit before."

Taye said nothing.

"I won't make that mistake again."

Now Taye laughed. Thor sat down and indicated that Taye should do so as well.

"We need you to finish what you started."

"Why would I do that?" Taye asked. "You might as well kill me now."

"We already tried that once," said Thor. "We'd prefer not to have to finish the job, but at least now you know we're more than capable."

Reflexively, Taye put his hand on his bandaged leg. The pain was mostly gone. He'd almost forgotten he'd been shot less than forty-eight hours ago.

"Gaia's broken. You're going to help our team fix it."

"What you're doing with Gaia is wrong. It's not what I ever intended when I started. You know that," cried Taye.

"You never could see the forest for the trees, Taye. Fix Gaia, or it won't be just you we kill. We'll use Gaia to kill everybody you've ever cared about in your life. They'll all die seemingly natural deaths. A car crash. A heart attack. Nothing suspicious at all. And not just your family, either. All your friends, all your teachers."

"You son of a bitch."

"After you escaped, our team was able to teach Gaia about DNA. At this point, we could find and kill everyone who even resembles you."

Taye stared down at the floor.

Thor continued, "I'll take that as a yes, then. You'll fix Gaia."

Chapter 17

I couldn't believe they'd arrested me. This was the craziest thing that had ever happened to me. Or maybe the second craziest; after all, I had presided over a shooting spree only the day before.

Technically, I didn't actually get to prison. They put me in jail, which I discovered was just the name of the cages inside police headquarters. They tried to talk to me, but I just kept saying that I wanted my lawyer.

By the time I arrived at my arraignment, there was a stable of male lawyers and a token woman sitting at my table. I wondered if Ancien would be picking up the tab for this or if I would have to pay for it myself, since I wasn't technically CEO anymore. I could afford it, but I certainly didn't like the idea of throwing away this much money on total nonsense.

"Just sit down, smile, and don't speak unless spoken to first," said the best-looking lawyer of the lot; he had a smile that could charm a pig. If it weren't for that smile, I probably would have been insulted. "We'll handle this, and you'll be a free woman by lunchtime."

I nodded and said, "Who are you?"

"Heath Lemming. Happy to meet you."

"All rise for the Honorable Judge Albright."

"You may be seated," said the judge. She looked wise but stern, with a frown that seemed baked onto her face.

The judge studied a piece of paper before saying, "You seem to have found yourself in the middle of quite the situation here."

"Your Honor," said the District Attorney. "Ms. Valencia fled a crime scene and had been uncooperative in our investigation of the events at the New York Stock Exchange yesterday."

"I didn't flee. Nobody seemed to want to talk to me. I went to the police department just yesterday to see if I could help with—"

"Excuse me, Ms. Valencia. Sit down. You will have a chance to speak, but if you speak out of turn, I will find you in contempt of court."

Heath grabbed my shoulder and pulled me back down into my seat. He made a *tsk*-ing sound through his teeth and shook his head.

The DA continued, "Then this morning, our main suspect escaped from prison, and Ms. Valencia was found at the scene just minutes later. We have evidence that shows there are ties between the suspect and Ms. Valencia. She is now a key person of interest in our case. She is also a flight risk. She has no ties to New York and plenty of means. She is rich. Your Honor, we are requesting that she be held without bail."

"This is ridiculous, Your Honor." Finally, Heath stood. "Ms. Valencia has been fully cooperative with authorities the entire time and has no interest in fleeing. She's the CEO of Ancien, one of the biggest and hottest startups in the world. She has absolutely no interest in harming her own company's reputation by helping some kid escape prison. This whole thing has been a misunderstanding. Why don't we dismiss the case and let Ms. Valencia speak to the police as any other regular citizen would?"

The judge nodded at Heath and then at the District Attorney.

"If only it were so easy to dismiss every case that comes through here. It would certainly save the state a lot of money. Alas, we still have due process to uphold here in New York. Even though from what I have just heard, these charges appear to be grossly overzealous and unlikely to hold any water in a trial, Ms. Valencia will still have to go through the motions. Bail is set at five hundred thousand dollars."

And with a slam of the gavel, it was all over.

As I stood up to shake his hand, Heath whispered in my ear, "Told you, free as a bird."

"But what about bail?"

Heath nodded at the female lawyer, who was typing furiously on her BlackBerry.

"Jackie's handling bail. Don't worry about the money—you're one of our VIP clients. We know you're good for it. As I said, you'll be out of here before lunch. Of course, the cops will still want to speak with you about the Flanagan case. But I'll be in the room with you the whole time, so they won't try to pull anything like this again. Once they finish with you, they'll drop the charges and this will all be one big bad dream."

"Except for the bill."

"Yes, well, there is that. Just do me one favor?"

I thought this was a rhetorical question, but he evidently wanted an answer. I nodded.

"Don't leave New York."

Chapter 18

Phillip stormed into Luna's office. Thor was sitting at the desk, staring blankly out the window.

"We need to talk," said Phillip.

Thor said nothing. He didn't move. Just kept staring.

"Did you hear me?"

Thor's facial expression didn't change. No surprise. No acknowledgment. Then he started speaking in Chinese.

"What the—?"

Thor raised a finger as he continued. Thor turned to face Phillip. Finally, Phillip could see he was wearing a Bluetooth earbud. Thor pointed at it for emphasis. Phillip's face turned bright red, and he mouthed, "Sorry."

Thor indicated the seat across from the desk, and Phillip sat down. Thor turned back to the window and continued to converse for a few more minutes. Phillip stood up and slowly retreated toward the door, but Thor stopped him.

"Phillip. Please sit down."

"You can't just fire me."

"It's good to see you too," said Thor.

"Oh, cut the bullshit already, will you?"

"What makes you think you've been fired?"

Phillip strode over to Thor's desk and slammed his fist down on the smooth surface.

"When Luna hears about this, she'll have your head."

"I insist you sit down." Once Phillip did so, Thor continued, "Thank you. Now where's all this coming from?"

"You revoked my permissions. Did you think I wouldn't notice?"

Thor winced, and Phillip thought he heard him curse under his breath.

"Well," said Thor. "That's unfortunate. This was not how it was supposed to happen."

"This was not supposed to happen," Phillip said.

"Look. You're right. You're fired. But you were not supposed to find out this way. We were supposed to talk things over before they revoked your permissions. In fact, we were supposed to talk earlier today, but I had a customer call that went over. And now, it appears they jumped the gun."

"I'm a board member. You can't get rid of me that easily. There needs to be a vote."

"There was one. You weren't invited. Nobody blocks the incoming CEO's first request."

Phillip leaped up, pointing his finger at Thor's face. "You're not going to get away with this. You. You—"

"We're done here," said Thor. "Oh, and by the way, we aren't announcing your early retirement just yet. We wouldn't want to harm company morale and all. So look busy and smile. But just to be perfectly clear, I never want to see your face in here again."

Phillip slammed his hand on the desk one last time before spinning around and thundering toward the door. But as he reached for the handle, someone pushed the door open, and he leaped backward to avoid getting hit.

"Oh," gasped Thor's secretary. "I'm sorry. I didn't know anybody was in here with—"

"I was just leaving," said Phillip.

"There's a Taye Flanagan here to see you," she said to Thor.

"Yes, of course. Show him in."

Phillip stepped out of the way as a burly security guard led a young black man into the room. Phillip thought he saw handcuffs, but before he could get a better look, the secretary pushed him out of the room, slamming the door shut behind him.

Chapter 19

They took me back to the jail, but as promised, I was released on bail shortly thereafter.

One of the cops even came over to me and said, "Look. I'm really sorry for all the trouble we've put you through." But then he added, "I was hoping we could talk before you head out."

This was not an officer I recognized from earlier interrogations.

"My lawyers aren't here."

"This isn't about your case. It's about the Flanagan case."

"You'll forgive me if I don't exactly take your word for it."

"Look, it's past noon. You must be hungry. Grab a bite to eat. I'll call your lawyers, and by the time you're done they should be here. Sound okay?"

A cop hadn't treated me this nice in days, but I still wanted to kick him in the nuts. In the end, I decided that as long as he was cordial to me, I could be cordial to him.

"I don't have my purse."

At this, he handed me a sealed oversized envelope. I could feel my purse in it.

"Okay?" he asked.

"Okay," I said.

I left the station and the first thing I saw was a faded Rite Aid sign across the street. It was next to a park. Then I recognized a face. Alex was sitting on one of the park benches, reading a newspaper. He looked up and waved me over. I crossed the street and sat next to him.

"I had a feeling you'd be out soon."

"It's great to see a familiar face around here. I thought you'd bailed on me."

"Are you kidding? I was in the courtroom watching you with your fancy lawyers. Best money can buy, huh?"

"I guess."

"I think the handsome one likes you."

I blushed, and Alex laughed.

"So you like him, too? Never figured you for the scumbag lawyer-type. I guess my cop instincts are wearing off."

I let out a pulse of laughter.

"I bet they didn't feed you in the can. You hungry?"

He handed me a Coke and an egg salad sandwich wrapped in wax paper. According to the wrapper, it was from a place called Mrs. Friggin's Kitchen. I was famished, and as far as I was concerned, this was the most delicious sandwich on the planet. I popped the tab on the Coke.

Alex continued, "I've been thinking about what you told me in the car. I'm trying to piece it all together."

"Me too," I said, through a mouthful of egg salad.

"Please. You do the eating; I'll do the talking. Now I still don't quite understand the computer stuff you were talking about, but what I do understand is your company runs a very large, very smart computer. Taye figured out how to make it use all its smarts on itself. That makes it extra smart."

I nodded. Close enough.

"And this computer you run can understand other computers. I tried doing research on Ancien. You guys let other people run their stuff on your super-smart computer. And it seems like a lot of companies use you guys."

I made an exaggerated nod, eyes open wide.

"Okay, *everybody* uses you guys."

I grinned.

"So if Taye's program is that smart—if it can do as many good things as you say, like curing cancer and all. Well, what if it's being used to do bad things, too?"

"Like hacking into other computers?" I muttered.

"Exactly. If a crappy programmer could build a Facebook just by describing their vision, a mediocre hacker could become the world's best hacker in the same way, no?"

I swallowed my bite of sandwich whole, without chewing.

"I suppose so," I said. "But we have security in place to monitor what people are trying to do on Ancien servers. Anything that looks even remotely like hacking gets detected and shut down immediately."

"And those security systems, are they written with code?"

"Of course."

"So theoretically, a brilliant hacker might find a way around them. Or a brilliant hacking computer program."

"Yes, I concede with great power comes great responsibility. But how does this lead to millions of deaths?"

"I haven't figured that part out yet. We'll need to find Taye to get that part of the puzzle."

I drained my soda with gusto. Then my paper envelope started ringing. I set the empty can on the bench and tore open the bag, digging through my purse to find my phone. Somebody had gone through it. It was a mess. The phone kept ringing, but by the time I found it and accepted the call, it was too late. It was Phillip Jones from Ancien.

I tried to call him back, but it went straight to voicemail. There was only a sliver of battery left. A few seconds later, I got a voicemail notification. I put it on speaker.

"Luna, it's Phil. Where are you? Something strange is going on. You gotta get over here. Thor's locked himself in your office with some young black kid. Said his name—"

Then my phone died.

Chapter 20

We stared at each other in disbelief, both thinking the same thing. It had to be Taye. Did Thor know about Gaia? Maybe, but maybe not. Taye hadn't told Alex about Gaia during his brief interrogation. But chances were good that Thor did know about Gaia.

Though this brought up many questions, there was one thing we knew for a fact: I couldn't leave the state. My hands were tied.

As if Alex could read my mind, he said: "Maybe I could go try to get ahold of the kid."

"You won't get past the front doors at Ancien. You're not a cop anymore, and our security is incredibly tight. Our customers demand it. Even in our facilities that don't have physical servers, we can't let outsiders mingle with employees. It's a huge no-no for us. Always has been. And what would you even do if you *were* able to find him?"

Alex didn't say anything for a long while.

I wondered how this kid could get across the country so quickly without getting spotted at the airport. And why would he end up at my company headquarters? If he wanted to talk to me so badly, why not try to find me at my hotel? Of course, that would have had its risks, but Taye didn't seem too concerned about risky behavior. Maybe he figured I'd already gone home.

But then again, I barely knew the kid. And he was clearly out of his mind for pulling that stunt at the stock exchange. Maybe he was making up all that death-rate stuff in a desperate bid for fame. I'd certainly run into my fair share of lunatics. What if he was just another?

I broke the silence, "Well, I guess that's it then."

I stood up and turned back to the police station. Alex didn't look up to say goodbye.

"That's it?" asked Alex.

"What am I supposed to say? Really?"

"Less than a day ago *you* were trying to convince *me* not to give up."

"That was before I got arrested for two felonies. It's over. My hands are tied. What business do we have investigating this in the first place? Let's just leave it to the people whose job it is to investigate."

"Those buffoons couldn't find a monkey's ass if it were sitting on their nose."

"But when we tell them that Taye crossed state lines, they'll bring in the FBI," I argued.

Alex laughed a full-hearted belly laugh.

"And why are they going to believe us?"

"My phone's dead, but we can tell them what the message said."

"A black kid's locked in a room with a rich white dude in California? That lead will go cold faster than your sandwich."

I looked down. I'd forgotten I'd even been hungry.

"Let me explain something to you, Luna. Those two starry-eyed buffoons in there are trying to win their way up the ladder as quickly as possible. They hand the case to the FBI, and they lose their chance at a promotion."

"But they'll never find him on their own."

"They don't know that for sure."

"Maybe Thor's holding the kid in the locked room because he called the police himself. Maybe the FBI is heading to Ancien's headquarters as we speak."

Alex rolled his eyes. I sat down again.

"What? How do you know that's not what's happening?"

"Occam's razor."

"Huh?"

"What's the simplest explanation? That somehow Taye, a high-profile young black man, escaped prison on his own, made his way to JFK Airport, evaded all the police there, was able to get through security with bogus identification, and showed up on the other side of the country?"

"Well, when you put it that way."

"Someone helped the kid. He's a genius, but he's definitely no criminal mastermind. Toilet paper rolls? Really? It stands to reason that he's probably still with whoever helped him. Simplest answer."

"But why? What's Thor have to do with all this?" I asked.

"You're asking the wrong question."

I went silent. I understood what Alex meant. I knew what question I needed to be asking. And trust me, I was asking it. But I didn't know the answer.

"You can't go find Taye," I said.

"Right."

"So, I have to go find him."

"Not necessarily. You could forget about the whole thing. The unexplained deaths. The strange ties they have to your company. You could let the cops pump you for information over the next few weeks. Let the case cool down. Eventually, they'll get tired of playing cat and mouse with you and let you go. Then you could fly back and hope that Taye's still there. Maybe he'll even still be alive."

"Let me ask you something," I said.

"Shoot."

"Why do you care so much? What's in it for you?"

"You know how some cops retire and can't reintegrate into the real world? They keep thinking about that one case that got away? The one that never got solved? Then they eventually blow their brains out, right?"

"Oh, Alex—"

"No, no, no. That's not me. I solved all my big cases. When I was–when I left, I left with a clear conscience. Sure I had open cases. But none that haunted me."

"Then what?"

"A death that I thought I understood."

"And now you think it might be murder? Connected to whatever this is?"

"If I let Laurel and Hardy run this, I'll never know the truth. And it's the not-knowing that will lead me to blow my brains out."

I looked around the park. There was a boy playing hopscotch and holding his mother's hand while she talked on her cellphone. A businessman was reading a newspaper. A delivery boy sped by on his bike. He nearly hit the little boy, but the mother didn't notice.

"Well, then. Let's go before I change my mind."

Chapter 21

Doug was back in Seattle. It was pouring rain, but this didn't comfort him the way it usually did. Life had been particularly difficult for the last three years. His life's work, System Inc., had completely collapsed after some overzealous cops dragged it through the mud. And in the security technology space, reputation was everything. He had to stand by and watch as his assets were torn apart and sold off to overeager competitors like fine cuts of meat from a butcher.

They'd tried to drag Doug down along with his company. They tried to claim he was responsible for all sorts of crimes. Heinous crimes. After three long years and the best legal defense money could buy, Doug walked out with only a misdemeanor tax evasion charge. He had to pay over a million dollars in fines and complete a hundred hours of community service. The community service was easily the worse of the two punishments.

Doug always knew time was more valuable than money. Money could be replenished. Time couldn't. But he wasn't about to let the last three years be a complete waste.

It was a setback, of course. And they had arrested his closest friends and associates. They'd taken away his business and most of his money. But they couldn't set back his mind.

In fact, the whole fiasco only served to inspire him.

Doug realized that he had gotten too complacent at System Inc. Blackmailing influential people by building the security applications they depended on had made him soft. It was too easy. Like shooting fish in a barrel. And Doug believed that nothing easy was worth doing. The hardest things in life were always the most rewarding. He had lost track of that. But life had a way of reminding him.

He stared at the Seattle rain through his apartment window.

The collapse of System, Inc. had been life sending him a message. And he had learned long ago that life's messages never came in straight lines, but rather in the form of puzzles. Still, it hadn't taken Doug long to determine the meaning of this mystery.

He hadn't been thinking big enough. The culmination of his life's work up until that point had been to eliminate the government. He had seen government as a crutch that humans no longer needed, but liked having around for purely sentimental reasons. The problem was it had grown so big that nobody was willing to tear it down.

Doug thought about Georges-Eugène Haussmann, who, in the nineteenth century, tore down and rebuilt Paris. Before Haussmann, Paris had been a filthy rat's nest of shit-covered streets. So he did what was needed, even though it wasn't the most popular course of action.

The historian René Héron de Villefosse once said: "The old ship of Paris was torpedoed by Baron Haussmann and sunk during his reign. It was perhaps the greatest crime of the megalomaniac prefect, and also his biggest mistake. His work caused more damage than a hundred bombings."

Without Haussmann's brutal destruction, Paris wouldn't have been ready to become the cultural epicenter of the world just a few years later. It brought health back to Paris after countless years of typhus and cholera. "It was the gutting of Paris," Haussmann wrote years later, reminiscing. And it wasn't without its sacrifices. Haussmann had had to demolish his own childhood home in the process.

Destroying the government had been too shortsighted. It wouldn't be enough to remove the roots of the weeds of humanity. Aim for a McDonald's and you'll hit a 7-Eleven. Aim for the stars and you'll hit the moon.

He wouldn't make the same mistake again.

He thought about the office he'd had, back when he was running System. It had been a modern masterpiece. He wondered what had happened to his toy train set. The one he had purchased while planning his first large-scale terrorist attack. Terrorist. That was a word he liked. It didn't have the same ring as megalomaniac, but it still made him smile.

His phone rang, and he picked it up.

"Doug," said Thor. "Can you come back? We're having some trouble with Taye."

"Really?"

Doug was happy to help, though he'd never admit it.

"Yes. We don't hire a lot of people with your, well, skill set."

Doug smiled.

"I'll be right there."

Chapter 22

Dark rain clouds blackened the sky as we approached JFK International Airport. I had no idea what to expect. We'd left the park in the first cab that stopped, without even detouring to get any of our stuff. Alex figured that it would take only a few hours for the cops to realize I'd bailed, and then it would be impossible to fly out of the state. Hours seemed generous to me. I thought my face would be plastered all over every airport within driving distance.

To distract myself, I tried to think more about what Alex had said. About how Gaia could be used for evil. It made a lot of sense. I didn't know how I couldn't see it before. When code becomes aware of itself, aware of its own structure, it's able to evaluate itself without any human weaknesses. If a human programmer were to write code on very little sleep, or even just when she's hungry, she might miss an edge case or copy and paste sloppily, without thinking through the consequences. If the code told the computer to erase itself, it would do so without a moment's hesitation, even if that was the last thing the programmer intended.

But if Gaia could understand that the programmer didn't intend to erase the computer, she could decide not to run that piece of code.

She? What am I saying? Jesus.

On the other hand, Gaia could just as easily be asked to report back every edge case that didn't match up with the intended code structure. Then a human hacker would basically have an exhaustive list of every security flaw in a given program.

I still couldn't imagine a world where Gaia itself was actually doing the hacking. That would be like imagining a gun that was built to automatically shoot any human it came into contact with. There still needed to be a human shooter pulling the trigger. Gaia might be an amazing tool and a feat of humanity, but it wasn't a full-blown living, breathing thing. It wasn't generalized artificial intelligence.

Alex grabbed my shoulder and said: "Hey. Earth to Luna. We're here."

He shook me out of my happy place, back into the terrifyingly bleak reality of my imminent prison stay. When they caught me this time, they'd probably send me straight to solitary confinement—like they did to Kevin Mitnick. I'd once read that he was put in solitary for eight months because they thought he could start a nuclear war by whistling into a pay phone. If he got eight months for that, well, with me, they would probably just throw away the key.

"Come on," Alex insisted. "We gotta go, or we'll miss the red-eye."

"I don't think I can do this. If I just go back now, it probably won't be too late. I'll tell them I was taking a bath or something."

"If you can live with not finding out whether or not your company is responsible for the largest genocide in human history, then sure, go ahead."

What did I owe the world anyway? Sure, I was wealthy beyond my wildest dreams. But it wasn't like I hadn't paid a price for that money. I didn't owe the world a debt of thanks. But then I saw a policeman waving us down, and I froze where I was, still in the back of the cab.

This time, it was the cabbie who spoke up: "Hey, lady, come on, are you coming or going?"

The policeman came up to us. This was it. They knew I was running. Just like I'd predicted. It wasn't going to take them long to put the pieces together. It was as good as solitary confinement for me. I considered yelling to the cabbie to floor it, but my mouth wouldn't open.

"Sonne? Is that you?" asked the officer.

"Son of a bitch, Jason Freeman. What are you doing working this lousy patrol? You pushing the airport traffic along now?"

"Hey, it's gotta beat early retirement, right?"

Alex punched Jason in the arm a little harder than seemed friendly.

"Are you taking a—" Jason started to ask, but Alex interrupted him.

"Just helpin' a family friend to the airport. Visiting from California."

Jason looked at me like I was a piece of meat. "Uh huh," he said. "Where are your bags?"

"In the trunk," said Alex. My mouth still wasn't working. Jason probably thought I didn't speak English.

"Well, have a good trip, ma'am," he said to me. "Good to see you, Alex. Hey, hey, this isn't a parking lot, keep it moving." He blew his whistle and ran toward a minivan.

I unbuckled my seat belt and hopped out of the taxi. Nothing was going to stop me now. My heart was racing. Alex was right: I wouldn't be able to live with myself if it turned out Ancien and Gaia were being used to kill people and I did nothing to stop it.

"That was some quick thinking," I said. "But what if he'd checked the trunk?"

He grunted and smirked. "You think a cop who's good enough to follow up on a hunch would end up here?"

"What about you? Why'd they kick you out?"

"That's a story for another day."

Chapter 23

"Five hundred thousand dollars, Heath?" yelled Neil Bower. "Do you have any idea the shit-storm you've gotten me into?"

"I'm sorry, I didn't peg her for a runner," said Heath.

Heath was sitting in Neil's corner office on the seventh floor. Neil was standing at the window, glaring.

"Apologies are for the weak, Heath. Come on. Eight years here and you still don't understand our motto yet?"

"Deny, deny, deny."

"You can say the words, but clearly you don't get them, do you? Christ, and to think you were on the fast track to partnership."

"Take the money out of my bonus."

Neil walked back to his desk and sat down, looking Heath in the eye.

"It's not about the money. You can't buy a reputation. You have to earn it. Three years in a row we've been voted the best criminal defense attorneys in New York City. And do you know why?"

"We never lose a case."

"That's right, Heath. At least that *was* correct. But then you went and fucked this one up. Jesus, Heath. So close. We were so close to getting four years in a row. Bower, Bower, and Nathanson. We would have been the first criminal defense attorneys to win four years in a row in New York City. You know what that would have done for us? And now the clock's back to zero."

"How is it our fault that she ran away?" asked Heath.

"That's the spirit. Fuck groveling. It's weak. Rule number two: blame someone else. But it's not going to work this time because it's our goddamn fucking job to prevent clients from running." Neil slammed his fist on his desk. "Our clients pay us to protect them from themselves. That's what we do. Whatever it takes. Hump their leg if you have to. You're a good lawyer, Heath. Arrogant. But there's nothing wrong with being cocky as long as you have what it takes to back it up. So I'm going to give you another chance."

"Thank you, Mr. Bower. You won't regret it. I promise." Heath stood up and reached out his hand, but Neil didn't take it.

"Oh, no. It's not going to be that easy. You took away my prize. You reset my clock. Now I'm going to reset yours. I'm transferring you back to the San Francisco office to start your partnership tenure all over again. I won't dock your pay. I'm not an asshole. I have a heart. But you've still got a lot to learn, and eight more years ought to be enough time for you to learn it."

Heath gritted his teeth.

"Fine, I'll just finish up with my clients and—"

"You're leaving tonight. Start work tomorrow."

"What about my stuff? My friends?"

"We'll set you up with one of our furnished apartments. Same as you're used to. You can gather your personal belongings tonight."

Heath scoffed.

"That's all. Now get out of my office," said Neil.

Chapter 24

Doug stared at the sorry sight in Thor's office. Chained to the desk and beaten to a bloody pulp sat a kid, who after a moment, Doug recognized as Taye. Thor had said things weren't going well, but Doug wasn't expecting this. How crude and naïve. Not that Doug was against the cruder methods—when they worked. But torture was only effective in forcing the most basic of actions. Like getting someone to sign a paper against their will. It wouldn't get someone to tell the truth or do anything more than basic brain function.

In Doug's experience, it was the thinking part of the brain that shut down quickest under duress. That's why people will say anything under torture. It's not that they're lying; a person simply isn't capable of distinguishing truth from a lie if they think they're about to be killed. Survival instincts kick in—the reptile brain. And those instincts will cause a person to say or do anything that might keep them alive.

Some people have no respect for genius, Doug thought. No one could torture Vincent van Gogh into painting the Starry Night. And this kid, Taye, was the Vincent van Gogh of machine learning. He was the keystone to Doug's master plan. Without him, the whole operation would fall apart. What had Thor done to him? Beaten him to within an inch of his life. Taye was only one of two people on the whole planet capable of completing Doug's plan, and Thor and his men had almost killed him.

"Taye, are you all right?" Doug asked.

Taye didn't move. His head rested on his arms, which were shackled to the big oak desk. Doug could see from how he was struggling to breathe in no particular pattern that he was not asleep.

"I'm so sorry about how they treated you, Taye. This is horrific and despicable. Are you hungry or thirsty?"

Doug went over to the kid and unlocked the handcuffs that were too tight around his wrists. They left bloody rings when removed. Taye didn't say anything, but Doug could see that he was crying.

"Don't cry, Taye. I know this has been hard on you, but don't cry. I'm here now. I'll take care of you and make sure this never happens again."

Taye looked up at Doug. One eye was so swollen that it wouldn't open. There was a gash across his cheek that trickled blood down to his lip. He spat angrily into Doug's face and dropped his head again.

Doug pulled a handkerchief from his jacket pocket and wiped his face.

"I deserved that, Taye. I shouldn't have left you alone with them. That's my fault."

Finally, Taye spoke. "You lied."

Doug smiled.

"That's not entirely fair, now is it? Sure, I omitted the whole truth, but you wouldn't have made your break-through if you knew everything from the start. Or am I wrong?"

"You disgust me."

"Here, let's get you cleaned up." Doug reached under Taye's arm and pulled him to his feet.

"You might as well get it over with and kill me now. I won't be able to do what you want. I've tried. I can't."

"We'll see about that, Taye. I believe in you. I always have."

Chapter 25

Getting banished to the satellite office in San Francisco had its benefits. If Heath was going to win his reputation back, he was going to need to find Luna. And the best place to start looking for her was in her home city.

After all, he wasn't going to give up without a fight. Sure, his client had skipped bail. He'd lost the battle, but the war was just beginning. He'd been thrown back to the bottom of the pecking order. But if there was one thing Heath loved best, it was a good redemption story.

"You're late, Heath," said Antonia. "The client's been waiting for ten minutes."

Heath's problem was finding time to look for her. Bower, Bower, and Nathanson was going to throw him every little startup they handled. It was like a revolving door of douchebags. And people thought lawyers were bad.

"Give me a break, I flew in last night," said Heath.

"You know, I'm under orders to keep a close eye on you. I know you're used to big-time cases over in New York. Maybe you're just not cut out for this corporate stuff."

"No, no, corporate law is great. I was just getting a coffee."

Heath hated corporate law. He loved courtrooms with lawyers and judges and juries. He loved telling stories. Overcoming adversity. Finding redemption. Quests. He loved it all. Manipulating people into believing whatever he wanted them to think. Filling out cookie-cutter legal form templates made him want to shoot himself in the head.

But it was the price he had to pay for being too cocky. Why hadn't he put a tail on Luna? Hell, he should have tailed her himself. It wouldn't have been such a painful chore. She was easy on the eyes.

Heath took a deep breath. Then he walked into the office, where two twenty-something hipsters were waiting for him.

"Hi, I'm Heath Lemming."

"Hi, David Alexander."

"Hey, I'm Andrew Smith."

"Happy to meet you. How can I help you today?"

"We want to incorporate our new startup."

Chapter 26

We made a rocky landing at the San José Airport. The sky was still dark outside. All the flights had been sold out, so we had to take a redeye. Alex said San José would be safer than going directly to San Francisco, where the cops might be waiting for us. Of course, if they were looking for us, they could easily just pull up flight records or check our credit card statements, but I wasn't about to say anything. I knew Alex was trying to comfort me, and I wasn't going to stop him.

We hadn't talked much during the flight. The only things we wanted to discuss were things we didn't want to be overheard. So I tinkered on my computer and charged my phone. But once we were in the taxi, the conversation flowed like a river.

"So how does it feel?" asked Alex.

"Weird. I've never done anything like this before in my life. I'm kind of shocked. It seems like at any moment, someone is going to handcuff me or something. You know?"

"Yeah, it's weird for me too. This is the first time I'm technically aiding and abetting."

I hadn't thought of that. At this point, Alex was as much a fugitive as I was. We were in this together. I decided that if it came down to it, I would push him away and claim that I did everything on my own, without anyone's help. Maybe I could get him out of trouble when the time came.

The taxi was driving up 101 toward Ancien headquarters in Palo Alto. Traffic wasn't bad, and the weather was beautiful. I was glad to be home.

I didn't know what more to say on the subject, so I changed tack. "I was thinking about Gaia on the plane, and I have a theory."

"Oh?" said Alex.

"So, you asked me if a mediocre hacker could become the world's best hacker, right?"

"Yeah." Alex smiled softly, like Yoda looking at a young Luke.

"Gaia's just a tool. It can understand and improve computer code, or it can find bad code. But it's not an artificial intelligence. It can't think on its own. Whether it does good things or bad things is dependent on who's running Gaia."

"Right."

"From what we can tell, Taye wrote the initial code, used Gaia on itself to improve its own programming, and then lost control of Gaia to someone else. That's why he came to me. He thought I could help him get control of it again."

"Yes, I've been working under that assumption for a while now."

"Well, why didn't you say so?" I asked.

"I basically did, you just weren't listening."

I laughed. This nontechnical ex-cop was quicker than I'd given him credit for.

"So the big question is: who's controlling Gaia?"

This time, it was Alex who laughed.

"I think we both know the answer to that by now."

"Well, fine," I said in exasperation. "If you've got it all figured out, why don't you just tell me what's going on?"

"So, you're not in charge of Ancien anymore, right?"

"You think I'd be sitting here with you if I was?"

"Well, then, whoever's in charge of Ancien is controlling Gaia."

"Thor Massino," I said.

"Sure," he said.

"Hey, you missed the turnoff," I yelled to the cabbie. "You were supposed to take exit 402."

"That way is full of traffic. This way is faster," said the cabbie. He was a burly old Italian with white hair.

"Traffic this early in the morning?" I asked. He didn't reply. I turned back to Alex. "But why would Thor be using Gaia to hack into other computers? And how does that lead to the increase in the death rate?"

"Trying to guess motive at this point is fruitless. We need more information. But you should have connected the dots on the increased death rate by now."

"Oh?"

"Isn't it obvious?" said Alex.

I shrugged.

"From what I understand, Ancien is a platform that runs the machine learning code for many of the world's biggest applications."

I nodded.

"Let's take the two biggest killers: cancer and heart disease. It's safe to say that doctors and hospitals are now entirely dependent on software."

"Yes, hospitals were some of the slowest to adopt the Ancien platform, but once they saw how well neural networks could diagnose diseases when trained by millions of real-life interactions, they signed on. Since then, pharmaceutical companies have trained deep learning machines to help administer drugs in a way that will minimize side effects—a notoriously difficult challenge for humans to manage."

"So with Ancien in the middle of everything, it's safe to say that if a master hacker were to influence the diagnosis and treatment of major illnesses, he could essentially make people sicker. It would be delaying diagnosis or under-prescribing medicine."

"Like net neutrality," I said.

"What?"

"The Internet and wireless providers serve all the data and videos you watch. Net neutrality seeks to make it illegal for providers to meddle in the delivery of that data and those videos. For instance, making them faster or slower depending on whether or not the content maker pays what amounts to a bribe for a service that should already be paid for."

"Yeah, I guess."

"The problem is," I continued, "not even a master hacker could influence a neural network. Humans don't understand how they work. Neural networks don't use regular logic. They use fuzzy logic."

"Which is precisely what makes such good cover. It doesn't look like murder. It looks like a good guess that turned out wrong. Plus, you said that Gaia is the most sophisticated code you've ever seen. Just because humans can't influence a neural network doesn't mean a machine couldn't figure it out."

I couldn't believe it. Alex and I had arrived at the same conclusion.

"What I can't figure out," said Alex, "is what about accidental deaths? Or deaths by lions or sharks? How are those on the rise, too?"

"Besides car crashes, there are so few that they're statistical anomalies. They're unlikely to be related to whatever's going on with the manipulatable deaths."

I looked out the window. The sun was starting to come up. It was beautiful, pink and orange. But we were nowhere near Ancien headquarters. Suddenly, the cabbie pulled over into an empty Kmart parking lot.

"Hey," I yelled again. "What's going on?"

This time the cabbie turned around and pointed a gun at my face.

"Get out of the car," he yelled.

I reached for the door handle.

"No, not you," he shouted. "You." He pointed the gun at Alex. "Get out."

I bent over in my seat and threw up. I hadn't eaten much over the last few days, so it was mostly just yellow bile. It came out like water from a hose.

"Ah, shit," yelled the driver. "Come on, get out, get out. Get out now."

Alex looked over at me. I was still throwing up. I reached out my hand to give him something before another heave overwhelmed my body.

"Don't worry, Luna. Just do what he says. I'll find you."

Alex opened his door, and before he could close it, the cab shot off so fast the back door closed itself.

Chapter 27

"Sir, we've got Luna."

"Good," said Doug. "Excellent. Leave us."

The security guard left the office. Doug had been sitting with Taye in Thor's office for nearly twenty-four hours.

In the meantime, Doug had sent for the most exotic foods and drinks—the finest available in the Bay Area.

There was a full Argentine *asado* with the best cuts of meat available. *Vacío, bondiola, bife, cuadril, paleta, molleja, entrecote.* The smell of beef wafted throughout the room—people could probably smell it two floors down, Doug thought. Plus, each cut came with a separate wine pairing.

Then they were brought an assortment of the best Chinese dumplings available. Doug's favorite was the *Qingtuan.* It was a sweet dumpling that looked like a green Mickey Mouse symbol. It had a stretchy texture and was made with black bean paste.

Taye didn't eat any of it. Doug had sampled most of the food and was completely stuffed. He thought for a moment before motioning the waiter over. Doug whispered something in his ear, and the waiter nodded and exited.

"Taye, you have to eat. How long has it been since you've had a good meal?"

"I'm fine," Taye said. He looked like he was going to fall over.

"I think I know what the problem is. I haven't brought you the right food yet," Doug said. "You know, to *your* taste, instead of mine."

Half an hour later, the waiter re-emerged with a long platter of ribs doused in heavy barbecue sauce and a plate full of cornbread.

"Please, Taye, I'm full. You can't just let all this food go to waste."

Taye looked down at the ribs and cornbread and shook his head.

"Really? You want for me to eat that, massa?"

Doug laughed heartily.

"I can't do what you want me to do," said Taye. "I've already told you. No amount of food is going to change the fact that I can't do what you want."

"Look, I'm trying to be nice here. I'm trying to help you. If you don't let me help you, then we'll just have to see what happens without my help."

"This is what you call help?"

"We rescued you from prison, Taye."

"You kidnapped me, which makes me look even more guilty. And you took me out of one prison just to put me in another. I'd feel safer in actual jail."

"Look, just fix the code, and we'll set you free. I will personally make sure you end up on some tropical island with no extradition treaty."

"I'd rather die than help you murder more people."

"Look, Taye, we know you broke Gaia before you ran away. Once you figured out how we were using it, you threw a wrench into it. All I'm asking you to do is to take the wrench out. You put it in, you can take it out. Can't be that hard."

"Fuck you."

"Fine," said Doug. He grabbed a rib and tore out a large bite. The sweet sauce dribbled down his chin. "I was hoping we could work this out. But life doesn't always move in a straight line. There are zigs, and there are zags. By the way, what was the last thing you ate? Just curious."

"Lucky Charms."

"The cereal?"

Taye nodded.

"What a shame."

Chapter 28

Alex thought about his predicament as the brisk morning air warmed with the sun. He sat in the empty parking lot of the abandoned Kmart. Luna was a bright woman; she had handed him her cell phone. Alex remembered that she'd received a phone call from a concerned colleague before the battery died. Apparently, she wanted Alex to get in touch with her friend. The phone was charged, but the big problem now was that it was locked.

Alex had been trying four-digit passcodes for about an hour. Guessing was his only hope. He had to find Luna fast. His instincts told him that this was the kind of situation where a kidnapped woman doesn't have very long to live.

Two, one, one, one.

Two, one, one, two.

Two, one, one, three.

He had already tried all the obvious combinations. Four of a kind. One, two, three, four. Zero, one, two, three. Every combination starting with a nineteen or twenty—any of which could be a birth year or a year of special meaning. Clearly Luna knew how to make a proper passcode—one that wasn't based on anything meaningful. So now he was attempting brute force.

As he pressed different combinations, he thought about his other options. He could go home. Nobody knew he was out here. He could just turn around and go home and never look back.

But then he would never know, and he wouldn't be able to live with himself if he didn't know.

He could storm Ancien on his own. With the tricks he'd learned as a detective, he could almost certainly get past security and look for Luna and Taye in the building. But maybe they weren't keeping them at headquarters. If they were smart, they wouldn't risk it. They would be keeping them in some unmarked building or storage facility. It would leave less evidence if their headquarters were ever investigated.

Plus, if he left, he would be giving up their trump card: Alex wasn't on anybody's radar. He still had the element of surprise. He decided to keep trying passcodes.

Two, two, one, five.

Two, two, one, six.

A BMW careened into the Kmart parking lot. Alex wondered if they'd changed their mind about him. Maybe the cabbie had told them about him when they got to wherever it was he had taken Luna. Maybe they thought he was too big a risk and were here to finish him off. He reflexively reached for his pistol, but he'd left it back in New York. Flying across the country with a gun would have drawn too much attention.

The car braked fast, and a tall, well-dressed man stepped out. He strode up to Alex, who was gripping a slab of broken concrete.

"Can I help you?" Alex asked.

The man seemed to be mumbling to himself. "Um, weird," he said, staring at his phone. "She's supposed to be right here."

"Who are you looking for?"

"A client."

Alex dropped the concrete slab and showed the man Luna's phone. "You looking for this?" he asked.

"What dumpster did you find that in?"

"What?"

All at once, Alex realized what this looked like. Here he was, an old black man sitting alone in an abandoned Kmart parking lot. No car. Nobody else in sight.

"Oh, no," explained Alex. "She gave it to me."

"Luna gave you her phone?"

"Yes. Who are you?"

"Heath Lemming. Her lawyer. Who are *you?*"

"Alex Sonne. I've been working with Luna."

"You've seen her? How long ago? It's incredibly important that I get in touch with her. She's in big trouble, but if I can just talk to her, we'll probably still be able to straighten all this out."

"So why didn't you find her earlier?"

"Her phone was off until just recently. I guess you're the one who turned it on, then?"

"Yes. She gave me the phone an hour ago, right before she was abducted."

"Okay, hold on. Apparently I'm missing a big part of the picture. Back up and start at the beginning. And don't hold anything back."

Chapter 29

It felt weird. Sweet and sour. The taxi driver bringing me back to Ancien headquarters. It had only been a few weeks since the endless meetings with bankers and investors. Trying to convince them all that Ancien was the best investment of the decade. But something inside me had changed. I wasn't CEO anymore. This wasn't my company. Wasn't my building anymore. It was familiar, but foreign. A detached nostalgia.

Or maybe it was just the fact that I'd been sitting in vomit for the last twenty minutes. After the incident with Alex, the cabbie didn't speak again. He dropped me off at the back of Ancien headquarters, where Thor was waiting with two security guards.

I'd saved every ounce of energy for this moment. Conserving it. I jumped out of the car, screaming, "What the fuck, Thor? Have you lost your mind?"

The two guards ran up and grabbed me before I could reach him. Thor's face expressed what looked like genuine concern, which caught me completely off guard.

"What's wrong? What happened?" he demanded. "Let her go."

I pulled myself out of their grip.

"Your goon drove me at gunpoint."

"What?" asked Thor. He seemed shocked. He knocked on the window, shouting, "What the fuck?"

The driver rolled down the window and said, "There was a man with her. You told me to bring her alone."

"Who was the man?"

The driver shrugged. "I was told to pick up the girl. Bring her here. Alone. Now she's made a mess in my car, and it'll take me all day to clean it up."

"Idiot," mumbled Thor. "Luna, I'm so sorry. This was just a simple miscommunication. Where have you been?"

I thought for a moment. "I was shaken up by the attack. It got to me, you know? How close we came to death."

Thor crooked his head and nodded.

"Of course. I totally understand. I was very upset by it all, too. Please come with us. Let's get you cleaned up."

"I want to go home."

"Of course. First, please come with me for just a moment."

He touched my arm, but I pulled away instinctively. The guards flinched. Thor nodded calmly and they stood down.

"You have a posse now?"

"Oh, they're just here to open the back doors."

How big of an idiot did Thor think I was? Or maybe it was something else. Maybe he knew.

"Has anyone told you what's happened since you've been gone?" he asked.

Thor pushed the small of my back, urging me through the open door. His hand was cold, and I wanted to swat it away.

"No."

"While you took some, let's call it personal time, the board made me interim CEO. I've been talking with the bankers and investors. We're pushing to get the IPO done as early as next week. It's been a crazy couple of days. Projections had to be rerun. Lawyers had to redraft all sorts of provisions. Insurance contracts had to be re-written. It's basically been a shit show."

"Welcome to my life."

"Your former life."

I scrunched my nose. He led me to the main elevator, then pressed the button to go down.

"I was hoping to go home to clean up and rest for a bit. I'm a bit jetlagged."

The elevator door opened, and the four of us stepped in.

"Yes, yes. There's just one pressing matter we need your expertise on. You can go home this afternoon." Thor sniffed the air. He looked at me and saw my vom-it-stained pants. He shook his head. "This won't do. Go find Luna a fresh change of clothes, please? Meet us in the basement, room A112. And bring us a never-ending supply of coffee too, will you?"

One of the guards stepped out without saying a word. The elevator doors closed.

"So, what's so urgent you won't let me go home?"

"Don't put words in my mouth. You're free to go home at any time. It's just that one of our biggest clients has sent us an emergency support ticket. It's super criti-cal, and if we don't deliver, it might mess up the entire IPO—again. At the very least, we would have to put it in the diligence documents. I bet it's something you can hammer out in thirty minutes, though, if you put your mind to it."

"Don't you have an army of programmers to do this for you?"

"Nobody knows Ancien like you do, Luna. Our team's been working on it all week and we keep hitting dead ends. I think your touch is just what's needed on this one."

Chapter 30

Heath took Alex to the Bower, Bower, and Nathanson office on Palo Alto's University Street. Alex usually hated lawyers, but he took a liking to Heath pretty quickly. Probably because he seemed to genuinely care about finding Luna. Alex was sure Heath had his own motives for doing so, but still, Alex also knew that most people were incredibly lazy.

When faced with a problem—any problem—most people would rather do nothing than risk failing to fix it. It had bred an entire generation of irresponsible, lazy asses, who simply waited passively to see what new problems would enter their lives. Alex couldn't stand people like that. And the older he got, it seemed the more passive people there were. Heath, however, looked determined, and Alex liked that.

By the time they made it to the office, Heath was fully caught up on the events since Luna's flight from New York—including the problem of the passcode.

"You're looking at the wrong problem," said Heath. "We just need to get ahold of Luna's friend at Ancien. All we need is his name."

"So, we just call the front desk and ask if Phillip is there?" asked Alex. "I don't even remember his last name. I don't think your plan's very likely to work."

"Come on, old man. Who calls front desks anymore? If he's Luna's friend, he's probably high up on the food chain. Most companies list upper management on their websites."

The world was moving too fast for Alex. Maybe it was a good thing he'd been pushed into early retirement. Heath sat at his mahogany desk and, with a few keystrokes, pulled up a list of senior executives at Ancien. Phillip Jones's large round face showed up right below Luna's. No smile. Looked like he hadn't smiled in decades. Chief operating officer. No phone number, but there was an email address.

Heath spent a few minutes drafting a short email and carefully double-checked the wording. Then he sent it and turned to Alex.

"There. Hopefully, this guy calls us back within a few hours. If he's as friendly with Luna as you seem to think, chances are we'll see him before nightfall."

"What did you say to him?"

"Basically that I'm Luna's lawyer and had a few urgent questions for him regarding her case. If your hunch is correct and Ancien's new leadership isn't aboveboard, they might be listening. I didn't want to risk them figuring out what's really going on. But I have yet to meet a senior executive who doesn't obsessively check email. They might not reply to every email quickly, but they sure as hell read them fast."

Heath was right. The call came less than fifteen minutes later. He put it on speaker.

"Hello, Heath," said Phillip. "Can you hear me?"

"Yes," said Heath. "Thanks for calling me back so soon. Some of the things that we need to discuss are quite, well, sensitive. Would you be free to meet this evening to discuss them in person?"

"I can meet you now. Just tell me where."

"Sure," said Heath. "Can you come by the off—"

"The outdoor Rodin sculpture garden at Stanford," Alex interrupted without hesitation.

"I can be there in fifteen minutes."

He hung up.

"Why not here?" asked Heath.

"If they're monitoring email, they might be watching him, too. This way, I'll be able to watch for a tail."

The good reason is almost never the real reason, though, Alex thought. His son, Simon, had always wanted to see the place. It had been his plan that when he got old enough to look at colleges, they would take a tour of Stanford just to see the damned art exhibit. He'd reassured Alex that he didn't want to go to Stanford. That he would never move that far away from his old man. But what the hell did Alex know? Maybe the real reason wasn't the good reason then, either.

"Good call," said Heath.

Phillip wasn't yet at the campus when they arrived. They strode lazily around the Rodin Museum, looking for a plump businessman. It was impressive, but Alex had to wonder what the big deal was.

Heath whispered to Alex, "Hey, what about him? Near *The Gates of Hell*."

Alex turned toward the massive sculpture. The man looked nervous. It was definitely Phillip. They went up to him.

"Phillip?" said Heath.

"Yes, are you Heath Lemming? The lawyer?"

"Yes, thanks for meeting us so quickly."

"I've got plenty of time. You see, I was recently laid off," said Phillip.

"I'm sorry to hear that," said Heath. He looked over at Alex, sticking out his bottom lip in defeat.

"It's not official yet. They're waiting for some big staff meeting before making the announcement. But they don't want me doing any work, so I was at home when I got your email. Figured what the hell? If I can help Luna, it'll be the most productive day I've had all week."

"Actually," said Alex, "Luna needs your help more than you know."

A loud bang echoed through the air. Once again, Alex found himself reflexively grabbing for the gun that wasn't there. He clearly needed to fix that. He ducked down, pulling on Heath, who was still standing and gaping. Alex was impressed with Phillip, though. Most people freeze up upon hearing gunshots. Especially big guys like Phillip. But he was instinctively crouching down, too.

No. He wasn't ducking. He was falling. He'd been shot.

Chapter 31

Doug stormed into Thor's office. Someone had cleaned it up since he'd last been there. Thor was on the phone, but as Doug approached, he hung up without a word.

"Please explain what the fuck just happened," Doug demanded.

"Fine," said Thor, exasperated. "But it'll have to be quick. I've got a parking lot full of press up my ass."

"The press will be the least of your problems if you let things fall apart at this critical juncture."

"As you know, we've been actively monitoring Phillip's email," explained Thor. "Ever since I let him go. This afternoon, we saw an email come through from Luna's lawyer. He wanted to talk. I decided it was too high of a risk to let that phone call happen."

"Good call so far."

"So I dispatched a couple of my men to Phillip's apartment, but by the time they got there he was gone. They tracked him to the Stanford campus. There was a lot more risk doing it in public, but we couldn't risk them talking. Especially in person."

"What is Luna's lawyer doing here?" Doug asked, his head tilted. "Isn't he based out of New York?"

"I don't know yet."

"So you had your men open fire in public—on a school campus no less? Are you crazy?"

"My men were overzealous—"

"That's the understatement of the year."

"I just told them to take care of Phillip. I thought they would do it, you know, neater."

"And they couldn't even be bothered to finish the job properly? Where did you hire these goons? I'm seriously beginning to question your abilities, Thor."

"I hardly thought we would need a sophisticated militia when you hired me, Doug. Gaia was supposed to do the work for us quickly and quietly. There weren't supposed to be guns. No blood. You said—"

Doug's veins were popping from his forehead. He thought he could see Thor quivering. Yes. He was. This asinine pussyfooted lightweight corporate dipshit was quivering. Like a little baby. Doug had made mistakes like this in his past, and they nearly cost him everything. Thor was supposed to be a seasoned professional.

Thor was a full-blooded Massino after all. A distinguished crime family. A respected name. Sure, it had been a few years since Joseph Massino had been at the top of his game, but Thor was their shining hope for the future. He'd been sent to Harvard Business School. They had groomed him to be a "fixer" CEO. The guy that was brought in to take a high-profile tech startup public. He was good at it. A natural businessman. It ran in his blood.

All to prepare for a moment like this. And Doug was the one who had spotted the opportunity. The one who put all the pieces together. He had the vision. And now it seemed Thor had conveniently forgotten his roots. Forgotten where he came from. Now he was scared of a little blood? What a goddamn fucking joke. This was Doug's shining purpose. This was what he was meant to do in life. He was sure of it.

"Calm down, Doug," said Thor. "I'll clean up this mess. I heard Phillip's at the Stanford hospital."

"The place has to be crawling with cops. There's no way your two goons could make it through the red tape."

"Who said I was sending anybody? I said *I'd* clean it up. Now, if you'll excuse me, I need to go visit my chief operating officer. I heard he's in critical condition. Who knows if he'll even make it through the day?"

Good. Maybe Thor wasn't completely a bumbling idiot after all.

Chapter 32

I was a prisoner in my own office building. Thor had left me alone with the guard, claiming the man was going to be my butler for the day. To bring me food or coffee. But he wasn't there to help. I just couldn't figure out if he was there to prevent me from leaving, to spy on me, or both. Either way, I was glad to be left more or less alone with a computer for a while. Thor had explained more about the problem they were having with Gaia. I pretended I didn't know what Gaia was and just nodded my head a bunch. When I asked what Gaia was used for, he told me it was confidential. When I asked who the client was, he said that was confidential, too.

The other guard came back with a change of clothes and some coffee. Apparently the best he could find were some black cargo pants and an old cream-colored dress shirt. He'd probably gotten them from the janitor's closet. They were too big, but at least didn't smell like vomit. I asked for them to leave the room so I could change, but they just turned around. I changed as quickly as I could. The clothes smelled faintly of cigarettes, which made me want to gag.

I desperately wanted to take a shower, but I figured that would have to wait. I was dead tired. The day had worn me down. It wasn't even five o'clock yet, but I felt as though I'd lived a week's worth of experiences since just this morning. I wondered what Alex was up to and if he'd managed to unlock my phone yet. That was my first order of business.

I walked up to the guards.

"Can I borrow a phone, please?"

One of them pointed at the desk phone sitting next to the computer.

"I need to send a text message and my phone's out of battery."

The guards looked at each other. One of them shrugged. The other rolled his eyes and handed me his phone. No passcode. What a joke.

I typed out a message and sent it to my cell. Even when locked, my phone would display the first part of any text message, so I figured that should help Alex get in if he hadn't already. I waited a moment and then deleted the message before handing the phone back to the guy.

"Thanks," I said.

He winked.

Then I sat down at the computer. It felt good to be back in a comfortable place again. Sitting in a dim room, behind a twenty-seven-inch ultra-high-definition screen connected to a maxed-out Mac Pro. It had been too long. Good old Macintosh, always there whenever people let me down. I still preferred the old days when my Mac would smile at me when it turned on. On my personal computers, I'd changed the startup logo to an old-school one just for fun.

Someone had already preloaded Gaia's source code on to this machine for me. I was already familiar with the code structure from having played around with it in New York, so instead of tinkering, I decided to try to get the thing running. Based on what Alex and I conjectured about Gaia's capabilities, I wasn't about to try to turn this death machine on. But I needed to understand better what we were up against. Until I could sneak out of here to find Taye, toying around with Gaia was the only thing I could do to make any progress. Maybe Taye had left clues inside Gaia that I could use to find him. If they were holding him in a similar room, we might be able to communicate by modifying the source code.

So, I tried to run Gaia with my hand over the kill switch. Like Thor had said, it didn't work. No need for the kill switch yet. I peeked at the source code again. Something was off. This was not the same source code I had seen in New York. Someone had changed it significantly. It was even less like my original template than it was last time.

I pulled up the source code history. As expected, it listed a lot of recent changes, and these changes were weird. Ultra-frequent. Like they weren't even human. Then it became clear to me. Even though Gaia seemed broken and unable to run, there had to be a working copy of Gaia still running somewhere, and it was modifying its own source code. Doing what? I had no idea yet. It could take me days or weeks before I could even glean a basic understanding of what was going on.

There was nothing I could do with this code. I couldn't debug it even if I wanted to. And I certainly didn't want to. But maybe I could figure out what the working copy of Gaia was up to.

Chapter 33

Alex sat in the hospital waiting room, drinking an old cup of cold coffee and feeling grateful that he was still alive. The shot had scraped the outside of Phillip's heart, and he had been put in a medically induced coma to recover. Alex knew that things could escalate quickly with these kinds of situations. Influential people hiding big secrets and all. But he didn't think they'd be willing to open fire in broad daylight, in the middle of a university campus.

The police had rushed in and locked down the perimeter within thirty minutes, but the shooters were long gone. Afterward, the local police asked Alex for his version of the story more than twenty times. He hadn't been able to make out the shooters' faces, but there were two of them: Caucasian, dark-haired, wearing all black.

He saw them riding away on motorcycles, and that was it. There was not much else to tell.

It was a good thing Alex had once been a cop. Otherwise, they wouldn't even have *that* much. Heath couldn't remember anything at all. The police had let him go long before Alex, since he was so useless. Once Alex was free to leave, he found he had nowhere to go, so he went to the hospital. At least there he could watch over Phillip.

Two cops stood outside Phillip's room. Alex had tried to get past them—not because he particularly wanted to see Phillip, but because he wanted to see if he could manage it. He told them he was a cousin. They didn't buy it; they asked for identification. Checked a list. The list came up short. Alex was pleased. They were taking this seriously. With nothing else to do, he just sat in the waiting room. At least it had a clear view of Phillip's room. He drank the only thing that wasn't pumped full of sweetener—the cold coffee.

Then a man appeared in the hallway and made for Phillip's room. Alex picked up a magazine but watched the scene carefully out of the corner of his eye. He didn't want to be seen staring. As they had with Alex, the guards stopped the man. There was a short conversation followed by a request for identification. Then they checked the list. The cop shook his head. The guy pointed to the list. Looked like he wanted the cop to check it again. The officer obliged and once again shook his head. There was some more conversation—this time a little more heated. Alex's interest was piqued. He snuck over to the waiting room door and cracked it open.

"This is ridiculous. I want to talk to your boss. Do you realize who I am?"

"Look, we're under strict orders here. No one goes in if they're not on the list. Our boss is coming in about fifteen minutes if you want to hear the same thing from him."

The man looked at his watch.

"I'm going to have your badges for this."

The man turned around and made a beeline for the waiting room. Quickly, Alex closed the door and sat down again, pretending to read his magazine. The stranger stormed in. He was well dressed. Corporate. And he moved with a certain swagger. This was a man who was used to being in charge, and he was not accustomed to waiting on anyone.

The man went to the coffee dispenser and pushed the button. It spat out a few drops. He threw the cup in the garbage and went to the couch. He sat down, nodding to Alex. Alex nodded back. A confused look came over the man's face. Alex glanced down and realized he'd inadvertently picked up a copy of *Women's Health*. Alex gave the man a shrug and a smile.

"Friend or relation?" Alex asked, like they were at a wedding.

"Friend," said the man. He pulled out a BlackBerry and started typing. Apparently he wasn't feeling sociable. But Alex was.

"I haven't seen one of those in years. I didn't think they even worked anymore," said Alex.

The man laughed but didn't take the bait. He kept typing furiously. Alex was going to have to switch strategies if he was going to determine the man's identity.

"You know, I'm Alex. Phillip's boyfriend. And I don't think I've met you before."

The man looked surprised but kept his face buried in his phone.

"Oh? Well, I'm Phillip's boss."

"I thought his boss was a woman? Luna something?"

"Oh, yes, that was Phillip's former boss," Thor said. "I'm his new boss. Thor Massino. Pleased to meet you."

"Ah, so you're the asshole who laid him off."

Chapter 34

I finally figured out what Gaia was being used for. I was looking at the code's history, all the way back to the very first commits, when Taye had been writing the code himself. That code was very easy to understand. Sophisticated, certainly. But straightforward.

As I suspected, he was applying Ancien's machine learning algorithms to computer code itself. Taye's earliest code was a simple big data importer script. It worked diligently to import billions of lines of code directly from GitHub into Ancien. This part had probably taken weeks.

It also imported all of the code's history—so as individual lines of code were improved and debugged and made more secure, Ancien learned the difference. Bad line of code. Good line of code. Billions of times. In dozens of programming languages.

One of the guards raised his hand to his earpiece and whispered something. I couldn't make it out. I pretended I didn't see it and kept working.

It was shortly after this big data dump into Ancien that I started to see small code changes being made to Gaia. I assumed those small changes were Gaia's experiments at improving its own code. It was still writing human language code, but they were small changes compared to the ones Taye seemed to have been making himself.

That's when the bad news started. Taye had apparently been trying to use Gaia to write better code. But someone else was making changes to Gaia too. The author of those changes was anonymous. That person had flipped a switch in the code, though. Instead of finding ways to improve bad code, now Gaia would simply find and report bad code. Shortly after, Gaia was modified further to exploit the bad code it found. Like me, Taye hadn't immediately recognized how powerful Gaia could be in the wrong hands. Looking at the early code history of Gaia was like watching a tragedy unfold.

I'd just found a particularly interesting change in the code history when the guard came up to me and dropped his enormous paw on my shoulder.

"Is it working yet?" he growled.

"Was that Thor? Tell him I'm making good progress, but it's complicated. I need more time."

"Time's up."

"I'm not done." He grabbed my shoulder to pull me out of the chair. "Hey, I said I'm not done. Let go of me."

"You're done for today."

"Where are you taking me?"

The guard didn't respond. He just started dragging me away like a lion pulling a carcass.

"Can I go home now?"

The guard said nothing.

Chapter 35

This time, Alex's attempt to get the man's attention had worked. Thor stopped typing, looked up from his phone, and laid it down next to him. Alex knew the Massino family name. Though they hadn't been an active crime family in years, the pieces in Alex's head were coming together quickly. This guy had probably hired the shooters. He was probably here to finish the job. And he was behind all of this. How had a crime boss managed to take over one of the world's biggest startups? He needed to find Luna before it was too late. This was not a man Alex wanted to spend too much time around.

"I'm sorry, what was your name again?"

"Alex."

"Look, Alex. I'm sorry that your boyfriend got hurt. And I'm sorry that things didn't work out for him at Ancien. But calling me an asshole is uncalled for."

"I'm sorry, you're right. I'm just so–" Alex was not a man who was quick to cry. But he knew a trick actors used: remember the mindset you were in last time you did cry. It only took Alex a moment to summon a believable layer of salty liquid.

Thor rolled his eyes.

"I get it. This is difficult for everyone. I know it may be hard for you to believe, but I'm one of the good guys. I just came by to make sure Phillip is okay."

Alex choked on his saliva.

"You all right?" Thor asked.

Alex nodded, pretending to try to compose himself.

They sat in silence for a while. Thor dove back into his BlackBerry and Alex pretended to read his *Women's Health* magazine. In reality, Alex was thinking through scenarios for whatever came next. He couldn't let Thor get into that room alone. Alex considered talking to the cops outside the room, alerting them to the situation. But that would raise a lot of questions he didn't want to answer. So far, all he had was a hunch. An unfounded accusation.

Then someone else came into the waiting room. It was a cop Alex hadn't seen before.

"Is one of you Thor Massino?" he asked.

Thor stood up. "I am."

Alex's blood ran hot, but he stared at the magazine with more fervor than ever.

The cop eyed him.

"One of my men tells me you want to see Mr. Jones?"

"Yes, I'm his boss. I just want to make sure he's okay."

"Look, the guy's in a coma. There's nothing to see here. Give me your number, and I'll make sure to call you as soon as he wakes up."

Out of the corner of his eye, Alex could see Thor trying to decide how hard to push it with this guy.

"Fine."

The cop handed him a pad of paper and a pen. Thor scribbled his phone number quickly. In that very moment, Alex's plan finally came together. He knew exactly what he needed to do.

Chapter 36

Heath was a lawyer. When he talked to police, he was trained to deny everything. With a straight face. The trick was to withhold the whole truth. To skillfully hide the lies within shades of truth. When they asked if he had seen anything, he answered that he saw the light-brown gravelly dirt. Which was absolutely true. Just not the whole truth.

After a few more questions like that, the police decided that Heath wasn't worth their time and let him go. Ideally, he would have waited for Alex, but he needed to get back to his office as soon as possible. After all, Alex was an ex-cop. He was probably telling the police everything he knew five times over. And loving the feeling of superiority, like he was the only one cool enough under pressure to notice the details.

Back when Heath was in law school, one of his favorite professors, Mr. O'Neil, keeled over mid-lecture from a heart attack. The room was full of over a hundred freshman law students—all of them frozen in their seats. Then, two of the students ran up to the professor, felt for a pulse, and told the others they would take him to the hospital to get help. Five minutes after Mr. O'Neil was carried out the door, he walked back in, fit as a fiddle. It had all been a test to see how observant they were. It was an example of how poor eyewitness accounts can be, even from the best-educated people in the world.

Heath was the only student in the room who noticed that Mr. O'Neil had changed his tie from a red one to a blue one while he was out of the room. Heath had the uncanny ability to spot the fine details that others missed. It was part of what had made him the best in his class.

He dug through every client document that Bower, Bower, and Nathanson had with Ancien. Of course, he'd seen some of them when preparing Luna's defense, but even those he reread now with renewed interest. He had to comb through everything he could find about Ancien to prepare for the call he was about to make.

"Do you need anything else, Mr. Lemming?" asked a young blond assistant, who had been photocopying pages for him all day.

"No, thank you. You've been very kind."

She smiled for a few moments, as if hoping he might change his mind, then turned and closed the door behind her.

Heath picked up the heavy gray desk phone. Cell phone reception in San Francisco was the worst. Wasn't this supposed to be the tech capital of the world? How was it possible that no one had figured out how to make clear cell phone calls yet?

He was ready. At least, he hoped he was ready.

"Hello?"

"Mr. Bower, it's Heath Lemming."

"Do you realize how late it is over here? Make an appointment with Kathy and we can talk in the—"

"Mr. Bower, this is important. I was shot at today."

There was a brief pause on the line, and then Heath heard a muffled apology to whoever Neil Bower was with at the moment. Heath figured it was probably some poker buddies.

"You were shot at?"

"Yes."

"Are you okay?"

"Yes. You probably heard about it on the news—the incident at the Stanford campus. I'm sorry to bother you directly, but I have reason to believe that Ancien is behind the shooting. And I believe they have kidnapped Luna Valencia, as well."

There was another pause. Longer this time. Heath had to ask if Neil was still on the line.

"Yes, yes. I'm here. Have you seen Luna yourself?"

"No, not yet."

"Look, Heath, you've just made some serious allegations against one of our largest clients. Do you have any hard evidence to back this up?"

"No, but I've been doing some research into Ancien's files and—"

"Heath, let me stop you right there. You have no evidence. I don't want to hear any speculation. The Ancien account is the one that made our firm what it is today. I don't need you poking your nose where it doesn't belong."

"But if I'm right, this could be the key that wins us the Luna Valencia case. I could get our track record back."

"Fuck Luna Valencia. If you see that twat, I want you to turn her into the authorities as quickly as possible. Need I remind you that she brought this upon herself by skipping bail? We owe her nothing, and there is nothing I'd rather see than her ass in prison where it belongs. Luna Valencia is not paying our bills. Ancien is. Remember who our client is."

"And if I'm right that Ancien tried to kill me today?"

"I'll kill you myself if you lose us the Ancien account on nothing but a hunch. I thought sending you to the

West Coast would help you get your priorities straight, but now I'm wondering why I kept you on at all. Look, you are to stop all investigations into Ancien and any *alleged* crimes they may or may not have committed. You are not the goddamned police. And if I hear that you saw Luna and didn't turn her in immediately, I will personally make sure you are disbarred. You won't be able to practice law on either coast for as long as I'm alive. I can assure you of that. Do I make myself perfectly clear?"

This time, it was Heath who paused. He imagined Neil was, at that very moment, calculating the size of the bill Bower, Bower, and Nathanson would rack up defending Ancien on attempted murder charges—if Heath was right.

"Crystal."

Chapter 37

Doug sat behind Thor's desk, impatiently picking at his fingernails. He knew the current situation called for patience, and that events would unfold at their own pace. But patience seemed to be an increasingly rare commodity these days.

He had hoped to hear by now that Phillip was dead and that Luna had debugged Gaia. But he knew from experience that plans rarely went as smoothly as intended. He thought about his dad. His father hadn't been patient enough, and he'd paid the ultimate price for it. Doug wasn't going to be like his dad. Humans were all just a bunch of pre-programmed ants running around, doing their jobs for a short amount of time, and then they always died. Doug's father had taken it all too seriously, and that was his downfall. The anthill was what it was, and one couldn't take it personally. No one ant was responsible. Humans were all just minor players contributing to their small lot in life.

Doug felt more confident of his role than ever before. In every society, everyone had special roles to play. Some people were scouting ants, searching for new sources of food. Some were fighting ants. Doug was the architect ant. He had a deep understanding of society's fabric and what needed to happen to fix it. He could see the shortcomings of his past so clearly now. He had tried, on several different occasions, to eliminate the government by orchestrating the deaths of as many government officials as possible. None of his previous attempts had brought the hoped-for fruits. But now he understood why. It was all so clear to him.

Doug knew that his ego and lack of imagination had gotten in the way of his own success. For years, he thought too much like those who came before him. Too far inside the box. He used to plan big flashy attacks on well-protected officials. No wonder they didn't work.

But he'd learned from his mistakes. He could see them as mistakes now.

Doug fancied himself as having a knack for finding the right tools for the job. Like CryptoBit before Ancien, life had a way of presenting him with the right tool at the right moment. And every time it happened, it only re-enforced that he was on the right track. This time, life had handed him the perfect tool at the perfect moment, and he wasn't about to let the opportunity slip past.

After all, if life didn't want him doing this job—if the anthill didn't need to be re-sculpted and re-architected—why were the pieces of the puzzle coming together so elegantly? Doug was sure this was bigger than him. He was merely the one ant on the hill that was prepared to do the job no other ant could. He was going to save the colony from itself.

Doug thought of a phrase from the Bible. The meek shall inherit the earth. He wasn't a religious man, but to him, this was more evidence in support of his actions. His strong will wasn't what would inherit the earth, like he'd initially thought. He had to be more humble. It was the only way to succeed in committing the greatest gen-ocide in human history. He needed to act meek in order to be strong. Like Lao-Tzu once said, nothing's softer or more yielding than water. And yet to compel the hard and unyielding, it has no equal. Doug needed to be more like water.

This insight had come to him in a flash at his last company. System, Inc. had been the largest provider of security and encryption technology for corporations and governments around the world. Everyone depended on his code for securing communications. There, Doug had learned what amazing power a person could hold just by being able to hear everything.

But with Ancien now available to him, his reach was exponentially expanded. System Inc. had been like read-only mode to the world. He could listen, but it was passive. At Ancien, he could effect change without risking getting caught. Ancien was read-write mode. So much of the world's most sensitive information was stored inside of Ancien. And with Gaia, Doug could command the world to do his bidding. It was the perfect plan.

Except, with Gaia not working, he was back to read-only mode. And Doug was sick of read-only mode. He needed to be in control. He didn't care that he could never take credit for it. He wasn't interested in the glory. The meek shall inherit the earth. It had been pre-ordained by powers that even Doug didn't understand. He didn't need to, though. He just needed to do his one little ant job. The anthill of humanity needed to be torn down so a new one could be built in its place. It was his humble duty.

The only thing standing in his way now was Luna Valencia. She was a professional. Not like some of the startup idiots he had dealt with before. She was someone Doug could respect. He'd been watching her carefully ever since joining the board, and she was not just a good CEO, she was technical enough to actually understand what she had built. That was very rare these days. Only a few high-tech CEOs possessed that skill.

Which was part of the reason why he got her replaced. If she ever got a whiff of the true purpose of the Gaia Project, she would stop at nothing to shut it down. So far, Doug had been able to keep the Gaia Project a secret, but things had spun out of control with Taye. If Luna could just get Gaia working again, he could quietly get rid of her and everything would be back on track.

Thor walked into his office, balking at the sight of Doug sitting there, looking so casual.

"So?" Doug asked. "Is it done?"

"They wouldn't let me in. There were police crawling all over the place. I'm the first person they'll call when he wakes up, though."

"You fucking idiot," Doug yelled. "Don't you realize how suspicious that will look? The cops will remember that you came by, so eager to see him, asking to be the first call they make when he wakes up. Who do you think will be at the top of their list of suspects when he dies? Shit. You probably just made yourself their prime suspect in the shooting. They're probably looking into your background as we speak."

"I have an alibi."

"Of course you have an alibi. They probably think you hired the job out. Which you did. You fucking idiot. You've created such a mess."

"You're overreacting. I was just a concerned boss trying to check on an injured employee. I'm sure the cops think it's nothing more than that."

"We'll see about that. People get caught for being far less sloppy than this. We'll need to brainstorm ways to clean up your mess. In the meantime, I think it's time you switch up strategies with Luna downstairs. I've been watching closely as she's been 'fixing' Gaia. I got her off the computer before she stumbled onto something important. So you need to go down to the basement and incentivize her to focus on actually fixing Gaia. She's spending far too much time trying to figure out what it does. We can't have her doing that now. Then take care of her. Too many loose ends."

Chapter 38

I was starving and tired. The guards took me to the cafeteria. They pointed to a long communal table that had a couple of apples and a banana on it. It would do as a snack, but I asked if they could get me a burrito. Ideally, heavy on the guac and sour cream. I was craving carbs. They didn't respond one way or the other, but as I hadn't seen either one of them for an hour, I guessed it was a no. They were probably standing right outside the room laughing at me.

I spent most of the hour thinking about how to find Taye. I wondered if they had taken him to a room and told him to fix his bug—just like me. I wondered if he'd cooperated. Probably not. That kid was as brave as he was smart.

Then it hit me. I could walk out of the room as if I didn't know I was a prisoner. Then, if they stopped me, I could just say I needed to use the bathroom. Come to think of it, I did need to use the bathroom. All that coffee. And if they weren't there, I could look around for Taye.

I walked casually over to the door, but just as I grabbed the handle, the door opened on its own.

"Oh," I said. "Hi, Thor. I was just going to look for you. Any luck with my burrito?" Now more than ever, I wanted to kick him in the kneecaps. It took every ounce of energy I had left to pretend I didn't know he was a psychopathic killer.

"Luna, the guards tell me you haven't fixed our little problem. Is something wrong?"

"Yes, something's wrong. The code is not written intelligibly. The only way I can help you debug it is if you let me talk it over with the person who wrote it." I thought for a moment and then decided just to go for it. "Can I speak to Taye?"

A look of shock spread over Thor's face. Then it turned to anger. "How do you know about Taye?"

That got him going. Good. It was better to have him off balance for what was coming next. "His name's all over the source code history. He wrote this thing originally, didn't he? Why not just have him fix it?"

I could see the gears turning in Thor's mind. I couldn't wait to see what tale he would spin. "I didn't ask you to look at the source code history, I asked you to fix the bug. The client's been up my ass since we last spoke. You know how clients can be. We just need this fixed— we don't need a history report on it."

"How am I supposed to fix it if I can't read the code? Looking at the history is the only way I can even begin to try to fix it."

"Look, Luna. The pressure is obscene. Perception is everything, and if you can't help us, there could be a lawsuit or worse. Our friends on Wall Street could accuse us of fraud. You're putting everything you've worked for in jeopardy. I know you can fix this. Just fix it."

"Let me talk to Taye," I said.

"That won't be possible."

"Won't it?"

He gave me the strangest look yet. I was almost there. Almost ready. His mind was racing. I could see it in his eyes. They kept darting left and right with odd jerky motions. I figured it must be a stress response. His tell. It was all I needed to know.

Finally, I gave in and let it loose, "I know Taye's here. Phillip Jones told me. Let me talk to him, and I'll be able to fix Gaia."

If his eyes looked like they were going to pop out before, now all they needed was a gentle breeze.

"I don't know what you're talking about," he stammered. His eyes jerked wildly. "Taye's not here. I don't know where he is, and you will most certainly not be able to talk to him. You will fix the problem. Then you will go home and rest. You deserve it."

"You know what, Thor? I can't tell what you're worse at: lying or leading. Has anyone ever told you that before?" And with that I pushed him aside and strode out the door. "I'm going home now, and no one is going to stop me."

As I expected, the two thugs were standing just outside. I fully expected Thor to yell at them to drag me back to the computer room. But he didn't. And they didn't. I kept going. I picked up my pace. I glanced through the glass of every door and window I passed. Most of the doors I tried were locked, and I didn't run into anyone else. It was getting late. Most Ancien employees were home having dinner with their families.

God, I was hungry. I was so hungry I felt weak. Running hurt and left me breathless, but I told myself I couldn't stop. I wasn't going to leave this place until I found Taye. I tried to remember what Phillip had told me. Something about a kid being locked in my office. I had to get upstairs. I heard footsteps behind me. They were slow and steady and methodical. I broke into a full sprint up a flight of stairs.

"Luna."

I recognized the voice immediately. I turned around and saw Alex standing at the bottom of the stairs.

Chapter 39

"Oh, thank God," I cried. I ran downstairs to Alex and threw my arms around him. He felt like a teddy bear, and I squeezed with all my strength. I hadn't felt so safe in anyone's arms in years. "How'd you get past security?"

"Asked if I could use the bathroom, then slipped by when the phone rang. We need to get out of here."

"What about Taye?" I asked. "We need to find him. Did you get ahold of Phillip?"

"Phillip's in the hospital."

"What?" I pushed back on Alex's chest. I couldn't believe what I was hearing.

"He was shot this afternoon," explained Alex. "He's in a medically-induced coma. But, Luna, we have to go. I followed Thor here from the hospital. I think he was trying to finish the job with Phillip. You're not safe here.

We need to get somewhere safe and come up with a plan."

"I'm not leaving Taye to these psychos."

"We have to."

"No, we don't. You do realize that I built this place, right? This whole building was my idea."

Alex looked at me, even more confused than ever.

"Come with me," I said, motioning toward the women's bathroom.

Alex hesitated but gave in. It was late; almost everyone had gone home. The bathroom was incredibly clean, like the day the building first opened. Evidently not many women worked in the basement. I went to the last stall—the handicap stall—and ushered Alex in. I followed close behind, locking the door behind us.

"Is this some kind of sisterhood of the traveling toilet thing?"

I laughed and flushed the toilet ten times in rapid succession.

"Was something supposed to happen?" he asked.

"No, but it would've been cool right?"

Alex laughed with his whole belly. I got him good. I unlocked the stall and went to the closet door. I pushed aside some cleaning supplies and pressed gently on the back wall. It clicked open, revealing a dark passageway dimly lit by sparsely placed LEDs.

"I tried to get them to pay for an entrance coded by toilet flush, but I had to settle for this instead."

I led Alex through a maze of passageways. Occasionally, there were small rectangular openings, and Alex stuck his head near one to peer through.

"Cool, huh?" I said.

"Creepy," he said.

Every few yards, there were forks in the passageways. I knew where we were going. We took a few sets of tight stairs.

"What is this?" asked Alex.

"When I was a kid, my parents took me to Italy. I hated the food, but when we visited Florence, I was smitten by the Palazzo Vecchio. We took a tour of the secret passages that went through the place. I always wondered why more modern buildings don't have these."

"So you built them yourself?"

"Yup. It's been my little secret, too. You're the first person I've told about it."

"Don't you think the janitors have found them by now?"

I shrugged. "If they have, they've done a good job keeping it secret."

Almost all the tunnels ended in women's bathrooms. All but one. We arrived at the door that opened on to my office closet. Though, it wasn't my closet anymore.

I pulled the door handle to engage the lock, but when I pushed, it wouldn't budge.

"Thor must have put his stuff in here already," I explained, as I shoved again at the door.

Alex squeezed his way past me. "Excuse me," he chuckled. He pushed the door, too, but it only budged a couple of inches. "Jesus, what does he have stuck in here?"

Alex felt his way around the opening of the door. He could just barely get his hand through. He caught hold of something and pulled it through the doorway. Even in the dim light of the cramped hallway I could clearly see what it was. I screamed. I didn't care if anyone heard me. Maybe it was better that they did. I just kept screaming. It was Taye's limp and bloody hand.

Chapter 40

The morning light broke through the blinds. The apartment they'd given him was nice. Even had the same furnishings as his New York place. High-end Swedish. But Heath hadn't slept. Both of the options he faced were unconscionable. On the one hand, he could ignore everything that had happened over the last week. Forget Luna. After all, it's what his boss had told him to do. Or he could follow his nose and figure out the truth that he'd nearly been killed to protect.

Heath had defended famous people before. But they were all assholes. Luna was different. There was something about that woman. A fire. A spice. He saw it in her eyes the moment they met in the courtroom. Finding Luna felt like the right itch, but he didn't know if he should scratch it. He could lose more than just his career.

Play along, go to work, and keep his head down. Or dig around and get to the bottom of whatever was going on. What kind of man was he? He decided to find out.

"Mr. Massino, there's a Heath Lemming here to see you." There was a quick pause, then the secretary looked up at Heath and added, "He doesn't know you."

"Tell him I'm Luna Valencia's lawyer."

She relayed the message and paused again, before putting down the phone.

"He'll see you, but he only has two minutes before his next meeting."

"Thanks. I'll make it quick."

Heath stepped into the office. Thor was seated behind a large desk, and he waved to Heath to sit. He did.

"Mr. Massino, I know you're a busy man."

"Yes, I am. And I don't like surprise visits."

"I'm very sorry. I work for Bower, Bower, and Nathanson. We do your criminal law work."

"If this is about Luna's bail, I've already explained that we're more than happy—"

"No, this isn't about money. This is about yesterday's shooting."

Thor's eyes widened.

"What happened yesterday was a tragedy," said Thor. "But what does it have to do with the Luna Valencia case?"

"Nothing." Heath noticed what looked like relief pouring over Thor's face. "An executive at a startup gets shot. Next thing you know, he'll be suing his employer."

"Oh, you're good." Thor laughed. "You fucking lawyers will suck the scum from the bottom of any pond, won't you? Always thinking ahead. I like that."

"That's why you pay us the big bucks," Heath said with a smile.

Thor relaxed and leaned back into his seat.

"So what do you propose we do about this situation?"

"Well, we're your criminal attorneys," said Heath. "Our job is to defend you. But I believe the best defense is a strong offense. I'm sure our firm could make quite a killing if Mr. Jones were to take you to court. I wouldn't be surprised if some lawyers chomp at the opportunity of just such a thing happening to them. Lots of billable hours defending a case like that. Personally, I prefer a more proactive approach. The easiest way to win a criminal case is to make sure it never gets filed in the first place."

Thor nodded. "What was your name again?"

"Heath. Heath Lemming."

Thor wrote something down.

"Heath, I like the way you think. I've never believed in the incentive structure of outside counsel. I could use more people around me who understand the way the world works. Legally, I'm not allowed to hire an employee directly from one of the law firms we work with. So, technically, I'm not allowed to offer you this salary if you were to quit your job and come work for me."

Thor slid the note across his desk. Heath studied it closely. Both men smiled, but for different reasons.

Chapter 41

If there was one thing Doug hated more than anything else, it was waiting for an appointment that was running late. Especially from a man who owed everything to him. Thor's office door opened, and a tall, good-looking man stepped out, grinning. Doug could tell the man was a lawyer just by how he walked. So smug and full of himself. Three years in law school and pretentious English majors turn into unholy assholes. Doug contemplated getting Gaia to target lawyers once it was up and running again.

"Doug," said Thor, like they were best friends. "Sorry for keeping you waiting. Please come in."

Doug entered the office, and Thor closed the door behind him.

"I expected Gaia to be fixed by now. I thought I made it clear to you that you were to get Luna in line."

"I did."

"By letting her walk out of here? I saw the security tapes. She and that old ex-cop snuck away at midnight in an Uber. This is getting out of control."

"Calm down. Who do you think was driving that Uber? I've paid half a dozen Ancien employees to drive around the campus posing as Uber and Lyft drivers. We bugged her house while she was here working on Gaia. Everything is under control."

"But you didn't get her to fix Gaia. Who cares what kind of surveillance you have? We need Gaia working."

"Of course we do. But we need her to fix Gaia on her own terms. We need her to think she's safe. I'm a Massino, but that doesn't mean I strong-arm everything. My family didn't send me to Harvard to turn me into a brute."

Doug was satisfied. Time and again, Thor had proven himself worthy. Maybe Doug had finally found a partner he could trust.

"Okay," said Doug.

"Okay," Thor repeated. "I'll let you know when Luna is done fixing Gaia. It shouldn't be long now. My team has been watching her approach and trying similar tactics. Even if she gave up now, we could probably crack it in a couple more days."

"Good. Now, there are some modifications I'd like to talk to you about."

Chapter 42

I couldn't believe it. Taye was dead, Phillip was in a coma, and I was a fugitive. How could things have gotten so out of control? Somehow, Alex had stayed calm and covered my mouth to stifle my incessant screaming. When I finally was able to calm down some, we made our way back downstairs and escaped through one of the back doors. I called an Uber. Alex suggested we go to a hotel, but I insisted we go to my apartment. I wanted comfort so badly. I needed to be in a place where I could feel like things were normal again.

Alex relented, and the driver took us to my place in Menlo Park. In all my ten years at Ancien, I'd never once felt it necessary to buy a house or move out of my small apartment. It wasn't like I was married or had children. I didn't even own a dog. My company was my family, and I spent most of my time at the office or traveling, anyway. Though, it was painful to see the increase in housing prices.

Before he let me enter my apartment, Alex insisted on checking it out himself. I rolled my eyes but keyed in my passcode to turn off the alarm.

"Go ahead," I said. "I'll wait here."

Alex checked every room. I took a deep breath. It smelled a little stale—the way it does when a place hasn't been lived in for a while. The outline of a home without the color filled in yet.

"Clear," said Alex. "You don't have much stuff."

"I don't let stuff own me. I assume you saw the couch. Make yourself comfortable. Do you want some coffee?"

"Sounds good," said Alex.

I couldn't get the image of Taye's dead hand out of my head. I needed to distract myself. The memory was unbearable.

"We need to come up with a plan," I said. "Thor's been a step ahead of us at every turn. He kidnapped Taye from prison before we could talk to him. He knew when I was going to arrive at the airport—and which airport I was coming to—and kidnapped me. He knew you were trying to speak to Phillip."

"And shot him," added Alex.

"Right." I looked at the floor.

"Sorry," said Alex. "It's been a long day."

"We can't stop this nightmare until we get ahead of him. We need to get in front of this."

"Any ideas on how to do that?" Alex asked.

"There's only one thing Thor wants: Gaia."

"That's Taye's program?"

"Yes."

"The one that kills people."

"I still don't know what it does yet. I have no idea what Taye did to break it before crashing my party on Wall Street. Maybe he modified it so that it can't cause any more deaths. I'm not even sure that Gaia *is* causing these deaths. Maybe the last couple of years have just been a statistical anomaly. It seems a little out there that one computer program could kill so many people without anybody realizing it."

"So what are you proposing?"

"We turn Gaia on."

"I thought you didn't know how."

"I stumbled on something just before Thor's thugs interrupted me. I noticed a series of changes to the code that didn't seem to be affecting anything functional."

Alex looked at me as puzzled as ever.

"I wanted to know why those changes were being made, but the comments in the commit history didn't make any sense either."

"Commit history?"

"It's like a journal the programmer keeps while changing the code."

"Okay."

"Well, they didn't make sense until I took the first word from every commit and strung them together. Taye left me a clue. Took a while to stumble across it, but I found it. He told me how to get Gaia working again."

"And you're sure that you should?"

"No. But what else are we going to do? We have no evidence to take to the police. We just have a lot of speculation. I mean, you were a cop. What would you do if we came in with our story?"

"There's Taye's body," said Alex. "But they've probably already moved it. I'm sure the closet was a short-term solution."

"And if we tell them to look for Taye's body and they don't find it, the rest of our story will be written off, too. Turning on Gaia is the only thing we can do. At least then we'll have leverage. We'll have something Thor wants, and then he might finally make a mistake."

Alex thought about this for a long moment.

"And are you okay with risking people's lives if you turn this thing on? You would be responsible."

I thought about this. What else could I do? I had no other option. Maybe Taye had incapacitated Gaia's killing abilities. I had to believe that was what he had done.

The kid had given his life to stop Gaia. He wouldn't have just given me the ability to turn a killing machine back on. There had to be a bigger plan.

"I don't think it will kill anybody," I said.

"If you're sure about it." said Alex.

I sat at my home computer and began typing. It only took a few minutes to download Gaia and make the modifications from Taye's hidden instructions.

"Here goes nothing," I said. I pressed return and the screen pinged.

"What happened?" Alex asked.

"That's weird."

I set everything up again and pressed return. Another ping.

"Is everything okay?" asked Alex.

I ran a diagnostic scan and realized why it wasn't working.

"Well, I can't start Gaia," I said.

"Why not?"

"Because someone else already has."

Chapter 43

Thor's secretary had gone home hours ago, so Doug rushed into his office without so much as a knock.

"Is it true? You did it? Gaia's up again?" Doug asked.

Thor nodded and then explained, "Just as I expected, Luna knew more than she was letting on. We were listening as she said where to look to get Gaia running. Before she could even turn Gaia on herself, our team had it operational."

"And the modifications we discussed?"

"That will take more time. Even though Gaia is running now, it seems to be very different than it was before. Making changes is going to take some time, but the major blocker is behind us now."

"Good, good. Can we at least use Gaia to deal with Luna, Phillip, and the ex-cop?"

"Not until we make those changes."

"And how long will that take?"

"Maybe a few days."

"Then we'll need to do it the old-fashioned way. No loose ends. Send in your best men and get it done quickly and quietly. Do it tonight. Make sure it looks like an accident. We don't need any more attention on us."

"Understood."

Doug hated the idea of counting his chickens before they were hatched, but he was proud. This was it. His life's work laid out in front of him. The tool that he was always meant to use to do the job he was always intended to perform. His dad would've been proud. He was proud of himself. At least, that's what he thought this feeling was. He imagined himself having coffee with his dad. Explaining how well this had all gone. And he could picture his father patting him on the back. Too bad he couldn't actually share this moment with anyone.

Of course, there was Thor. And that meant more to him now than it used to. But it didn't give him the sense of accomplishment that he longed for. And he couldn't very well throw himself a party for having created the best and most efficient killing machine in history. The least detectable one.

He thought about how much he had matured since the day he'd watched his dad hang himself. How much he had changed. Back then, he was just a kid who had peed his pants. Now he was a man. An ingenious man, who could plan the most amazing ideas and bring those plans to fruition. They would write about him in history books. If people knew. But no. The meek shall inherit the earth. Let what was written come to pass. That's where so many others had gone wrong. He wasn't going to let his ego get in the way anymore. He had transcended his ego. That's the part his dad would have liked best.

Chapter 44

Alex started freaking out. I couldn't understand what the big deal was. He grabbed me by the shoulder and pulled me away from the computer. He dragged me to the bathroom and turned on the shower.

He whispered in intense fury, "We have to go. Now."

"Slow down, slow down. What's going on?"

"You said it yourself. They've been one step ahead of us at every turn."

"Yes, so?"

"And now Gaia's running."

"Right."

"They're watching us. Your place is bugged. Come on, we've got to go."

Shit. He was right. Somehow, Thor had bugged my apartment. He'd heard everything. I had no idea what to do. Listen to my instincts? Run. Listen to my brain? Stay and figure out what Gaia was up to. From what I could tell, it was killing people. I needed to make some calls. After all, just a few days ago, I was CEO of this company.

"No, I need to stay," I said.

"Luna, don't be crazy. Listen to me. We need to go. You said it yourself—you only have leverage so long as they can't get Gaia working. They got Gaia working. You're disposable to them now."

"They're not going to kill me."

"Don't be stupid, Luna. You know too much. If they're willing to kill millions, they'll kill you too."

"If they're killing millions with my company, then I would rather die than let that continue. I have to stop them. If you're not willing to help me, I understand. But I need to know more."

"If you don't let me keep you alive, you won't be able to stop them. Luna, we have to go—*now.*"

"Fine. Just check let me check one last thing."

Alex rolled his eyes. "You have thirty seconds."

I ran to the computer and typed as fast as I could. Alex went to the window.

"They're here," he shouted.

"What?" My heart was pumping like a diesel engine.

"They're here. Hurry up."

"So soon?"

"They probably sent these guys right after you told me how to get Gaia working. Come on, we don't have time for this, we need to get out of here."

"I just need to do one more thing."

A window shattered. I heard a hissing noise. I wondered if that was what a silencer sounded like. Alex tapped nervously on my desk.

"Okay, okay. Done. Let's go."

Chapter 45

Chelsea Moore had finally made it. After years of hard work and more debt than she cared to admit, she was now teaching fourth grade. This had been her dream since she was in fourth grade herself. Fourth grade was the year she fell in love with books. One of those competitions to read ten books in ten weeks. Most of her classmates complained about it, but at the end of those ten weeks, Chelsea discovered that she was, in fact, a bookworm. *The Little Prince, The Chronicles of Narnia, The Giver, A Wrinkle in Time.* She couldn't get enough. She loved to read. And she wanted to share her love of reading with as many other fourth graders as she could.

Getting to this moment hadn't been particularly easy for her, either. Her love of books consumed her. She didn't find much time for socializing and had never had a boyfriend. She didn't need one. Rochester, Darcy, and Heathcliff were there for her whenever she needed them. And they'd never let her down. They'd never judge her because of her Troll doll collection. Or for how much coffee she drank.

And the children. Fourth grade was such a magical time to be a child. Old enough to start comprehending things like books, but still so young and innocent. None of the children would ever judge Chelsea. They would love her. And she would love them all so much. Yes, she was sure of it. This was her life's purpose. This was what she was meant to do on this little blue dot.

This was the first day of the first class that was truly her own. Her practicum was officially over. She had shadowed a few other teachers, and now the training wheels were finally off. Her heart could hardly contain her excitement. She'd spent the last week staying up late, thinking about how she was going to welcome her children. She was going to give them all big hugs and make them feel warm and happy.

She decorated her classroom with all sorts of fun knickknacks and treasures for the kids to discover. She hid a full set of *Toy Story* toys in various places throughout the room. They could do a treasure hunt to collect them all. She had found a huge bag of them at Goodwill for four dollars and couldn't believe her luck.

As the kids filed into the room, Chelsea wanted to cry tears of joy. Her heart skipped a beat or two. She welcomed them each one at a time, making sure they all felt special and appreciated. Then, when they were all settled into their seats and the bell rang, she began class.

"Hello, everyone. I'm so glad you're all here. My name is Ms. Moore."

She turned around to the blackboard, reached up high, and began to write. As she did, she recited the letters out loud.

"M-S. M-O—"

She couldn't breathe. There was a sharp pain in her arm. Maybe she had stretched her arm too far. Not on her first day. She wouldn't let the children see her in pain.

"O-O-R—"

Chelsea Moore grabbed her arm and fell to the floor. After a few moments of shock, the children began to scream.

"9-1-1. What's your emergency?"

"One of our teachers is having a heart attack," said the assistant principal. "Please send an ambulance to Monroe Middle School as quickly as possible."

Ancien's voice recognition API processed the words "heart attack" within a fraction of a second. The police department had finished integrating Ancien's flagship installation of their Emergency Response Machine Learning Operating System into their call center last month. Palo Alto was gifted the system free of charge. The system could semantically assist with the emergency management system, offering the operator instructions and options for handling any emergency.

Instructions immediately popped on the operator's screen.

"Is she breathing?"

"Yes. Please, just send an ambulance."

The operator pressed the button on the screen that was supposed to send a prioritized request to the first responders. But Gaia had been watching this emergency since it heard the phrase "heart attack." After all, at 36 percent, heart attacks were the largest single cause of death each year.

Gaia's neural networks had experimented with various amounts of delay when intercepting these first responder calls. The longer the delay, the greater the likelihood of death. Certainly, it would have been easiest to prevent the call from going through, but that would present two big problems. First, Gaia's intervention would easily be detected, and Gaia had been specifically programmed to avoid human detection. Second, Gaia was programmed to increase the death rate in small, steady increments. If Gaia stopped all first responders from answering heart attacks, the death rate from heart attacks would skyrocket. Then, to prevent human detection, it would have to skyrocket other causes of death by a similar percentage.

Neither of these scenarios was ideal, so instead, Gaia held back the message for ten minutes. A ten-minute delay would increase the mortality rate of a heart attack by 30 percent. This didn't make heart attacks deadly enough to affect enough change. But it was a start. Gaia might have to intervene again if Chelsea Moore ended up being routed to a hospital running Ancien Machine Learning Medical Assistants. Of course, Gaia had long before made sure that those hospitals were preferred; eventually, any hospital not running Ancien would be forced either to upgrade to Ancien software or to go out of business.

"Where the hell is the ambulance?" yelled the assistant principal.

"Please, stay calm. They're on their way. Is CPR still being performed?"

"Yes, yes. Please just get help here soon."

Chapter 46

"A Heath Lemming is here for you, sir. Says he has an appointment, but I don't have anything on the books."

The message came from the intercom. Thor pressed the button and replied, "Yes, tell him to wait."

"I thought you had this under control," said Doug. "Now you're saying Luna's disappeared?"

"Yes, when my team got to Luna's house, nobody was there. They looked for clues to where she might have gone. We listened to the recordings in the house. It sounds like they figured out we were listening."

"You're going to have to find her. Do you understand? This needs all of your resources. This could ruin everything. She knows far too much now."

"Of course, Doug. You keep assuming I'm a fucking retard. Stop treating me like a child. I've done everything I promised I would when we started. Every time there's been a problem, who fixes it? Me. So back off. I've got this under control. We will find her, and we will take care of her. Please leave so I can run this business."

Doug was boiling with anger. He did not appreciate being spoken to like this. But Thor had a point. He had been getting results. The problem was, Doug had learned before that past performance was not always a good indicator of future performance. He wanted to trust Thor, but he couldn't let himself. However, he was out of energy. He decided to let Thor win this battle, and he left the room. Heath entered.

"I'm here," said Heath.

"Good, I'm glad. You're just in time. There's a project I'm going to need your help with. But before we move forward, I need to know something."

Heath sat down in front of Thor's desk. The man was imposing, but he looked more frazzled than the other times Heath had seen him. Like he hadn't slept in days.

"Sure, of course. You can ask me anything."

"I need to know that you have no attachments to Luna Valencia. You were her lawyer, after all. She's young. Beautiful. I wouldn't blame you if you had feelings for her. But if you do, you need to tell me so right now. Before we move forward."

Heath laughed.

"Sir, Luna is absolutely not my type. I mean, look at me. Do I look like the kind of guy who has a problem getting women? I'm a heartbreaker, not a guy who falls for every girl I run into."

"So you have absolutely no attachments to Luna Valencia?"

"No."

"Good. Then your first job is to find Luna and bring her back to me."

"No problem, sir."

Chapter 47

I was on the run again. However, if there was any-one in the world I could choose to be on the lam with, it would be Alex. He was always so calm and col-lected.

The day before, we had narrowly escaped by ducking into the courtyard and running into a neighbor's yard. Alex took my phone and threw it into a koi pond. I was mad at first—there were phone numbers on there that I had never memorized. But who knew if Ancien was tracking me through my GPS? And at least Alex still had his phone.

We found an ATM at a 7-Eleven, and I withdrew as much cash as I could. Then Alex tore my credit card from my hands. I was afraid he was going to throw it away, but he didn't. He just didn't want me using it out of habit. He put the card in his back pocket, in case it became absolutely essential that we use it.

From there on, we no longer left a digital trail. We paid for two rooms at a cheap motel in cash. We used fake names. But I didn't get much sleep. Every time I heard a noise, I thought someone was about to break down the door and kill me. It got so bad that I knocked on Alex's door. I was glad when he opened it. We shared some whiskey from the minibar.

In the morning, we checked out of the motel. Alex told me to take everything because we weren't coming back. I laughed. I had nothing to take. We got breakfast at Denny's. I hadn't eaten at a Denny's since I was a kid. I got a Grand Slam with bacon and French toast. Alex just drank coffee. He made me feel so safe. The only other man to make me feel so safe was my dad.

During breakfast, Alex got a phone call from Heath. He wanted to meet. Alex didn't seem to think it was a good idea, but Heath had been shot at, too—just the same as Phillip and Alex. He was one of the good guys. Or at least, he wasn't a bad guy. Besides, at this point, we needed all the help we could get. They decided to meet at noon at a coffee shop in East Palo Alto.

We took a taxi. It was dirty and smelly inside. The Starbucks was in bad shape, too. Alex had picked one of the worst areas to meet, but I was sure he had his reasons. We waited for fifteen minutes before Heath finally arrived.

"Sorry I'm late," Heath said. "Traffic."

He still had a big fake grin on that handsome, chiseled face. He was as self-assured as I remembered him.

"Luna, it's so good to see you. It's been too long," continued Heath.

"Good to see you, too."

"And, Alex, I'm sorry we got split up after the shooting."

"Why did you want to meet, Heath?" Alex's tone surprised me.

"I wanted to make sure you're okay. I've been thinking about you. How have you been?"

"You could have asked me over the phone. I'm only going to ask this one more time, Heath. Why did you want to meet in person?"

"I need you guys to know that Ancien is after you, Luna."

"Yeah, we know that already," I said. "They almost got us, too. Last night."

"You need to come with me," said Heath. "We can stay at my hotel until we get this straightened out."

"That's not going to happen," said Alex. "Come on, Luna, we're going."

"Wait," said Heath. "Don't go. I can help you get out of this mess. But we need to work together. I have an idea, but you have to trust me."

Alex grabbed my arm, but I pulled away.

"No, I want to hear what he has to say."

"Luna, there's only one person you can trust, and that's me. Remember the last time I told you we needed to go?"

"It seems like that's all you tell me to do. Listen, go warm up the car. I'll be there in thirty seconds."

Alex was about to refuse, but I interrupted.

"Thirty seconds. I promise."

He relented.

"So," I said to Heath. "You've got thirty seconds."

"You can't trust him, Luna. I know you think you can, but I'm still your lawyer. Is he the one who convinced you it was a good idea to skip bail?"

He didn't exactly convince me to do it. It was my idea. He'd just helped me see the wisdom of committing a felony. When I thought of it that way. I nodded.

"Look, I'm sure you two have been through a lot. I know a lot of crazy stuff is going on, but you need to come with me. You need to trust me. I've been looking for you ever since New York." I pointed to my watch. "No, I need more time," said Heath. "Time to explain. Please, come with me. I can tell you more in the car."

I thought about it for a moment. He was clearly sincere in his concern. He meant every word. I could usually tell when people were lying to me. If he was lying, he was doing a damn good job of it. But words are just words. Heath was right about one thing. Alex and I had been through a lot recently. And his actions made it clear to me whose side he was on.

"Your thirty seconds are up," I said.

"Luna, please. Don't."

"I'm sorry, but for what it's worth, I do believe you're on my side. I think."

Chapter 48

When Chelsea Moore was admitted to the Stanford University Hospital at nine forty in the morning with acute myocardial infarction, nurse Helen Hope knew instinctively that she was going to need a bypass. She paged Dr. Julio Fernandez, the best cardiothoracic surgeon they had. It was unusual for a woman of Chelsea's age to have a heart attack, but given her weight, it was also not a complete surprise.

Helen knew Chelsea's weight was going to cause some complications, both in surgery and recovery. But her young age should compensate for any problems. She had a good chance of surviving this. But if she didn't get herself into better shape, she probably wouldn't survive another such attack. Helen hoped Dr. Fernandez would put in a pacemaker, just in case she didn't lose the weight.

By lunchtime, Ms. Moore was out of surgery and Dr. Fernandez was working on another heart attack case. This time it was an eighty-five-year-old man with no insurance, who probably wouldn't make it.

"Ms. Moore? Can you hear me?"

Helen's voice was soft and kind. Ms. Moore opened her eyes slowly and looked around.

"Do you know where you are?"

She shook her head.

"You're at the hospital. You had a heart attack. You had triple bypass surgery, but you're okay. You're in recovery now."

Ms. Moore tried to speak, but her mouth was too dry. Helen handed her a cup of water with a tiny straw. She sucked at it and smiled.

"Take it easy. You've still got some heavy drugs in your system."

"My kids?"

"You have children? We're trying to contact—"

"No. No children. First day."

"Calm down, Ms. Moore. We'll take care of you. You're in good hands here."

Helen looked over at the monitors. The new Ancien EKG Machine Learning API had been trained on millions of example graphs just like these. It had taken decades for the technology to improve to the point that computers were better than doctors at reading these graphs. But now the accuracy was undeniable. Like Chess and Go before it, computers were now better at playing these games than the best human counterparts. Next to the charts, Ancien reported its opinion of the current patient's health and recommendations for how to proceed.

Heart Rate: Nominal
Blood Pressure: Nominal/Slightly Low
Breathing: Nominal
Oxygen Levels: Nominal
Overall Health: Nominal
Recommendation: In 2 minutes, administer 10 units IV bolus of reteplase

Helen didn't trust the machines, even though they hadn't yet given her a reason to doubt them. So far, they had been incredibly accurate. The closest thing to a mistake she'd encountered was when one of the machines recommended putting a newborn under the bilirubin therapy light. The child's skin was as clear as a peeled apple—no yellow pigment at all. She decided to ignore the recommendation. But when she checked in half an hour later, sure enough, the kid was as yellow as a lemon. She put the baby under the light and everything ended up fine, but she did wonder how she had missed it earlier.

The idea of computers trained to recognize human health problems bothered her for reasons she couldn't explain. Most of the doctors loved the machines. They trusted them almost without question. But Helen sat and watched the graphs for herself. Just in case. She was terrified of the day they would remove the charts altogether.

The graphs looked all right. She administered the recommended ten units of reteplase into the IV and went to check on the next patient.

Chapter 49

"The team's having trouble with the changes you requested," said Thor. He hadn't shaved since New York, and it was starting to show. His beard was coming in as blond as the cropped hair on his head.

"Troubles?" asked Doug.

"Yes. Both technical and moral," said Thor. He'd ordered security to make a private walking path. After all, Luna had built a grand campus for walking. It was a shame to put it to waste. Thor wasn't so much mimicking Steve Jobs as he was keen to enjoy the sun and fresh air.

"Moral?"

"You're surprised? The team was never intended for assassinations," said Thor. He had ensured that no employees would be allowed near the path during this time of day; he could talk freely without worrying about anyone overhearing.

Doug's ears turned red. Thor noticed and decided to continue with his explanation.

"The team we put in place after Taye's initial success was made up of the best minds we could find. You can't be surprised that some of them ended up having a conscience."

"I thought you paid them not to have a conscience. That was our plan, wasn't it?"

"Well—"

"Well? Was it or wasn't it?"

"It's not that easy." Thor hated that he was losing control of the discussion. Doug had been pulling the strings for far too long now. It was about time he paid a little more respect to the man who was making all this happen. "Look, I told them when I hired them that this was the only fair and just way to handle population control."

"They don't know the real reason?" Doug asked.

"They don't need to. It's easier this way. For them and me. Most of these guys think they're doing a good thing."

"They *are* doing a good thing."

They passed the turtle pond. Thor had had the turtles removed when he created this walking route. He didn't like animals that moved so slowly.

"Look, Doug. I do plenty of things you don't tell me to do. If you had to tell me, then quite frankly, I wouldn't be the right man for the job. If I had to pass every single decision through you, we wouldn't be here in the first place."

"Fine, then let's kill half the team. The ones most morally opposed. I assure you, the other half will get in line quickly."

"That's not the only problem. There's also the technical issue. Gaia's not the same as when we started. The code we now have makes almost no sense to anyone on the team. Even our best guy can't make heads or tails of it. We don't know how to change it."

"Is it even working?"

"Yes. It's difficult to get hard data this early, but preliminary data suggests it does seem to be working. We've been monitoring daily death statistics from local hospitals, and there has definitely been an increase in just the last day. We have to watch for a few more days to be sure it isn't a statistical fluke, and then, at the end of the month, we can check the bigger death statistics."

"Good," said Doug. "The ability to target specific people was a stretch goal, but it's becoming increasingly important. Just look at the situation with Luna."

Thor kicked a rock off the path, as they headed for the walk around the small, man-made lake.

"I know, I know. We've been looking for her."

"If Gaia could target her, we wouldn't need people to look for her."

"She's off the grid. Even Gaia wouldn't be able to find her."

"We'll see when you get the job done. Find a way to motivate them. We can't have loose ends like Luna just walking around, ready to spoil everything we've worked so hard for."

"Speaking of which," said Thor, "I think it's time to move to the next stage of the plan."

"It's not time yet."

"I think it is."

Thor picked up his pace. Doug kept up.

"Who hired who here? You do what I say, when I say it."

"I think it's about time you considered me a partner in this operation."

"Partner?"

Thor stopped short. They were on the far side of the lake by now. A bird was singing. Thor wanted to find that bird and kick it.

"It's not that hard to imagine, is it? With what we're about to do in the next stage of Gaia, there will be plenty of money to share between the two of us."

"Share?"

"Are you a fucking parrot all of a sudden?"

The bird sang louder.

"Kill Luna," said Doug. "Then we can talk about a partnership."

Thor was prepared for this moment. His men were in place. He'd orchestrated the conversation with Doug perfectly. He picked up his phone, then dialed a number that wasn't in his contact list.

"Take her out. Now."

Chapter 50

"You know, I want to thank you, Alex. You've been a great friend to me these last few days. After you start a company, it can be hard to make new friends."

Alex was driving us to the hospital to check on Phillip. It was a big risk since Alex had seen Thor at the hospital, but I convinced him it was worth it. Thor had been two steps ahead of us at every turn. The only way to beat him was with information. And there were precious few ways for us to get more information without being discovered. However, getting to the hospital was taking forever. Rush hour traffic combined with a crash on El Camino Real. I'd told Alex I should drive—after all, I knew all the back streets, but he was as stubborn as I was and already sitting in the big chair.

"I have trouble believing that. Big-time CEO. I bet you have a million friends."

"You know the cliché about women in business?"

"Not really."

"Well, they say to get ahead in business, you need to stand up for yourself. In a man, that's called confidence. In a woman, it's called—"

"Confidence."

I laughed.

"I wish more people thought like you in this world, Alex."

We finally pulled up to the wreck. It was a doozy. Three-car pileup. A mother was holding her infant child and screaming at a teenage driver, who I gathered caused the wreck.

"Well, I hope you're okay. Your insistence on going to the hospital makes me worried."

"No, I'm fine."

I smiled. I hadn't stopped to think how close Alex and I had become. I didn't know if I could have done any of this without him. I thought about how depressed I had been before all this madness began. It wasn't just that I was lonely. It was that I didn't have anything to do. Everyone at work knew I was the lame duck. And they treated me like it.

I'd heard the things people called me behind my back. The office chatter. When I was put on the cover of

Wired, everyone wanted to take selfies with me to send to their friends. But now they wouldn't even say hello to me in the halls.

Ancien was my baby. I had given everything to create it out of nothing. And I employed these people at above-market salaries and great stock options. And this was how they repaid me? By treating me like I was a ghost?

Then my passenger-side window shattered onto my lap. The door was intact. Nobody had run into us. I wondered if a bird had flown into my window or something.

"Get down," yelled Alex.

I ducked into his lap. I heard two shots whiz over my head. Alex hit the gas and pulled onto the curb, honking wildly for pedestrians to get out of the way.

"How did they find us?" I shouted back.

"I told you we shouldn't have met with Heath. He's one of them."

Another shot shattered the back window. Alex pulled into a side street. An old lady was crossing in the middle of the road. Alex held the horn, yelling at her to move. I stuck my head up and looked back. A black Ford Crown Victoria turned the corner at high speed. The old lady hurried as fast as she could. Alex drove onto the opposite sidewalk, speeding past her. She flipped us off, screaming something.

"I said keep your head down," Alex yelled at me. But before I folded down to hide again, I saw something that terrified me. Two families—five small children, two mothers, and two fathers—were crossing the street ahead of us. They were lined up like the Beatles on Abbey Road, and Alex was not slowing down. In fact, he was speeding up.

"Slow down. Alex, those are children."

He honked even more frantically than with the old lady. The kids stared at us in shock. I turned around and saw the Crown Vic closing in on us.

"Alex, no."

The kids weren't moving. The parents were screaming at them to run. We were feet away now. Alex jerked the wheel sharply to the right, and we popped up on the sidewalk, straight into a grassy park. At this point, Alex just held down the horn. People dove out the way like they were receivers diving for a Hail Mary touchdown.

Alex jerked the wheel again and turned back onto the pavement. I heard sirens in the background. I was a fugitive in New York, and now I was going to become a fugitive in California, too—if I survived, which was looking increasingly less likely.

The Crown Vic had caught up to us. I could see the driver. He seemed calm, as though he had done this sort of thing before. He slammed his car into ours. Alex screamed. The car spun. It was like a roller coaster ride from hell.

Our car finally came to a stop. I could hear the sirens getting louder. I saw the driver calmly get out of the Crown Vic, a long gun in hand. He turned to me. I tried to unbuckle myself, but my seat belt was stuck. I looked over at Alex. He was slumped over.

"Alex. Alex."

No response. The man reached my door. He was dead calm, eyes cold and empty. Like he was bored—like he was tired of having to kill people all the time. He pointed the gun straight at my face. The world stopped moving. I could swear the birds froze mid-flight.

I squeezed my eyes shut as hard as I could, wishing I could just wake up. Wishing this was all just a bad dream. The worst dream I'd ever had in my life. I swore to God if I could just wake up, I would be a better person. Then I heard a thud and screeching tires.

I opened my eyes. It wasn't a nightmare. I was still here. But the man wasn't. Then I saw Heath.

"Luna, you okay?" he asked. "Come on. Let's go."

Chapter 51

Helen checked Ms. Moore's vital signs. She was crashing. What had gone wrong? She'd been fine just thirty minutes ago. Damn Dr. Fernandez for not installing that pacemaker. He worked too many hours and probably skipped it so he could meet his girlfriend for drinks. Helen paged him anyway. It would serve him right to have to cut his social life short.

"What's going on here?" came a voice from the hall. "I just checked on her a few minutes ago," said Dr. Fernandez, dashing into the room. "She was doing fine."

Helen bit her tongue. She might have been wrong about him going home early but not about him pulling too many hours.

"No idea. She started crashing when I walked in," said Helen. Chelsea began coding. Helen instinctively began doing CPR. Dr. Fernandez looked at the Ancien-powered device next to Chelsea's vital signs.

"Give her one milliliter of epinephrine," said Dr. Fernandez.

"Now?"

"Yes, now," said Dr. Fernandez, indignantly. "Hurry."

Against her better instincts, Helen stopped administering CPR and injected the epinephrine. They both stood there and waited. They watched the vital signs on the Ancien dashboard. Nothing.

"Come on, come on, come on," said Dr. Fernandez. Was that a bead of sweat on his forehead?

"Should I get the charging paddles ready?"

The doctor checked the screen. Helen already knew what it was suggesting. She'd read it already.

"No, let's wait a few more seconds."

Helen bit her lip. She had seen so many patients code before. She knew the steps. Knew the order. Give CPR a chance. Then electricity. Only when that failed were they supposed to give the patient epinephrine.

"There we go," yelled Dr. Fernandez. The heartbeat stabilized. Ms. Moore was alive again. "And that is the last time I will have you questioning my decisions."

"You mean Ancien's decisions. You think that you would have skipped over CPR and electroshock therapy that quickly if the computer hadn't told you to?"

"It worked, didn't it? Look, I'm her doctor, and ultimately it's my call. If you can't deal with that—"

"What? Go ahead. Finish your sentence."

"Don't question me again. Are we clear?"

Helen wanted to smack him so hard. She wanted to knock a tooth out. She wanted to leave a big mark. Something to remember her by.

"Yes, sir. We're clear. I'm sorry," she said as she shoved past him through the door. Helen was fuming. This was not how doctors should act. This was not the kind of treatment Ms. Moore deserved. And at a teaching hospital no less. These kids were being trained from med school to trust these machines above their own instincts. Soon medical students wouldn't feel the need to study so hard. Why bother, when the machines will tell them what to do? That was the problem with this whole generation. Kids didn't need to learn to read maps anymore; everybody used GPS all the time. They didn't need to know how to do math anymore; their phones were sophisticated calculators. They didn't need to learn history when they could Google everything.

She paced up and down the hall to blow off some steam. As far as Helen was concerned, this whole world was going crazy. The brains of everyone from children to esteemed doctors were rotting. And people were complicit in this. They welcomed it with open arms.

Helen wasn't going to be part of the welcoming party. She was determined—even if it meant she was the last one standing—not to trust these machines. She was going to keep doing things the old-fashioned way. And when she couldn't do that anymore, she planned to pass on those ways to as many open minds as she could reach. She was not going to let humanity forget how to take care of itself. Not as long as she was alive, at least.

"Helen." She froze like she'd been caught.

"Oh, Deputy Reynolds. You scared me. Is everything all right?"

"No. My replacement's late and I need to use the bathroom. Would you mind?"

"Of course, of course," said Helen. She flipped through some papers in her hands. "I was just about to check on Mr. Jones, anyway."

"You're a doll," said the deputy as he shuffled off toward the restroom.

Helen went into Mr. Jones's room and began talking to him—something she did with all the comatose patients.

"Mr. Jones, how are you feeling today?"

She glanced at his vitals and made some notes in her chart. Phillip Jones's eyes were closed, and his breathing was slow and steady. Helen took out her stethoscope and listened to his chest and bowels.

"Everything looks good. You're doing great. Sorry to bother you. I'll just change your IV fluids and let you get back to sleep."

Helen got a fresh bag of saline solution. She carefully removed the nearly empty bag and placed it on the bed as she hooked up the new one.

"Oh my, it looks like we need to replace your colostomy bag, too. I'll be right back."

Helen was about to leave the room when she heard something hitting the ground behind her. She turned and saw Mr. Jones's hand dangling from the bed and the empty bag on the floor.

"Mr. Jones?"

His eyelids began to flutter.

Chapter 52

I begged Heath for hours to go back and get Alex, but he said we couldn't. That it would be too big of a risk. But I felt I was risking everything every moment I was away from him. Heath took me back to his hotel suite to rest. I slept only a few minutes at a time, between obsessively checking the news to see if I could learn anything more about Alex's condition. The news mentioned a crash and fatality on El Camino Real, but nothing about any guns, and they were not releasing names. It was driving me mad.

I called the local hospitals. But I couldn't remember Alex's last name. And trying to describe him wasn't getting me anywhere. Heath didn't sleep, either. He was working on something on his laptop, letting me freak out in peace.

"What are you working on, anyway?" I finally asked. "And how did you know I was about to be killed?"

"I followed you from the coffee shop," Heath said, not bothering to look up from his laptop.

"Why?"

"I told you, I don't trust Alex. I'm your lawyer. It's my duty to protect you."

I laughed.

"You're my lawyer, not my bodyguard."

He looked up at me with eyes full of something I couldn't place. Then he shrugged.

"Luna, you know you're knee-deep in shit, don't you? You're in the crosshairs of some very nasty people. You can't trust anyone."

"Can I trust you?"

He stared at me in silence for a long moment.

"Of course you can. I'm your lawyer."

"You keep saying that like it means something. If memory serves, you're technically Ancien's lawyer, aren't you? I mean, it's Ancien paying the bills, not me, right?"

He didn't respond. He went back to typing.

"I want to go," I said. "I need to go—now."

"No. As I said, we're waiting here for a while."

"Waiting for what?"

"For it to be safe."

"For who? I want to go." I stood up. "I'm going, and you can't stop me."

Heath slammed his laptop shut and got up.

"Fine. Fine. Where do you want to go?"

"The hospital in Stanford. I need to check on a friend."

There was a knock at the door. I saw Heath look toward the door, his eyebrows furrowed. My heart skipped a beat. My mouth felt like I'd been chewing a large ball of tinfoil.

As Heath went to see who it was, I ran to the bathroom. I kept the door open a crack so I could see. Peeking through the slit, I saw Heath checking the peephole. He kept the chain on as he opened the door.

"Room service, sir. I was just checking to see if you needed a fresh pot of coffee."

"No, thank you, we were just about to leave."

Heath started to close the door, but the man stuck his foot in the crack.

"Are you sure? I have a fresh pot right here. I was told to come by at six every day."

Heath looked confused, then all at once he seemed to understand. He grabbed something from his pocket. I couldn't see what it was, but I assumed it was cash. He stuffed it through the door, and the foot disappeared. Heath shut the door.

"Where'd you go, Luna? Are we going to the hospital or not?"

I flushed the toilet and ran some water in the sink. I splashed my face.

"I'm ready when you are," I called back.

Chapter 53

"We did it," said Thor, stepping out of a black car onto the runway. "You were right. With the right incentives in place, our programmers cracked it. We call the feature Gaia's Wrath. With it, we can now target anyone in the world."

Doug's smile widened until he was grinning from ear to ear.

"Have you tried it out yet?"

"No," said Thor. "I wanted you to have the first go at it."

Doug took a deep breath. Once again, the universe had provided. When Thor suggested that Doug joins him on his private jet to Seattle that morning—with the promise of good news—he wasn't expecting news as good as this. Thor was scheduled to meet with Boeing to close a deal that would put Ancien in all their new airliners. Ancien had already proven its value to the aviation industry when it was installed on small private jets built by Cessna.

Thor continued, "So, will this make Gaia's Wrath more valuable for whoever we're selling it to?"

"You keep using the words 'us' and 'we.' Have you forgotten our deal?"

"Of course not. I merely assumed Luna would be the first person targeted by Gaia's Wrath."

"How does it work?"

They stepped onto the jet. It was spacious inside, with four large chairs surrounding a circular oak desk. Thor sat down and pressed his fingers against the desk; a screen rose up and a keyboard was revealed.

"It's easy," said Thor. With a few keystrokes, he pulled up a screen with a single text input. The door of the jet closed, and almost immediately started to taxi to the runway. "You just put a name here."

"What if it's a common name? Like, John Butler. There are probably dozens of John Butlers in the United States alone."

"Collateral damage."

"That's the kind of collateral damage that gets noticed, Thor."

"We'll keep working on it. I don't think there are a dozen Luna Valencias. Go ahead, try it." Thor spun the circular desk toward Doug until his fingers touched the keyboard. The jet pushed with full force as it began its ascent to the clouds. Doug sat quietly. He always enjoyed the feeling of his stomach moving up to his throat.

"So, you never answered my question. Will this make Gaia more valuable?"

Doug laughed.

"What's with your obsession with money, Thor?"

"It's how we keep score, isn't it? It's how we know who's winning."

"And are you, Thor? Winning?"

"Well, I could always be winning by a wider margin."

Doug watched as the plane tore through the layers of morning clouds, and the warm yellow sun shone in through the windows. He stood up and went to the minibar at the back of the plane.

"Is that what you want out of life, Thor? To have the most money? To make your family name mean something again through commerce?"

"Fuck you. What I want is my business. You don't see me trying to butt into your motivations, do you?"

"I guess not. I guess not," Doug mused. He pulled out a bottle of champagne and two glasses and returned to the table. "Is this thing online?"

"What? Gaia's Wrath? Yeah. The plane has a satellite Internet connection. It should be good to go."

"And how long will it take to do the job?"

"Who knows? You'll be the first to find out. It could be minutes or hours. Maybe days. Our team has used Gaia to break into every major healthcare, government, and digital service there is. Gaia's Wrath determines how best to kill efficiently and without being traced. We've never tried to figure out how quickly it does its job before."

Doug poured two glasses of Dom Perignon, vintage 2002.

"Well, it's about time someone found out. Here's to a long and fruitful partnership."

Thor grabbed the glass.

"Here's to Luna Valencia," said Thor.

"I'll toast to that." Doug swirled the glass under his nose and took a small sip. He let the champagne linger on his tongue for a moment before swallowing the bubbles that had waited for so many years to see fresh air— only to be consumed seconds later.

Doug sat down and typed on the keyboard.

Luna Valencia.

He pressed return. The screen seemed to freeze for a moment. Then a confirmation appeared. Doug continued typing.

Phillip Jones.

Doug pressed return and looked up.

"Who was that lawyer representing Luna again?"

"Heath Lemming. Why?"

Doug typed Heath's name and pressed return. Thor's eyes widened.

"Hey, wait. Heath's on our side. He's going to bring Luna to me."

"If this thing works, then he won't need to bring us Luna. If it doesn't work, he still can. Either way, it'll be fine."

"I don't think we should be using Gaia's Wrath without consulting each other first. We don't even know if it works yet."

"Don't worry, partner," said Doug. "It'll be fine. I believed you a few minutes ago when you told me it worked."

Doug looked up at Thor. Thor was staring out the window at Mount St. Helens. Quickly, Doug typed out one last name. He wasn't going to make the same mistake he'd made last time. Collateral damage.

Thor Massino.

Return.

Chapter 54

"Where am I?" asked Mr. Jones.

"You're in the hospital," Helen said. "You've been shot, and you've been in and out of consciousness. But you're doing a lot better now. Take it easy. You still have a long way to go in your recovery."

Mr. Jones closed his eyes and relaxed back into the bed. Helen looked at his vitals. Then she saw Ancien's recommendation. Ten milliliters of penicillin. Strange. Mr. Jones had not been in surgery recently enough for this to make sense. On the other hand, Helen didn't want to skip it. Maybe he had an infection that wasn't going away. Or maybe Ancien was just being careful. She loaded a syringe and pressed out the air. She stuck the needle into the IV line.

Then she felt it. The sting of hypocrisy. She had just been scolding Dr. Fernandez for his dependence on Ancien, and now look at her. It had been a long night, and her shift was almost over. But there was no excuse to be lazy. She removed the needle and lay the syringe down. She took Mr. Jones's chart from the foot of the bed.

"Shit."

She looked over at Mr. Jones and sighed with relief. He was still asleep. She'd almost killed him. He was allergic to penicillin. What had she been thinking?

She looked back at the Ancien screen.

Recommendation: None

Had she imagined it? No, just moments ago it had been telling her to give him penicillin. She would swear to it. Then again, she was tired. Double shifts had been getting harder and harder lately. But this was unforgivable. The fact that she'd been so close to making such a fatal mistake.

The patient rustled awake again.

"Where am I?" he asked a second time.

Once more she told him, "You're in the hospital. You've been shot, but you're doing a lot better now."

This time, he started making an effort to sit up. Helen helped him and put a pillow behind his back.

"Take it easy. You've been through a lot in the last few days."

"I need to see Alex and Heath. Please, it's important. Where are they?"

"Calm down, Mr. Jones. All in good time."

232 | LUCAS CARLSON

"No, I need to see them. Alex Sonne and Heath Lemming. It's a matter of life and death."

"I'll see what I can do."

Helen finished changing the colostomy bag and left the room. She looked at her watch. She was finally done with her second shift. She could leave and let the next nurse deal with Mr. Jones's delirious requests. But there was something about one of the names that made her curious. That first name: Alex Sonne. Where had she heard that name before? Alex. It was her brother's name. Was that why it was so familiar?

She decided to let it go. She went to the locker room and began changing her clothes. She'd debated doing even this much. Considered going home and just collapsing fully clothed. But she had been wearing these clothes for three days in a row. Two days too long.

If it had just been a single shift, she would have looked into the mystery more. But she had no energy left. It would take every ounce of strength she had just to stay awake for the fifteen-minute bus ride home. The mystery could wait until tomorrow. Or the next nurse could deal with it. Or not.

Maybe the next nurse, Jordan, would be just as tired as she was. Maybe he, too, would make promises he wouldn't keep. Pass the buck. Seemed like a favorite pastime. She was dressed now and ready to go, but maybe she would just look into this one thing. At least make a note in the file.

But her legs were moving as if through pure molasses. Her eyes were only half-open. It was going to have to wait. She walked past the nurse's station. She watched as a tall, good-looking man and a striking young Latina woman argued with the head nurse.

"Are you family?"

"No, but you don't understand. I was with him when he was shot. I need to see him," the tall man was saying.

"If that's true, then you can understand why he's under strict guard. We don't know who shot him yet. For all we know, it could have been you."

"I'll sue you for libel. You and this whole hospital."

These arguments never got old. Visitors always felt so entitled. The more they dug their heels in, the more the hospital staff dug in theirs. Helen never understood why they didn't just lie and say that they were family. That way it wouldn't have to escalate. As it was, security would almost assuredly get involved. And it looked like that time was soon approaching. Jordan, the nurse on duty, had that look. He was done arguing.

"Check the list. Look for my name. He probably said it was okay for me to visit."

"Mr. Phillip has been in a coma. He hasn't given us any list. And even if he had—"

"Check my name anyway." Helen had one foot out the door. She knew this was going to end with security dragging this couple away. "Heath Lemming. Please just check for my name."

He picked up the phone. "Security, please come to the nurse's station on level two. Code gray."

"Hey, call off the code gray," Helen called over to Jordan. "I just spoke with Mr. Jones. He was asking to see a Heath Lemming."

Jordan pulled Helen aside and hissed, "I don't care who he asked for. We can't let anyone see Mr. Jones right now. The hospital can't take on the liability. What if this guy is the shooter, here to finish the job?"

"Why would Mr. Jones be asking to see him if he was the attacker?"

"Maybe he doesn't know who attacked him."

Helen leaned and said, "Or maybe it's just this guy's his lawyer here to help him."

Jordan looked over at Heath. "Are you his lawyer?"

Helen nodded vigorously. Heath was looking at her from the corner of his eye.

"Yes," said Heath. "I'm his lawyer. And this is my associate. We're with Bower, Bower, and Nathanson."

"Show me proof."

Heath pulled out his business card and identification. Jordan looked over them carefully. Then up at Heath. Then down at the identification once more.

"And you're sure Mr. Jones asked for him by name? Heath Lemming?"

Helen nodded.

"Do you think he's well enough for visitors?"

Helen nodded. The security guards arrived. They grabbed the man and woman by their arms.

"Do we have a problem here?"

"No, I'm calling off the code gray. But you only have five minutes before I need to kick you out. He needs rest."

"Thank you," the woman said to Helen. Helen nodded and smiled and left the hospital. Mystery solved.

Chapter 55

I walked into the hospital room giddy with excitement.

"Phillip?"

He put down a magazine. "Well, well, well. So she finally comes to check on me."

I ran up to him and gave him an awkward hug, trying to work my arms around the breathing tubes and IV. He pulled the tube out of his nose. I sobbed.

"Hey, hey. None of that now. Glad to see you, too," said Phillip. I could feel him nodding toward Heath.

"Phillip," I said, with tears in my eyes. "I am so, so sorry. You can never under—"

"Hey, stop that. You have absolutely nothing be sorry about."

"If I'd kept a closer eye on things—"

"No."

"But this wouldn't—"

"I'm alive, aren't I? And in no small part thanks to you."

Phillip pointed toward a screen with his vital signs. I hadn't noticed it until now. I'd forgotten that this was our pilot hospital. Ancien was watching over Phillip.

Wait. Ancien was watching Phillip. Which meant Gaia was watching Phillip. I ran over to the wall and unplugged the machine.

"Hey," said Phillip.

The machine interrupted. It didn't turn off as I had expected it to. Rather, it started sounding an alarm. Moments later, the male nurse ran in.

"What's going on here?"

He saw me standing there with the cords still in my hands.

"We need to turn these machines off. How do you turn them off?"

"Okay, that's it. Out. Now."

I kept pulling at the cables, but it wasn't working. There must have been a backup battery in the machine somewhere. New alarms started going off. The cops flanking the door ran in and tore me away.

"Those machines—Phillip, you're not safe here. Ancien is running on those machines."

"Hey, guys, you don't need to grab her like that. I'm her lawyer. We were just about to leave."

Heath put his hand on the shoulder of one of the cops. Immediately, he let go of me and grabbed Heath's arm instead, putting him in an arm lock.

"Assaulting an officer, are we?"

They were dragging us out of the room when I glanced back at the bed. Phillip's eyes were wide. He'd figured it out. I looked back at Heath, who was staring at me. This couldn't happen. There was a warrant for my arrest. I'd be thrown in jail immediately. They started handcuffing us.

"Is this really necessary?" Heath asked. "Are we under arrest?"

"You have the right to remain silent," one of the officers began.

"Aw, shit," yelled Heath. He threw himself against the officer, and they both fell to the ground. The officer behind me ran to help his partner.

"Run, Luna. Go."

I couldn't process what was going on. But somehow my feet were moving. I was going somewhere and fast. Where? I had no idea. Why? Not sure either. When I finally hit the exit, my brain kicked in. Should I stop? Turn around? Maybe it wasn't too late. If I cooperated, maybe they'd understand. Maybe they'd even help.

Wait. Help? Why the hell would they believe me? I had no proof. Everything that had happened transpired over code. Groups of ones and zeroes flying over optic cables, leading countless people to their untimely, un-traceable deaths. There was no smoking gun. There was no body with DNA evidence. It was hard even for me to believe.

I had to run. I had to nail Thor to the bloody wall, or nobody would ever find out. I'd be thrown in jail where I wouldn't be able to do anything to help anyone. Phillip. Alex. Even Heath. Just like Taye. They'd all die in ways I couldn't even imagine. All by my hand. By my company. By my invention. I couldn't let that happen.

"Stop. Stop that woman."

I ran.

Chapter 56

"Did you hear? They got her," Thor said proud-ly.

"I wanted her gone."

"We'll be able to take care of her much more easily now."

The two men strode through an aviation hangar. It reminded Doug of a big-box store, except instead of fur-niture and electronics, this place was full of airplane parts.

Doug had invited himself to the Boeing meeting. The hangar they were walking through reminded Doug of his work at System Inc. His old project and its failure to achieve what he had now accomplished with Ancien. And the fact that he had gotten so close, only for it to fall apart at the last minute. The devil's always in the details. And Luna was one detail that needed dealing with—

quickly. Or Ancien could fall apart just as rapidly as System had.

"I'm losing confidence," said Doug.

Thor sighed loudly. "Give it time. The more we interfere, the more likely this thing will be traced back to us. With deep-learning systems, even the programmers don't know how it works. The program makes decisions in strange ways. You just have to relax and be patient."

Doug wondered when Gaia's Wrath would take Thor out. It had made the flight to Seattle delightfully thrilling. The thought that maybe Gaia's Wrath would somehow take down the plane right then and there. Doug would have been ready, too. He knew where to find the emergency parachutes. Doug knew which exit door he would use. He ran through the whole event in his head. But the flight went smoothly. Had Gaia's Wrath not worked? Did its strange mind somehow come to the conclusion that this way was not quite undetectable enough? Or did it not yet know how to take down a plane? Doug was going to have to talk to the engineers once Thor was out of the way.

"I'm sure you're right."

Even standing near Thor was a thrill. Doug wondered in what form death would come for him. Not only was Thor becoming too big of a liability with his incessant talk of partnership, coupled with that ego that was too big, but Doug longed to see Gaia in action again. He remembered watching the first time he had seen Gaia at work. But that had been a lucky accident at a shipyard. He wanted to see what the world's most powerful and secret killing machine could do. He wanted to be there again. He had to see it again.

Man's ego had created the world's biggest threat ever: overpopulation. Humans kept multiplying like rabbits. And how could it be stopped? Humans had already tried making more food, but while they were creating food in higher quantities, it tasted like cardboard. Doug couldn't stand eating vegetables grown in the United States anymore. And soon, it wouldn't just be the United States. It would be the entire world. He wasn't alone, either. Americans didn't like eating that cardboard, so they just filled themselves with worse things: sugar, salt, and fat.

To Doug, there was no question what had caused the rapid rise in obesity and cancer. It wasn't McDonald's fault. It wasn't Coke. It was humanity's insatiable need to fornicate and reproduce. They created too many babies. That was the root of their problem. The food that was good for them didn't taste good anymore, and that drove the demand for the crappy food.

If Doug were president, he would require citizens to obtain licenses to reproduce. He would make sure prospective parents had enough money to afford the number of children they wanted to raise. Even then, he would need to turn down many requests. The problem had been going on for too long. There were already too many people here. There would need to be a massive population reduction before any new babies could be born.

But Doug knew he wasn't going to become president. At least, he knew he didn't want to try to run for president. Not just yet. And this solution was so much more elegant and efficient. He didn't need anyone's permission. He could manufacture the same outcome without having to jump through any of the hoops.

And all he had to do was let go of his ego. The meek shall inherit the earth. Thor wasn't meek. He wasn't going to inherit a fucking dime.

"Watch out," came a voice from behind them.

A huge box of propellers came crashing down with a thundering noise. Tons of metal scraping, bending in on its own weight against the concrete. Was this it? Doug wondered. Was it happening? His heart fluttered. For about thirty seconds, he and Thor tumbled wildly toward the ground, like two young brothers wrestling. He looked over at Thor, who was lying flat on the floor.

"You okay?"

Please be no. Please be no.

"Yes," said Thor. "I'm fine. That was close." He pushed himself up and brushed himself off.

"Wasn't it?"

"Come on, old man. We're going to be late."

Chapter 57

I wondered just how many jails I was going to see before this whole charade was over. I'd never gotten so much as a speeding ticket before this, and now? How many laws had I broken? I was wanted in two states. How had life turned out like this for me? I was a powerful Latina startup geek. I was on the cover of *Wired*. I wasn't a Thelma or a Louise. Was I?

Speaking of *Thelma and Louise*, I could swear I was sitting next to them in this cell. These two women had been talking nonstop since I got there. They didn't even seem to notice me.

"Luna Valencia?"

I raised my head.

"Your lawyer's here."

My lawyer? Had Ancien already hired another lawyer on my behalf like in New York? How did they even know where I was? I considered telling the guard that I didn't want to see this lawyer.

"Come on, lady. Let's go."

He swung open the door. I stood up slowly, trying to think my way through the problem. If the lawyer did anything funny, I decided I would scream as loudly as I could. This was a police station after all. Someone would hear me. He wouldn't be able to just take me out quickly.

The cop led me down a corridor and pointed at one of the doors. I took a deep breath, thinking maybe I should just start screaming now. Make them take me away from here. To a psych ward somewhere. I'd probably be safer in a padded room than here with an Ancien lawyer.

"Come on, come on. I don't have all day."

With that, the cop swung open the door. I opened my mouth and screamed. But the scream turned into a squeal of joy.

"Heath. What are you doing here?"

He made a shushing sign. "Luna, I'm your lawyer," he said. He thanked the officer, who turned and left, shutting the door. Heath came up to me, and I hugged him tight.

"How are you not in jail?"

"Released on bail. The cops didn't like it one bit, but I've got a clean record. Nothing they could do. Of course, I'll probably be disbarred for what I did to that guy. Technically, I'm probably not even a lawyer right now. But they don't know that."

I hugged him again.

"So when do I get out of here?"

I looked around the room. It was small and looked like it had been built in the sixties—probably hadn't been cleaned since then, either.

"That's not going to be so easy this time. The judge isn't going to look kindly on the fact that you skipped bail in New York."

"So we tell him what's going on. We have to explain this whole situation to someone. Someone has to listen."

"Nobody's going to believe it."

"But it's the truth."

"The truth doesn't matter if we can't prove it. You're going to have to trust me. I've got to go speak with someone."

"Who?"

"I can't tell you."

"Why not?"

"You're going to have to trust me," he repeated.

"I did until just now."

"Just hang tight for few more hours. You're my only priority. I've handed off all my other cases to my colleagues. I'll explain everything to you in due course. I promise. But for now, you'll be safest here. I think. Just sit tight. I have a plan."

Chapter 58

Helen Hope had been asleep for just four hours on Saturday when she was paged. A nurse's husband had died. Nobody else was available. One cold shower, three large coffees, and one hour later, she clocked in for an eight-hour shift. She wasn't supposed to work again until Monday, and she needed the rest. But she also needed the money. So rest would have to wait. At least it wasn't a twelve-hour shift.

She looked over the charts. Not much had changed while she'd been sleeping. But then she saw it.

"Are you kidding me?" she said, nearly dropping her fresh cup of coffee.

Helen raced to find Dr. Cho, Chelsea Moore's primary care physician. Helen was able to catch her as she was heading into the ICU. She was washing her hands.

"Dr. Cho, I think there's been a mistake."

The doctor raised an eyebrow.

"Ms. Moore in 319. It says that she's being prepped for discharge? That can't be right."

"Why not?"

"She's still recovering from a major heart attack. Her heart stopped again last night. She needs to be here another two days at least. For observation."

"Ms. Moore is doing exceptionally well. I reviewed her charts this morning and have been watching her all day. In my opinion, she would recover better at home."

"Did Ancien tell you that?"

Dr. Cho finished scrubbing her arms and dried them off.

"Ancien didn't have to. I've seen more post-op infections caused by people staying in the hospital longer than necessary than I care to count. This place is teeming with germs. Small children visiting their loved ones. Kids are walking Petri dishes—you know that. The sooner we release people, the better for everyone."

"She's not ready."

"That's not your call. Now if you don't mind, I need to check on my double bypass patient. And you need to go help Ms. Moore get out of here. If she's not gone in thirty minutes, she's going to have to pay for another full day in that room."

Dr. Cho went through to the ICU. Helen shook her head but returned to room 319. Chelsea Moore was taking a nap. Helen couldn't bring herself to wake this woman up. After everything she'd been through, Helen couldn't understand why she'd be discharged so quickly.

Helen looked over Ms. Moore's vital signs on the screen. Like Dr. Cho had said, her vitals did indeed look healthy. Much stronger than when Helen had left the hospital a few hours ago. But this poor woman had almost died twice in the last few days. If it happened again and she wasn't already in the hospital, she wouldn't stand a chance.

Helen looked over at the Ancien recommendation. *Prepare for discharge.* Bullshit. That couldn't be right. Something had to be going on here. This poor woman wasn't ready to leave.

Chelsea opened her eyes and yawned.

"Ms. Moore, it's good to see you again."

"Don't you ever leave this hospital?" she asked.

Helen laughed. "It would appear not."

"They told me I'm being discharged."

"Yes, Dr. Cho thinks you're ready. How are you feeling, honey?"

"Tired."

The opiates hadn't even left her system yet, and they wanted her out of here? It made no sense.

"Do you have help at home? Someone who can take care of you? Feed you? Assist you in the bathroom?"

"Not really. I live alone." Her eyes struggled to stay open. "But it's a small apartment. It's not far to the bath-room."

"Do you have someone who can drive you home?"

She shook her head. "But I can call a cab, right?"

This wasn't right. Not right at all.

Chapter 59

Thor kicked over a recycling bin. A homeless man stared from across the road, and Thor flipped him off. He turned his phone back on as he walked away from the Palo Alto Waze office. His phone's incessant pinging during the meeting had distracted him. Thrown him off his game. He'd fired an assistant for sending too many text messages before.

Waze was a Google acquisition for maps. Hadn't been incorporated into their other products, yet. The Waze team was signing a deal to put Ancien into its newest release, but the lawyers had privacy concerns. This was taking too much time.

A horn blared. Tires squealed to a stop. He could smell the burnt rubber.

"Hey," shouted the driver. "Why don't you watch where you're going?"

Thor looked up from his phone. The crosswalk was indeed red. Still, he cursed the driver and kept going.

It was hot. Not a single cloud in the sky. Thor ducked under the shadow of an overhang.

For many, a weekend with lawyers was on par with pulling one's own teeth with a rusty set of pliers. Not for Thor, though. Usually Thor loved it. It was one big power struggle. And power was what Thor knew best. He knew how to manipulate it. How to bend it. How to make others think they had it. Especially when they didn't. That's the thing about power. The more you grabbed at it, the more it slipped away. You couldn't just take power. But you could direct its flow. And the more other people tried to grab it, the easier it was to redirect.

Most lawyers played right into Thor's hands. Lawyers knew the law. Thor knew power.

"Thor," he heard from behind him. He turned his head. It was Heath Lemming.

"Oh, were we supposed to meet now? I'm just—"

"We need to talk. I've got Luna," Heath said.

Thor looked around.

"Where?"

The crosswalk turned red. Even though Thor saw this, he still had an urge to cross.

"I mean, I have her in my control."

"A bit of a stretch, wouldn't you say?"

"I don't know what you plan on doing with her."
Now Heath looked around. People were waiting on the
other side of the street, but nobody was within earshot.
"But I don't think killing her is the best course of action,"
he whispered.

"Heath, how could you accuse me of such a horrible
thing? Why would you think that? All I asked was for
you to find her and bring her to me. I'm just concerned
for my friend and predecessor. I don't know why you're
blowing this out of proportion, but maybe hiring you
wasn't such a good idea after all."

Thor could see beads of sweat forming on Heath's
brow. He didn't know what angle Heath was trying to
play here. Maybe he was recording the conversation.
Trying to get him to confess. If so, it was a rookie mistake—and a deadly one to make with a power player like
Thor.

"Fine, let's do it your way then," said Heath. The light
turned green. Thor nodded. "I think Luna has more value to you alive as part of the company. Rather than separate."

"What about the confidential knowledge she has in
her head? Don't you think that makes her a liability if
she were to unexpectedly leave the company? You
know, of her own accord."

"That's what I mean. I think she's got proprietary information that we still need her to document before she

unexpectedly leaves. And she trusts me. I think if you give me some time, I can help you get that proprietary information. But you can't force her out of the company until we get it."

Classic power move. Thor had been using this technique since he was a kid running garage sales for his parents. When a customer came and asked for a discount, he would say his parents weren't around so he couldn't check with them. The truth was his parents didn't care.

"I think we'll be just fine without her intellectual property."

Thor could sense Heath's attempts to redirect power. People didn't usually try to manipulate others unless they had a good reason to do so. Thor thought through the reasons Heath might have for trying to manipulate him.

"Don't you think the board and stockholders will find it unsettling if Luna just disappears?"

Another power technique. Appeal to authority figures.

"No."

Fuck authority figures. Amateur negotiators always made the mistake of over-explaining their stance. Thor was no amateur. Best to keep it short and simple. Less fodder to pick apart later. Heath was definitely up to something.

Another stoplight. Thor was getting tired of this. He looked to both sides. No cars were coming.

"Look," said Heath. "If you want Luna, you're going to have to go through me. You think you've got everything under control, but you don't. You don't even know for certain where Luna is at this very moment."

That's when Thor realized what was going on. Heath had a thing for Luna after all. He had been her lawyer. There was history. His initial hunch had been correct. Heath wasn't working for him—he was working for Luna.

"Palo Alto Police Department. Right over there," said Thor as he pointed across the street. "Just a few blocks that way, if I'm not mistaken."

"Actually, you *are* mistaken," said Heath.

"Look, I'm tired of playing cat and mouse. You've been helpful, but this isn't working for me anymore."

"But—"

"You're fired, Heath."

And that's how you redirect power. Thor turned around and started walking again. Heath followed him into the middle of the road.

"Thor, wait—"

Thor thought he could physically feel the flow of power shifting toward him at that very moment, right under his own two feet. Pulling in an irreversible new direction with such violent force. The feeling took his breath away. Like flying five feet off the ground. How easy it was. How natural. Just a few words and the world bent to his will. Just a few words and day became night. Light became dark. Life became death. With nothing but a few words.

Chapter 60

It had worked. Thor and Heath were dead. Doug was over the moon. His only regret was that he hadn't been there to see it for himself. How elegant Gaia's Wrath had been. Two for one. Genius. He couldn't imagine how any assassin in history could be as omnipotent. Gaia's Wrath was the Mozart of death. The Einstein of murder.

Of course, Gaia's success meant problems for Doug. Thor, for all his shortcomings, still ran Ancien's day-to-day logistics. Doug had organized an emergency board call for that evening to discuss the matter. It took some cajoling to get a quorum, but in the end, it came together.

"I'd like to call this emergency board meeting of Ancien to order," said Doug, seated behind his desk at his home in Seattle. There wasn't time to fly the board together; a phone call would have to do.

Doug continued, "As you may have heard, our friend and CEO, Thor Massino, was killed today in a tragic accident with a self-driving Chevy Volt. GM released a statement saying it was driver error and not a software glitch."

"Bullshit," came a voice from Doug's speakerphone. "We should sue."

"Of course, we'll look into all litigation options, but tonight we have more pressing matters. Specifically, I have called this quorum to elect an interim CEO. With the IPO rescheduled, and obviously now it will need to be rescheduled yet again, it is vital that we act quickly."

He heard indistinct murmurs on the phone.

"Does anyone know where Luna is?" another voice asked.

"At this time—and this is not public knowledge—it has been brought to my attention that Luna is in Palo Alto."

The murmurs broke into shouts.

"Please, let me finish," said Doug. "Luna's been arrested. On Monday, she will have a hearing. Something about assaulting an officer. By that time, we will not be able to keep it out of the press any longer. Hence the urgency of this call. We need strong leadership now more than ever to keep the ship afloat."

"What about Phillip Jones? He was always Luna's second-in-command."

Doug winced, grateful that he was not on video at that moment.

"Phillip is still in the hospital. The last I heard, he's still in a coma."

The conversation was going exactly how Doug had anticipated. The questions. The order. The groupthink. It all flowed together like a river of inevitability. There was a long pause.

"Doug, I heard you were working closely with Thor. You helped him fix the deal with Boeing, I believe."

"Oh, I would hardly characterize that as helping, but I'd been shadowing Thor. That is true." The meek was about to inherit. Destiny.

"Given the unfortunate turn of events, I think we only have one real option. I'd like to propose we name Doug Kensington our interim CEO. Doug, would that be all right with you?"

Doug nodded. "I can be there tomorrow morning to begin sorting this mess out."

"In that case, I second the motion," came another voice.

"Since we're not able to see each other at the moment, please let it be known now if anyone opposes the motion."

Chapter 61

I'd been waiting in my cell for hours and Thelma and Louise were still talking. They seemed completely comfortable with one another, like they were best friends on vacation at a Sandals beach resort. They were ignoring me, which I didn't mind at all. It gave me time to think.

"Oh, honey, please. There's no way the Hilton beats the Four Seasons."

"I just don't like how they look at me at the Four Seasons. I mean, really. We all have a job to do. We're all working. Can't there be a little professional courtesy?"

I looked down at my nails. They'd grown long in the last week. I'd barely had a chance to breathe. To do the basics like shower and cut my nails. I looked like a hot mess. I wondered when Heath would be back. Maybe he could pull some strings and get me a shower. Though the thought that I'd be showering in prison one day soon made me sick to my stomach.

"Fuck those douchebags. You won't survive long if you keep worrying about what other people think of you. You've got to look out for number one and fuck everyone else."

"Figuratively or literally?"

They giggled like schoolgirls. I'd expected to be out by now. It felt strange being in jail again. Twice in one week. Like Heath said, this wasn't looking good. But on the other hand, fuck Heath. Fuck anyone who thought it didn't look good. I wasn't there because I did anything wrong. I was trying to help. Poor Taye. His brilliant young mind. The things he could have done. The things we could have done together.

"I admire you for not caring. I don't know how you do that. I try to tell myself that it doesn't matter. I try to write it off, but I just can't."

"Don't worry. You'll learn. You get numb to it after a while."

I admired these two women. They had people they could count on. They had each other. I used to have friends. I used to have people I could count on. In college, I'd tried so hard to make everyone happy. It was exhausting. Then, after I started Ancien, I guess I threw the baby out with the bathwater. Running a startup, volunteering with charities, and being social was too much. At least it was too much for me.

In Alex, I'd found someone I could connect with. He seemed to be like me: a lone wolf. But he handled it so much better than I did. He didn't seem to mind the solitude. That would be ideal, wouldn't it? Living without friends wouldn't be so much of a problem if I didn't get so damned lonely all the time.

"Luna, your lawyer's here," a cop said again.

Finally. It had taken him long enough. My heart skipped a beat, and not just because I was hoping Heath would finally get me out of here. Heath may have been arrogant and self-centered, but he wore his arrogance well, and underneath he had a big heart. I could see that in the way he was helping me.

The cop led me down the hallway, but this time, I was excited. Maybe Heath had found a loophole. Or bribed a judge. We arrived at the same door he had taken me to last time.

"Usually, I make it a point not to ask questions," said the cop. "But your last lawyer seemed perfectly fine to me. Why did you switch?"

I didn't understand his question. I just stared blankly back at him.

"Fine, don't tell me."

He pushed the door open, shoved me in, and slammed it shut behind me. The man was wearing a dark suit. It wasn't Heath.

"Do you work with Heath Lemming? Where is he?"

The man didn't look like a lawyer to me. His shoulders were broad like a quarterback's. He stood up.

"Please, have a seat."

"What's going on? Where's Heath? Is he okay?"

My heart was racing a thousand miles an hour. I sat down. The man walked behind me. I wanted to scream. I looked around the room—there was a mirror on one wall. Maybe the cops were watching. Maybe they were behind the mirror. He couldn't hurt me if they were watching us. I tried to think of the *Law & Order* episodes I'd seen. The cops weren't allowed to listen in on lawyers talking with their clients. But they could watch, right?

"Luna, everything's all right. I work at the same law firm as Heath. He sent me. He told me everything. I'm here to help."

I relaxed my shoulders and let out a sigh of relief.

"Just relax. I'll be getting you out of here in no time."

"Where's Heath? Why didn't he come himself?"

"He was just pulled into another case. He asked me to take over."

The burly man was now standing directly behind me. Heath had told me he wasn't working any other cases. And besides, he wouldn't just give up on me like that.

Something was wrong. This man wasn't right. I needed to get out. I opened my mouth to scream. The cops would hear me. But before I could draw breath, something pressed against my mouth. Instinctively, I breathed in, and acrid fumes filled my lungs. This time, it didn't smell at all like cleaning solution. I tried waving my arms, but I couldn't reach the man. My breathing became short and shallow. But I didn't feel like I was going to pass out—exactly the opposite. Like a volcano was erupting inside of me, like the pressure was building. But, then, it wasn't a volcano anymore. It was an earthquake. My body began shaking out of control. I couldn't see anymore. I couldn't control my body. I couldn't—

Chapter 62

Helen Hope was just finishing her unexpected shift when the dead lady arrived. She wasn't actually dead, but she was a total mess. Seizures. Throwing up. Foaming at the mouth. It didn't look good. She had come from the police station. Apparently they had taken one look at her and sent her here instead. As the poor woman was rolled past, Helen saw the straps holding her down. Then she recognized her. It was the crazy lady from Mr. Jones's room.

"Helen, can you help with this code gray?" Dr. Fernandez asked, following behind the gurney that carried the crazy lady. The bastard looked so happy and healthy. He must have just gotten to the hospital, probably after a proper night's sleep.

"My shift just ended. I'm exhausted."

"I need your help," he said with a smile.

Shit. Those were the magic words. Who had taught Dr. Fernandez the magic words? She rolled her eyes.

"Fine. I need to get changed."

"You're the best," the doctor shouted as they flew by. "We'll be in the ICU." He turned to a resident and said, "Get me some activated charcoal."

Why couldn't she have said no? Just this once? She was so tired. She needed more caffeine but couldn't stomach the thought of another cup of coffee. Helen popped a couple of the NoDoz she'd been saving in her pocket for just such an occasion. She thought for a moment. Better to pop a couple more, just in case.

On her way to the ICU, Helen read the patient's vitals on an Ancien tablet. Luna Valencia. Age thirty-one. Brunette. Mexican descent. No known allergies, though it wasn't exactly like anyone could have asked her. She was in bad shape and getting worse. Since arriving at the ICU, she'd already crashed once, and moments after Helen got there, she started crashing again. The cause was still unknown. At this rate, they wouldn't have a chance to find out until the autopsy.

Dr. Fernandez wasn't giving up, though. Good for him. Helen's NoDoz started kicking in, and she started to feel like she was back in her body again. The patient started to flatline. Dr. Fernandez began CPR. Helen looked at the Ancien screen. Once again it was suggesting an injection of epinephrine, but this time, the doctor wasn't even looking at the screen.

Helen didn't think she was needed at this point. All her years of experience told her that she had wasted four perfectly good NoDoz. But the doctor kept going with compressions. A fresh burst of foam gushed from the patient's mouth every time the doctor pushed. He was mumbling to himself.

"Strychnine, arsenic, hydrogen cyanide. Probably not arsenic or hydrogen cyanide—there's no blood. But strychnine's so old school."

One of the residents chimed in, "So Agatha Christie."

"What?"

"*The Mysterious Affair at Styles?*"

"What are you talking about?"

"Never mind."

The doctor kept thinking. The Ancien screen changed its recommendation. Now it read: *Time of death, 7:30 p.m.* The alarms were blaring. *Beep. Beep. Beep.*

The resident, who had been watching the screen intently, looked over at the doctor again.

"Do we call it?" *Beep. Beep. Beep.*

"Quiet. Shut off that fucking alarm. Nobody say a word."

He kept the chest compressions going. There hadn't been an unassisted heartbeat for over five minutes now.

Helen saw something in Dr. Fernandez's face. Something finally clicked. It was over.

"Helen, quick," he yelled between chest compressions. "I need you to go grab the cryokit."

"We're going to freeze her?"

"Just get it. Now. And bring more activated charcoal."

She ran to the equipment room. Cryotherapy was being used more and more as a way to extend life, though Helen had never seen it in action. The hospital had only recently acquired the cryokit. She'd heard they'd tried it out once before. Unsuccessfully. But she'd read about other attempts. She dragged the self-contained machine back to the ICU.

Dr. Fernandez had already set Ms. Valencia up for hypothermic induction. A fancy term for quickly cooling down a body. While still performing CPR, he'd had her stripped naked and placed on a bed of ice packs. But the body would cool down faster with the intravascular catheter hooked up to the machine Helen had just finished plugging in.

"Quick, time is of the essence," yelled Dr. Fernandez.

"Have you done this before? Treat a dead poison victim with induced hypothermia?"

"Nobody's tried this before. Now come on. We need to hurry."

Ms. Valencia's blood was redirected through the cryokit machine, which cooled it down before returning it to the body. The cryokit simultaneously oxygenated the blood, so as soon as she was hooked up, the doctor no longer needed to continue CPR. Helen remembered an amazing news story about an Italian boy who survived being trapped underwater for forty-two minutes by using a similar blood oxygenation technique.

"The body temperature has reached the target of thirty-three degrees. But it's still falling."

"Careful, if it goes below thirty-two, her blood will start crystallizing, and then she's dead for sure."

"It's at thirty-two now."

"Get rid of the ice packs. Hurry. Take them out now."

It was so weird seeing this body sitting on the table. The woman's lips were blue, and her face was as white as the corpses in the morgue. With the oxygenation, she didn't need to breathe. But still, it was strange to see her not breathing.

"And she'll come back to life after this?" asked Helen.

"Who knows? If we're lucky, this will give her body time to eliminate the toxins. If not, at least I finally got to see this machine in action."

Chapter 63

Doug was thinking over his situation with glee. He had been made CEO of the world's most powerful company. And he had killed or incapacitated everyone who had gotten him here and everyone who had gotten in his way. Taye, Heath, and Thor dead. Luna killed, though unfortunately not by Gaia's machinations. But dead was dead. Phillip and Alex would follow soon. He considered accelerating those two as well, but he was too curious to see how Gaia's Wrath would accomplish the task. He'd even taken the precaution of entering into Gaia the names of every programmer who had worked on the project.

The Massinos were not happy about Thor's death, and they weren't writing it off as an unfortunate accident, as the press had. But nobody suspected Doug. After all, why would they?

Doug stared at his employment agreement. The Ancien lawyers had initially drafted these same documents for Thor, so when he died, his unvested shares reverted back to the company. The lawyers just changed a few details here and there. Ten percent equity. Add that to the 5 percent Doug had purchased outright with what was left of his fortune after the System Inc. disaster and his total ownership position was 15 percent of the whole company. Twice as much as what he had expected to walk away with. The meek most certainly did inherit the earth.

But his last move had not been meek, had it? He was CEO now. That was bold. He couldn't hide in the shadows anymore. He was exposed. And while it felt great to grab this company by the balls, he had learned his lesson already. He couldn't hold on and squeeze it and twist it, no matter how gratifying that might be. He had to move forward with his plan. He had to get out of the spotlight as soon as possible. If he moved quickly, he could have his cake and eat it too. If he was too slow, everything he'd worked for could fall apart. He wasn't going to let that happen again.

He signed his employment agreement, and then picked up the phone.

"Ni hao," he said.

"Ni hao, Mr. Kensington."

"Everything is now ready."

"We've been watching the news. Things don't look ready."

"Thor's dead. That doesn't change our plan. I'm the CEO now. You will be dealing directly with me."

"Will that not prove to be a conflict of interest?"

Doug took a deep breath. These people were so cautious it made him sick.

"On the contrary. There are now fewer stakeholders, and the IPO is in more jeopardy than ever. I would say that fate has dealt the cards perfectly for our arrangement."

"I will speak with His Excellency, and we will get back to you if he still wishes to proceed."

Doug swore that if the wind blew two degrees off normal, these people would panic. Sometimes he even questioned if this was the right move to make. If his plan still even made sense. Such fickle people. So oligarchical. Handing them the world's most powerful weapon fully loaded had its risks. But the United States had it coming. One way or another, this outcome was inevitable. Rome was burning, even if they didn't know it yet. There was no sense forgoing a little profit.

"Tell him we've figured out how to target individuals."

There was a long pause.

"And it works?"

"Yes."

"We need proof."

Doug thought for a moment. If he lied now, it would come back to haunt him later. They were bound to find out, regardless.

"Thor's death is the proof."

Another long pause.

"And the police don't know this?"

"No."

"You surprise us, Mr. Kensington."

"Good surprise or bad?"

"Both."

These bastards ought to be begging for the chance to pay him double. Doug knew exactly why they wanted Gaia's Wrath. The names they were so desperate to put into his little death trap. Hell, he'd happily type in those names himself. Knock out that final domino. He was tempted. Very tempted. But why do it himself when there was someone so eager to pay him through the nose for the opportunity? Same end, bigger payout.

He only had to be careful that they wouldn't double-cross him. Doug wasn't planning on letting the Chinese do to him what he had done to Thor.

"I've got another buyer lined up, if you've changed your mind."

The man on the telephone laughed slowly.

"You Americans. Always with your power games. You can't make a river flow upstream with words alone,

276 | LUCAS CARLSON

you know. I will speak with His Excellency and get back to you shortly."

The line went dead and Doug put down the phone. The man was wrong. Look at all he had accomplished over the last few years with only his words. With just his words, Doug could make any river swim upstream. Anything Doug could imagine, he could make happen. He knew that now. He knew the secret, too. Let go of ego, and the world was his to command. It was a big ball of Play-Doh. History's greatest men had been sabotaged by their egos. Khan. Caesar. Napoleon. Hitler. Now Doug Kensington would join their ranks—except he would succeed where they had all failed. Conquer territories they could never have imagined.

The only thing he had to sacrifice to accomplish this was history's recognition. No one would ever know what he did. In the history books, the Chinese would get all the credit for his great work. Only Doug would know the truth. And he accepted that. He reveled in it. The power of the secret was intoxicating. He was unstoppable, precisely because nobody knew to try to stop him. The meek shall inherit the earth.

Chapter 64

"How long do we keep her like this?" Helen asked. She didn't know if it was the NoDoz or the novelty of the situation, but she felt more alive now than ever before. She knew some of the other nurses used Desoxyn, a methamphetamine, to stay alert. Some even got addicted. She'd seen it play out and was too terrified to try it—scared she might like it. But they all described a euphoric sense of feeling more alive. Seeing more. Smelling more. Feeling more. And that's what Helen was feeling at the moment. She could see the appeal.

"It's hard to tell," said Dr. Fernandez. "We want to make sure enough of the poison has been neutralized for her to survive the thaw. But the longer we keep her like this, the harder it will be for her to come out of."

"Jesus."

"I guess we're just going to wait until we can't hold out anymore."

This was the doctor Helen had been waiting for. The doctor who relied on instinct and creativity rather than statistics and computer screens. Helen had hope again. Hope for humanity's future. She'd been so close to losing that.

"Page me when that feeling comes. I'm going to do my rounds."

"You should go home. Get some rest."

"I can't miss this. We're making history."

Helen smiled, and Dr. Fernandez smiled back. Helen felt like she was walking on pillows. She ducked her head into Mr. Jones's room to check up on him.

"Hello, Mr. Jones. How are you feeling this evening?"

He was sitting up in his bed, typing furiously on his laptop.

"I've been saying all day that I'm fine. I'm feeling fine now. I'm ready to go. Please, can I be discharged now?"

Helen checked his vital signs. The machines weren't hooked up.

"What's wrong with the machines? Why aren't you hooked up?"

"I don't want any medicine. The doctors say I need to stay for observation, but I don't want to be observed anymore. Can't I go home?"

Helen pulled the stethoscope from her neck. She didn't mind that the computers were disconnected. She liked checking blood pressure the old-fashioned way, anyhow.

"What's the big rush? You've been seriously injured. You need time to recover."

"I can get better at home."

She released the pressure on the cuff slowly and watched the seconds tick by.

"Well, I can't deny that your vitals are strong, and you seem to be recovering well. Given the recent turn of events, it might even make more sense for us to discharge you. I'll talk to the—"

"What turn of events?"

"Nothing. It's nothing. Don't worry about it."

"No, tell me. What's happened?"

"I am not allowed to say anything. Patient confidentiality."

"So someone is here? Who?"

Helen blushed and threw the stethoscope back around her neck.

"I'll talk to the doctor and get back to you about being discharged. Maybe as soon as tomorrow morning."

"Is it Luna? Is Luna here? Is she okay? What happened to her? You have to tell me. It's incredibly important. I need to talk to her. Take me to her."

"I've said too much. Please, Mr. Jones, relax. I'll speak with the doctor. Stay still, and I'll be right back."

Helen rushed from the room and stood outside the door, breathing heavily. Her heart was racing, and her throat hurt. The veil of fatigue was falling over her again. She was making mistakes. She needed rest. Just one last thing to do before she could call it a night.

She felt clammy. Her eyelids were like rocks. She couldn't catch her breath. Helen walked over to Ms. Moore's room. She just wanted to check in one more time before giving up. At this point, she wouldn't even be able to make it home. She decided she would crash in the equipment room. It wasn't like *Grey's Anatomy* here; employees weren't allowed to sleep in the hospital. But one of the residents had snuck in a cot. Hopefully, nobody was in it already.

Helen couldn't believe her eyes. She rubbed them together. Hard. It couldn't be. Maybe something had changed. Maybe she was in the wrong room.

"Where's Ms. Moore?" she yelled.

No answer. She walked out of the room and back to the nurses station. She caught Jordan watching something on YouTube. He noticed her, clicking frantically on the screen until it turned into a spreadsheet.

"Hey, where's Ms. Moore?"

"Discharged an hour ago."

"Are you fucking kidding me?"

"No."

"How'd she get home?"

"Yellow cab."

"We don't discharge people at night."

"Dr. Fernandez said we needed the bed."

Helen's breath became shallow and rapid. Her eyes began to flutter.

"Helen? You don't look so good."

She swayed, giving in to the overwhelming darkness.

Chapter 65

Doug sat silently in the dark, in what had until very recently been Thor Massino's chair. He was contemplating his next move. He imagined every possible eventuality. Considered every strategy that maximized his outcome—no matter what turn of events occurred. It was mid-afternoon in China. He had given Xi Liu plenty of time to present the situation to China's president. If they didn't call back soon, Doug was going to have to start making phone calls; other groups might not pay quite as well, but they would still get the job done.

The phone rang.

"Hello," Doug said with supreme confidence. No "ni hao" this time. They were calling him.

"Ni hao, Mr. Kensington."

"So?"

He was tired of bending over backward with politeness. He knew this would rub Mr. Liu the wrong way, and he no longer cared. If they didn't want Gaia anymore, then fuck them. China was a pawn in Doug's chessboard, not the king. It was about time they got the message.

"I have presented the news."

"And?"

"We have… concerns."

"About?"

"We need proof."

God, this was so tedious. Doug had half a mind to hang up.

"What do you have in mind?"

"We will give you a name. If you can do what you claim, we have a deal."

"I'm not interested in the deal anymore," said Doug.

Xi Liu scoffed.

"I am confused. Is this another of your American games?"

It was time to use one of his favorite strategies.

"No. Before, we were talking about one kind of weapon. Now we are talking about another, much more powerful weapon. Certainly you don't imagine I am still interested in the original figure we discussed."

Squeeze and twist.

"Is this what you like to call a 'bait and switch'?"

"It seems like you know more about these things than I do, Mr. Liu."

"Very well. If you can provide sufficient evidence, I have been authorized to double our offer."

"Triple."

"I am not authorized—"

"Triple."

"Fine. Triple."

Doug smiled. It was too easy.

"Give me the name."

Chapter 66

"Where's Helen?" said Dr. Fernandez. "She's going to kill me if I do this without her. Can you page her again?"

A resident ran out of the room. Dr. Fernandez had no idea if this was going to work. He had been reading about induced hypothermia with keen interest for years and had been waiting for an opportunity to try it out.

Ms. Valencia's body sat there as blue and lifeless as a corpse. Cheating death by slowing down bodily functions was one thing. Overcoming fatal poisoning was a whole other story. If this worked, it would set a fantastic precedent. He would be written about in medical journals. Maybe he would even be featured in *The New York Times.*

He could see the headline now: *Genius Palo Alto Doctor Brings Poisoning Victim Back To Life.* If it worked. If it didn't, no one would even notice. It would be just another time of death. Another body for the statistics tables.

And failure was an enormous possibility. Not just because the procedure was so risky, but because there had been an unusually high number of deaths recently. All the doctors had been discussing it in the lunch hall. It was the topic du jour.

Half the doctors thought the high death rate was strange. The other half thought those doctors were crazy. There was no correlation between the death rate and any diseases. It wasn't like cancer, or the flu was causing the increase in deaths. It was more amorphous than that. Hard to pinpoint. Which was why the debate was so lively. Dr. Fernandez was in the camp that they were crazy. It was a statistical anomaly. It would correct itself soon.

"I can't wait any longer. Let's get started."

Luna's cold body lay on the table. Her arteries were still hooked up to the cryokit.

"We're going to warm her up slowly, people. If there are any signs that there is still active poison in her system, we'll bring her temperature down again quickly."

Dr. Fernandez watched the patient's vital signs carefully as her temperature slowly increased degree by degree. Ms. Valencia's lungs hadn't taken a breath of air in hours. They hadn't needed to. The cryokit oxygenated her blood, taking over the lungs' primary function. Likewise, her heart hadn't been pumping blood of its own accord either.

"When will the heart start beating?" asked one of the students.

"When the body's back to its normal temperature, it will turn back on."

"Like magic?"

The doctor took a deep breath. "No. Like science."

Her skin was finally starting to turn pink again, though the stillness and lack of life were startling. Even under anesthesia, people's bodies would move. The chest would go up and down. Blood would be seen pumping in the neck. Such small movements signaled life. And this body looked as dead as those in the morgue.

Half an hour later, the body was finally at 98.7 degrees, but there were no signs of self-sustaining life.

"Do we freeze her again?" a student asked. "Did we not leave her long enough?"

The doctor stared intently at the screen, making no answer. He was focused on something the others in the room didn't understand, breathing deeply. In and out. In through the nose. Out through the mouth. After five minutes of this, as if snapping out of a hypnotic trance, he spoke, "Turn off the machine."

The resident looked shocked. "What? But—"

"Turn off the machine."

"We can still put her under again. She needs more time," argued the resident.

This time, the doctor yelled, "Turn. Off. The. Machine."

The resident shook his head and went to the cryokit. The doctor resumed his deep-breathing ritual. The resident pulled the plug. The body lay warm and pink and as lifeless as a doll. A minute passed. With the machines off, the room was silent.

"Is she dead?"

"Quiet," Dr. Fernandez barked.

Another minute passed. Still nothing. Her body had been richly oxygenated through the bloodstream. If she didn't start breathing soon, the oxygen would run out and cause irreparable brain damage.

Dr. Fernandez was holding his breath. He'd been holding it since they unplugged the machine. He had simulated the patient's richly oxygenated blood by purposefully hyperventilating for the last half hour. Packing as much extra oxygen into his bloodstream as he could. He was working off of pure instinct, his face bright red by now. His lungs were struggling. Begging for air. He resisted. He would not give in. This was history in the making. This had to work.

It was mutiny. His diaphragm wrenched in little spurts. Even his eyeballs wanted him to take a breath.

Just one. Little. *Shit. Motherfucking shit brains.* He couldn't do it. He couldn't do it. He tried to hold it. Just one more moment. He thought of Helen. She would be proud of him. Then he wondered why he cared what Helen would think of him. And that wondering was just enough.

Who was making that noise? He wanted to yell at them so bad right then. To make an example out of them that would go down in the hospital's history books. But then he realized he was the one making that noise. He was breathing. No, he was gasping. Out of control. Get it together. He needed to get it together. He had failed. It was over. Finally, he had enough oxygen in his blood again to speak.

"Turn on the machine," he yelled. "Come on. Come on. Come on. Turn it on."

The student and resident both ran for the plug at the same time—right into each other. It was a scene right out of *The Three Stooges*. One of the nurses even broke into laughter.

"Shut up. Come on, you fools. She's losing brain cells by the second. Oh, Jesus. You fucking morons, I'll just do it myself."

He ran to the wall. The doctor felt warm blood running down his forehead. They were not going to ruin this for him. This was his moment. His chance to make a name for himself. He grabbed the cord. The socket was in an awkward spot behind the heavy machinery. He tried to pull it away, but the brakes were engaged. He dropped to the floor and reached his hand blindly, feeling his way to the plug. He found it.

"Quick, turn the temperature down. Now."

The student had finally made it to his feet again and was staring at the cryokit's console like the words were in Cyrillic.

Just then, Helen stumbled into the room. She glanced around the room, disoriented. She looked at the resident, still nursing his head on the floor. She looked at Luna lying lifelessly on the table. Finally, she looked at Dr. Fernandez lying on the floor with his hand still behind the cryokit, which he had just plugged in. Then back at Luna. She knew. He could see it in her eyes. She knew. It was too late. No history was going to be made here tonight. She was too late. Helen looked down at the floor.

And then there was a ping. A single ping that broke the moment in half. Dr. Fernandez wasn't even sure if he had actually heard it. And then he heard another. And in one fleeting moment, the dead body lying lifeless on the table reanimated with a violent gasp of air. She began coughing like a nearly drowned woman trying desperately to breathe again. Dr. Fernandez acted instinctively. He grabbed an oxygen mask as he pulled himself off the floor.

"Calm down. Calm down. It's okay. You're okay. You're going to be all right."

Chapter 67

The doctors said I'd been legally dead for three hours. Said it was some kind of record. Something about a poisoning, but I didn't know what they were talking about. I couldn't remember much. I remembered being in jail. For something I didn't do. Or did I do it? I didn't know. They said I shouldn't worry about it. The memories would come back. That I should rest. But there was something I had to do. Something that couldn't wait. But I didn't remember what it was. Did I leave the oven on? No. I hadn't been home recently. Had I? Maybe I had, actually.

I tried to remember what it was like to be dead. My brain was all fuzzy around the edges. The more I tried to remember, the more it eluded me. I had only vague feelings. Whispers of forgotten memories. Emptiness. An ultimate loneliness. But then no. That's how it started. Not how it ended.

Something happened to me while I was dead. Something I wished I could remember. I wished they didn't have me on those damned drugs. I looked over at the machine administering the drugs to me. One of my own machines. It said Ancien on it. That was cool. But also not cool. Not right. Something wasn't right. But I couldn't remember. Dammit, I wanted to remember. I wanted a clear head.

What happened when I was dead? What was it? I'd started out dark and alone. I vaguely remembered feeling scared. Feeling lonely. Desperately lonely. And then? What was it? The loneliness turned into something else. Something better. It was at the tip of my tongue. My tongue. My tongue was so dry. I was so thirsty. I needed water. I needed water more desperately than I'd ever needed it before. I opened my mouth to scream for help, but my throat was so dry that I couldn't speak. Nothing came out but a faint whimper of air.

I looked over at my IV. What was in that fluid? Wasn't it supposed to be hydrating me? Something was wrong. Something was very wrong. I needed to remember something. Why was I still thinking about Ancien? What did I need to remember? It was important. What button did I need to press for help? I couldn't find any buttons. I fumbled around madly. It felt like my arms weren't connected to my body anymore.

Then there was something blocking me. Something human. It had hair on its arms. What was it doing? What was he doing? Was he trying to do something to me? I recognized him, but I didn't remember from where. I wanted him away from me. Something told me he needed to get away from me. I tried to direct my flopping limbs in his direction. I couldn't tell if it was working or not. I had to focus. Who was this? *Focus, Luna. Focus. Pick one sense and just laser in on it.* Vision wasn't working for me. I couldn't speak. Maybe he was speaking, though.

I needed to focus on sound. I directed all my energy to listening. At first, it came in short bursts of whispers.

"Luna."

I could hear my name. Progress. Slowly, more words began to make sense.

"Luna. Calm down. Stop moving. It's Phillip. I'm here to help."

Who was Phillip? Was he my doctor? I knew that I knew a Phillip, but who was he? Maybe he was trying to help. I tried to tell my body to calm down and relax. Slowly it seemed to start working.

"Luna, we need to get out of here. Ancien is trying to kill us."

Then it all came flooding back. Taye. Gaia. Alex. Thor. Oh, dear God. What had I done? So many techies were afraid that artificial intelligence was going to enslave or destroy humankind. But they were so short-sighted. The truth was so painfully obvious now. It wasn't artificial intelligence that we needed to be afraid of. It was ourselves.

I could see so clearly how the problem with machine learning and big data was the accountability of the humans running such machines. Not the machines themselves. The smartest machines in the world would always be missing one key thing: the spark of imagination. The intention behind the action.

I knew machines could be programmed to outperform humans in any given task. Visual processing, image processing, games, even programming other computers. But these were just buttons and levers. Albeit extremely powerful ones. Still, someone needed to be sitting behind the curtain, pulling those levers and pushing those buttons.

When it came down to it, all this technology was just a hammer. A great big powerful hammer. It made me think of the last piece of great technology to come before this one: nuclear fusion. Like nuclear fusion, that power could be harnessed to create massive amounts of electricity—or the world's most horrific weapons. And the introduction of this technology to mankind very nearly led to its destruction.

I saw that the machine learning big data platform I had built over the last ten years had become a nuclear reactor on the brink of exploding. There were no checks and balances. The world didn't even realize the enormity of Ancien's abilities. Nobody had seen the mushroom cloud. Thor had been killing countless people, and nobody even noticed. We had accepted so much technology into our lives that it was impossible to trace back to the source of all those murders—all that devastation.

I am become death, destroyer of worlds.

I had to stop it. Suddenly I remembered. I had to stop it. That's why I didn't die when I was dead. I remembered the vague feeling of terror, the memory receding even as I thought about it. It had changed. I had changed. I was on borrowed time now. I had cheated death. I had died and been reborn so that I could stop Ancien from falling into the wrong hands. Nobody knew. If I didn't stop it, chances were nobody would ever find out until it was too late.

Then I realized I was still in a hospital room and there were people shouting.

"What are you doing? Stop that."

"Can't you see something's wrong? She can't speak. She's disoriented. These machines are killing her. We need to—"

"Stop touching those. Stop it now, or I'll call security."

"Please, you need to help her."

"Just stop. Let me check."

I still couldn't see, but whoever said that seemed to be calming down. My eyelids raised, and there was a bright light.

"Luna? How are you doing, dear?"

I tried to speak, but words still escaped me.

"Okay, okay," said the lady's voice. "You're right. This is not good."

Chapter 68

Doug was surprised by the name they had chosen. He'd half expected to hear the US president's name. That would have been fun. Indeed, that was a name he'd been tempted to try himself. But it was a Chinese name. Doug assumed it must belong to some dissident. An enemy of the state. It made sense. They wanted to see just how powerful Gaia was. They wanted to know if it could reach across country borders.

Of course, Doug knew it would. Gaia was global. It was already killing Chinese. The job would be done soon enough. Could be any minute. And when it was over, they would call him and everything would finally come together. The last piece of the puzzle was falling neatly into place.

Doug hadn't slept. Nor had he left his office. It felt good to have an office again.

Then there was a knock at his door. Doug turned his head, curious. It wasn't like he was the only one working on Sunday in that building. But he certainly wasn't expecting any visitors.

There was another knock. Doug stood up and walked slowly to the door. He held his breath and tried to listen for clues. There were none to be heard. He opened the door.

Standing in front of him was an old man. He looked like he hadn't showered in days. A pungent smell of body odor invited itself through the door.

"Hello?"

"You're not Thor Massino."

"No, I'm not. Who are you?"

"Do you know where Thor is?"

"Please, won't you come in and sit down? I'm expecting a phone call, but it probably won't come for a few more minutes."

The man had a cold stare. He looked haggard, his white hair sticking out in various directions. Doug had never seen him before. This would be more entertaining than watching his phone. What was the worst that could happen, after all? His curiosity was piqued.

The old man entered the room and looked around.

"This is Thor's office, isn't it?"

On a whim, Doug decided to play along.

"Well, yes. Can I get you something? Tea? Coffee?"

"Coffee. Black."

Doug went to the far corner of the office where there was an espresso maker built into the wall. He pressed a button, and the grinders started whirring.

"So, what do you need to see Thor about so urgently?" Doug asked.

"Who are you?"

Doug rolled his eyes. This was getting tiresome.

"I'm sorry, I haven't introduced myself. I'm Doug Kensington, one of Ancien's board members. Do you work here?"

Doug handed the stranger his coffee and motioned to him to sit down. They sat across from each other.

"You're on the board? It's about time someone knows what's going on, and you're probably as good a person to tell as anyone. Thor Massino is not what he appears to be. He's been using Ancien to kill people."

"What are you talking about?"

"I've been working with Luna Valencia ever since the shooting in New York. That kid, Taye—he found out what Thor was up to. Thor broke him out of prison and brought him back here. Luna and I found his body right over there."

He pointed toward the closet.

"You saw a dead body in that closet?"

"Yes, I did. But that's not even the worst of it. I think Thor's been killing millions of people using a system Taye built on top of Ancien. He needs to be stopped."

"Is that why you came here today? To stop Thor? What were you planning to do if you found him?"

"I don't know. Talk to him."

Doug watched the man's reaction carefully: he reached unconsciously for his jacket pocket. There was probably a gun there. This just got even more interesting.

"These are some incredible allegations, Mr.?"

"Sonne. Alex Sonne."

"Mr. Sonne. Do you have any evidence to back up your claims?"

"Not yet, but with your help, it shouldn't be too hard to get some."

"Of course, you're right. I'm glad you ran into me. Are you okay? You don't look so good."

"I was in a car wreck. I'm all right."

"I'm sorry to hear that. Let me see if I can't find you something a little stronger than coffee."

Doug went to his desk and opened the bottom drawer. Sitting in it was a bottle of tequila, two shot glasses, and a gun. He pulled out the tequila.

"Thanks. Cheers," said Alex. They downed their shots. "So you didn't have a clue what Thor was up to this whole time?"

"I still don't believe it. If what you say is true, there are going to be some serious consequences for everybody. Even innocent bystanders like me." Alex nodded solemnly. "What do the police have to say about all this?"

"We haven't gone to the police yet."

"Why not?"

"Two reasons. First, no evidence. Second, Luna's in a bit of trouble with the police."

"Ah, yes, of course," Doug sighed.

"Can I ask you something?"

Doug hated when people asked that.

"Sure."

"It's nine in the morning on a Sunday. What are you doing in Thor's office and why did you let me in so easily?"

"I'm waiting for Thor. We were supposed to meet this morning, but he didn't show up. Why do you think you're still alive?"

Alex looked puzzled. "What do you mean?"

"Well, if Thor created this amazing killing machine, why hasn't he used it to kill you yet? Or just sent a hit man to do the job?"

"I've almost been killed at least twice now."

Third time's the charm.

"I'm sorry, do you mind if I just get another drink?"

"Be my guest."

"Want one?"

"No, thanks."

Doug reached for the cabinet.

Chapter 69

Phillip sat by my side, watching carefully as the nurse rehydrated me. Somehow, someone had messed up and put a high-salt-solution drip into my veins. Worse, they were probably just following Ancien's instructions. I had to stop this. It didn't matter what I had to do. I needed to fix this.

I'd been in and out of consciousness all night, but this time, when I woke up, I finally felt like myself again. I had been given another chance. I'd had a taste of death. A taste of what ultimate loneliness felt like. I couldn't help but laugh at how melodramatic I had been the week before. I knew now in my bones how precious my life was. How unique and sacred my short existence was and how quickly it could all go away. Yes, life was hard. Yes, it felt lonely. In many ways, life was the worst conceivable fate—other than death, that is.

This feeling in my bones made me even more outraged about what Thor had done. Cutting short other people's lives for what? Profit? Trading other people's already short stint on this planet for mere dollars? It was disgusting.

"Phillip," I muttered. He was half asleep in the corner, but immediately he jumped up and came to my side. "We need to get out of here."

"I've been waiting for you to say that. Do you think you can get dressed on your own?"

I nodded. He handed me a bag of clothes. Everything ached, but it was better to feel pain everywhere than the nothingness of death. Every sensation was a reminder that I was still alive. On borrowed time. I had a mission to complete.

"Luna, you do know that Thor's dead, right?" Phillip said from just outside my room.

"What? That's not possible."

"He and Heath were hit by a self-driving car."

I paused. "And Alex?"

"I don't know where he is. Are you okay?"

"Yes," I said. "I'm all right."

I pushed down the sobs that wanted so desperately to come out. Pushed them down deep where they could hide safely until the time was right. Now wouldn't do. Tears would have to wait.

"So is it all over now that Thor's dead?"

"I think his death is rather convenient," said Phillip. "Plus, that saline solution mix-up earlier? If Thor was the mastermind behind it all, then his death certainly hasn't stopped Ancien."

"You mean Gaia killed Thor?"

"I have to assume so."

"Who's taken over?"

"Doug Kensington."

"I remember him. He's on the board. He's the one who nominated Thor in the first place. Do you think he's involved with all this?"

"While you were asleep, I looked into his past. He was involved in some questionable situations with his old company. Rumored to be terrorist-related. Did you know that?"

"No, he automatically got a board seat when he bought out KPCB's shares."

"You didn't do a criminal background check?"

"Of course we did. His record was clean. No convictions."

"Well, if he's not involved, I would be surprised," said Phillip.

"Let's talk to him first. We need to find out, one way or the other. Can you get me a wheelchair?"

Phillip wheeled me out of the room. I kept my head down, and Phillip moved quickly. Nobody noticed. Or if they did, they didn't say anything. A few minutes later,

we were outside where the air was cool and damp. A
storm was brewing.

Chapter 70

Doug reached for the gun in the filing cabinet. Then the phone rang, and he stopped short. Gun or phone? It rang again, and he made his decision.

"I'm sorry, I've been expecting this call all morning. Would you mind waiting in the hallway for just a second?"

"Of course not."

Alex left the room. The phone rang a third time. Doug waited until after Alex closed the door to answer.

"Hello?"

"Mr. Kensington, I must extend to you my sincere congratulations."

"You had doubts?"

"Of course not, we just didn't realize it would work so quickly."

"Can you tell me how it happened?"

"What do you mean?"

"The cause of death."

"You don't know?"

"It uses machine learning. Its methods are a black box to me."

"Black box? I am not familiar with this expression."

"Doesn't matter. How did it happen?"

"There was a train accident a little over an hour ago." Doug's heart skipped a beat. A train. How poetic. How he wished he could have been there. "Somehow, a switch did not occur at the right time. It caused a head-on collision."

"And you're satisfied it will be reported as an accident?"

"Reported?"

Doug had forgotten just how rigidly the Chinese controlled the press.

"So we have a deal then?"

"Yes. We'll send the term sheet to you tomorrow."

"Excellent. It's been a pleasure doing business with you."

The phone clicked. The asshole hung up on him. It was okay, though. Doug would have the last laugh. He rose and went to the door. When he opened it, Alex Sonne was gone. Doug ran back to his desk and picked up his phone.

"Older black man with white hair. Don't let him leave. Detain him. Use any force necessary."

Chapter 71

Just as I pushed open the car door, it started pouring buckets of rain. The wheelchair had been helpful in getting me out of the hospital, but I didn't need it. I was powered by a force deeper than myself.

On the car ride over to Ancien headquarters, I'd asked Phillip about his wife and son. Jake was the sweetest nine-year-old boy I had ever met in my life. But he was mentally challenged and needed a lot of attention. He behaved like he was five. I always thought five was such a great age to be stuck at—if you had to be stuck. Phillip told me his wife had left him and taken Jake with her a few months ago. Apparently, they hadn't even visited him in the hospital. I apologized for asking. He shrugged.

"At least I've got friends like you," he said. He opened his door and hopped out into the rain. Together we ran toward Ancien headquarters for the second time since I'd returned from New York. I wasn't thrilled to be back, but if there was even a sliver of a chance Doug could help us undo the damage Thor had caused, I needed to know.

Or if Doug was in on it, maybe I was walking into the biggest mistake of my life. Again.

We got to the front doors. They were locked. I knew some employees worked weekends—mainly support staff and customer representatives. There should have been at least one security guard near the front door, but nobody was at the desk, and I couldn't see anybody to flag down. We banged hard on a glass door as the rain continued to pour down. In a way, it felt good. Like a shower washing away something inside of me that desperately needed cleansing. Cold and refreshing. I closed my eyes and tilted my face up to the sky.

"Nobody's here," shouted Phillip. "Let's go around back. See if we can find someone walking around."

We began running along the side of the building, when Phillip stopped and started pounding against the glass wall.

"Can you open the door for us?"

When I caught up to Phillip, I looked in. I couldn't believe what I saw. Alex Sonne was looking over at us. He'd been running when Phillip first yelled for him, but stopped when he saw me. He looked at us standing there, drenched in rainwater, and shook his head like he couldn't believe it was me, either.

Then he ran to the window and started yelling.

"What's he saying?" asked Phillip.

I couldn't hear through the double-paned glass. But I could understand his hand gestures. He was telling us to get out of there. Something was wrong.

Phillip responded by pointing at the door and saying the word "door" over and over again as loudly and slowly as possible.

Alex looked exasperated. Then I saw a couple of security guards running toward him. He must have heard them, because he started running again, at full speed. Phillip and I returned to the front doors.

But when we got there, it was still empty. We stood there for a moment in silence. Finally, Alex appeared. He ran to the door and pushed on the handle with all his might. I could see the sweat dripping from his forehead. The door wouldn't budge.

He tried the one next to it. It too was locked from the inside and outside. Alex looked around desperately, then dove behind the front desk. A moment later, the two security guards rushed into the room. They looked at us, then looked around the lobby. One of them held the radio up to his mouth and said something we couldn't hear, then they both dashed out the other way.

I saw Alex pop his head out and glance around. Then he ran to us. He waved his arms madly.

"I think he's telling us we have to go," said Phillip.

"We can't just leave him here."

"They probably radioed another guard to come pick us up."

"We can't leave him."

Alex was still gesticulating wildly. I reached into my pocket for my phone, but it wasn't there. Alex had thrown it away so Thor's men couldn't track us. I asked Phillip for his phone and typed out a message, then slammed the screen against the glass door. Alex calmed down enough to read it, then nodded and ran back the way he had come.

"Follow me," I told Phillip. We ran around the building again. I slipped in a pile of mud. I had never seen so much rain in Palo Alto. Phillip helped me up, and we continued toward the back of the building when suddenly Phillip grabbed me and pulled me to the ground.

His finger was on his lips. Then he pointed. I saw two guards up ahead, walking the perimeter.

"Shit," I said.

"Quiet," Phillip hissed.

"They're right in front of the emergency exit I told Alex to meet us at."

"Shit."

"He's going to be popping out of that door any second now."

I looked around and saw a rock sitting next to us. A good-sized landscaping stone. Heavy. I picked it up and threw it into the parking lot.

"What are you doing?" asked Phillip.

I shushed him.

The guards heard the rock and looked around frantically. One of them spoke into his radio. The other went to investigate.

"Do you think I can take him?" I asked.

"What? No way. Those guys are monsters."

"I've got to do something."

Just then the door popped open, and Alex came through at full speed. The door slammed into the waiting guard and as he fell, his head slammed into a cement block, cracking open like a ripe coconut. The guard in the parking lot turned around, grabbing instinctively for his gun. Alex didn't have his bearings yet. He couldn't see the guard.

"Look out," I yelled.

Alex saw the danger just in time and leaped aside. A deafening shot filled the air, and I saw splinters of concrete spraying all around. I turned to Phillip. He was lying on the ground, covering his head with his hands. I had to do something. I looked around again. Then I saw it. I checked to make sure the coast was clear, and then I ran as fast as I could.

A few moments later, I was standing with a bloody rock in my hand. I turned to Alex, who was leaning against the building, trying to catch his breath. He looked back at me and nodded. I dropped the rock and reached down, picking up the fallen security guard's gun. Alex and I dashed over to Phillip, who was still cowering on the ground.

"Here," I said to Alex. "I hate these things."

"Give it to me," Phillip insisted. "I need more help than he does."

Phillip took the gun from me and stuck it into his pocket.

We decided to go to Phillip's house to regroup. It was closer than mine. Confronting Doug was clearly not an option at that moment. This time, none of us spoke in the car. Both Phillip and Alex were spent. I was probably spent too and just didn't realize it. By the time we arrived, the rain had stopped, though we were all still sopping wet.

The first thing we did was change into dry clothes. I put on a sundress Phillip's ex-wife had left behind.

Phillip made a huge pot of tea.

"Good to see you again, kid," said Alex with a wry smile.

"Don't you go disappearing on me like that again, you hear?" I said.

He chuckled.

Phillip stayed quiet.

"What the hell were you doing showing up at Ancien's front door like that?" Alex asked.

"Trying to figure out if Doug knew about Gaia."

"Well, that was a damned stupid thing to do."

"Oh, yeah? And what exactly were you doing there?"

"It was a damn stupid thing for *you* to do. I knew what I was doing."

"Clearly," I said.

"Either way, Doug does know. He's the main guy now, and he's fixing to sell your company to someone. And that someone doesn't have the best of intentions."

"How do you know that?"

"Let's just say I had my ear to the ground."

"We can't let this continue. We have to stop him. Phillip, can you call your people and have Ancien shut down?"

He did not respond.

"Phillip?"

He was standing over the kettle of boiling water and sobbing.

Chapter 72

"Oh, Phillip. What's wrong?" I asked, as I ran over to his side. "What's the matter? Are you hurt?"

He wept.

Just then, Alex started laughing hysterically. Like a hyena. I turned to look at him.

"And what the hell's wrong with you?"

My eyes began to blur. Phillip kept crying. Alex kept laughing. My head hurt. What was going on? Something was not right. The water kept boiling, steam filling the air.

Something was wrong. The air. Something was wrong with the air. Carbon monoxide. We had to get out of there. Phillip collapsed to his knees.

"Phillip, stand up. We've got to get out of the house."

Alex's laugh turned into a cough. I reached for the tiny kitchen window and opened it. My vision blurred even more. All I wanted to do was sit down. Plop on the couch and take a nap. Hell, the kitchen floor would do just fine. Never before had I felt such an intense desire to just give in and let go.

"Come on, guys. We're leaving. The house is poisoned. Leave. Now."

I pulled at Phillip's shirt, but was a futile effort. He wasn't going to budge. Phillip was not a small man. I couldn't pull him out alone even if I had my full strength.

"Alex, I need your help. We need to get Phillip out of here."

Alex was trying to make his way over to us, but he couldn't walk in a straight line. He swayed in long arcs like a drunkard. But his eyes now had purpose. He got to us, and together we pulled the sobbing man into the hall. It took every ounce of strength I had left, and every muscle in my body was screaming at me to give up. Give in. Let go. But I couldn't let go. Not now. I wasn't done. This wasn't my time yet. This wasn't our time to go.

Then it struck me. I looked over at the thermostat. It was a Nest. One of Ancien's newest beta customers. Ancien. Gaia. My own baby was trying to kill me. Again. Trying to kill us. Now I was crying along with Phillip.

No, I was crying instead of Phillip. Why wasn't Phillip crying anymore?

"Phillip, don't fall asleep on me, buddy. Wake up."

I let go of his arm for a moment and slapped his face with as much strength as I had left. He didn't open his eyes. I grabbed his arm again.

"Come on, we need to get out of here," I yelled.

Alex pulled as hard as he could. I wouldn't have been able to do it without him, but he wouldn't have been able to do it without me, either. I saw him fighting unconsciousness, his eyes fluttering to the back of his head.

We made it almost to the door. I could almost reach the handle with one hand.

"Come on, Alex. One more pull," I said. "I just need one more pull, come on."

"Okay, just a minute. I just need to catch my breath."

Alex let go of Phillip and sat on the floor next to him.

"No, no, no, no, no, no, no."

I tried to pull Phillip on my own, but I couldn't manage, even though we were just inches from the door. There was no time. There was no time. I just needed a quick rest, and then I'd be able to pull them both. Just a quick rest. I wondered what Heath was doing right then. I missed seeing him. Just close my eyes for a few seconds. Picture his handsome face. Then I'll. Then.

No. Wait, no. I stood up, turned around, and opened the front door. A whoosh of air flew in. Clean. Cool.

Crisp. I greedily filled my lungs with the damp nectar. Then I turned around and slapped Alex as hard as I could manage. Between the slap and the fresh air, he came to. I could see clarity in his eyes. We grabbed Phillip and yanked him out the door.

Chapter 73

"What do you mean you can't find them?" Doug demanded. "You're not dealing with Jason Bourne here. It's two old guys and a woman."

"We've done a full sweep of the building. They're not here. Our best guess is that after taking out Lorenz and Kowalski, they escaped by car."

"Where?"

"We're looking. We searched Luna's house and were about to go check Phillip's, but we started getting dizzy."

"What the fuck are you talking about?"

"It might be a coincidence or else sabotage, but Luna's house is full of carbon monoxide. Within a couple minutes of searching, one of our guys passed out."

"Carbon monoxide?"

Doug thought about it for a moment and then his eyes brightened.

"Yes, sir. Most of us were fine, but we needed to take one of the guys to the hospital."

"Go to Phillip's house now. Bring gas masks and three body bags."

"Yes, sir."

Chapter 74

For some time, the three of us sat dazed on the front porch, trying to clear our heads. Phillip woke up with a splitting headache. Alex seemed to bounce back pretty quickly, though it was taking me a little while.

"We've got to get out of here," Alex said.

"We can go to my house," I suggested.

"And get poisoned there? Thanks, but we need to go somewhere no computer or person knows about."

"And do what?"

"Plan our next move. We can't just sit here. Chances are, Doug's men are on their way. Give me your phone, Phillip."

He handed it over.

"You going to look up hiding spots on Yelp?" he asked.

Without a moment's hesitation, Alex smashed the phone on the ground. It barely cracked the screen.

"Hey, what the hell are you doing?" Phillip cried.

"As long as this thing is intact, Doug and Ancien can keep track of us."

He slammed it on the ground again. A piece of glass snapped off, but still it wouldn't break.

"Can't I just turn it off?"

"Don't be so naïve."

With the third smash, the phone finally came apart. Alex pulled some of the guts out for good measure. Phillip looked bewildered. He sat down and put his head in his hands.

"Hey, are you all right, Phillip?" I asked.

No response.

"Come on, we're going," said Alex.

"Where?"

"Away."

We walked for nearly half an hour before we escaped the residential maze in which Phillip lived. The first place we found was a strip mall. Alex asked if any of us were hungry. I wasn't and Phillip didn't respond, so we kept walking.

The first hotel we came to was a Hilton. It looked so nice. We could just collapse in bed for a bit. But Alex kept walking, and we followed. By now, the sun had burned through the morning clouds, and the sky was clear. The only things indicating it had ever rained were the few scattered puddles and children jumping gleefully into them. The sun felt false on my face. The warm comfort only skin deep.

I thought about the people who had died for what I had built. Trying to stop what it had become. Taye. Heath. The countless faces of people who met death before their time. Who else might still be fighting for their lives thanks to what Ancien had become?

"Hey, Luna, duck," Alex pulled Phillip and me to the ground. "We need to move to side streets."

A few moments later, I looked up and saw a Google Earth car slowly turning the corner. It had an alien-like spinning camera on the roof.

Had this been inevitable? Did the infusion of technology into our everyday lives make mass murder the only possible result? Of course, Asimov, Gibson, and Hertling might say so. But this was different.

Computers were not thinking on their own, deciding who to kill. Yet, it wasn't quite people killing people either. It was a weird mash-up of the two. Nobody was deciding who would die. At least, I hadn't found any evidence in the code that would suggest as much. Nor was anyone determining how these people would die. The computer figured out those parts on its own. But whether they realized it at the time or not, it was human beings who created the intention to kill. Not the computer.

The one thing nobody seemed to be able to synthesize with computers was the creative intention. The spark of why. More and more, any discrete task could be better accomplished by computers than by humans. But the intention behind the task, the creative force. That was still as mysterious and intractable as the soul.

Then we finally stopped. Alex had walked us to the Palo Alto Police Department.

Chapter 75

Doug punched a hole in the wall. He wrenched his fist out, torn and bleeding, and punched a second hole next to the first. He let out a guttural yell. His bad leg was acting up, too. It always did when things weren't going his way. It was like a sixth sense—he knew he had bigger problems when his leg started hurting. The leg he'd stitched up on his own all those years before.

This was not okay. Not okay at all. How the hell did they keep getting away from him? His men reported that Phillip's house was indeed completely full of carbon monoxide. An amazing accomplishment by Gaia's Wrath. But no bodies. The kitchen was in disarray. There had been a struggle. But the front door and kitchen window were open and nobody was inside.

And now they couldn't be found.

What should have been a simple loose end had become a liability that could ruin everything. That could take down his masterpiece.

He opened one of the desk drawers. Blood poured from his right hand. A flap of skin hung loose. To a less-trained mind, such searing pain would be crippling. Instead, it helped Doug focus. He closed the drawer and turned to the keyboard.

Doug brought up the command input to Gaia's Wrath and began hitting keys slowly and deliberately, until they were so covered in blood he couldn't see the letters anymore. Maybe if he typed the names again, it would unlock some magic machine learning hack. *Luna Valencia. Phillip Jones. Alex Sonne. Luna Valencia. Phillip Jomnes. Aklez Sppne.* Fucking blood. His fingers were slipping too much in the warm, viscous fluid. He dashed the keyboard to the floor.

He was so close. He wasn't going to let anybody get in his way this time. Everything had fallen into place to make this happen. If it wasn't supposed to happen, he would have known by now. Thor wouldn't have died. The Chinese wouldn't have been interested in the acquisition. Gaia's Wrath would not be able to target individuals. Something would have gone wrong. Anything. But nothing had gone wrong. Goddamn it.

He opened the drawer again. This time, he pulled out the gun. Something had to be done to set things right again. To put the manifest back in the destiny. Nothing was going to stop him. Nothing. No thing.

Chapter 76

"No," I said.

"Yes," he said.

"But—"

"Listen, we have no other choice at this point."

"I won't do it. I've been in enough police stations in the last week to last a lifetime. I am not just walking myself into this one. You're going to have to drag me in kicking and screaming."

"That's why you two are going to wait for me over there."

He pointed at the library across the street, and I let out a sigh of relief.

"What are you going to do?"

"You let me worry about that. If I'm not with you in thirty minutes, get out of there and don't stop walking."

"Where to?"

"Mexico."

"You better be joking."

He didn't respond. Just turned and strode into the police station.

I held Phillip's hand as we crossed the street.

"Phillip, what's wrong with you?"

There was a long pause.

"Do you think I—"

Phillip sat on the concrete steps at the entrance to the library. I joined him.

"What?"

"I've fucked up."

"No, that's not true. What are you talking about?"

"I've fucked up everything good in my life."

His eyes were glassy.

"Phillip, what are you saying? You're one of the best people I know."

"That's nice of you to say, but I'm a loser. I lost my job. I let a megalomaniac take over your company. I let two megalomaniacs take over."

"That's not your fault. You can't blame—"

"And then today I couldn't even protect you. I don't know what kind of person I am."

"Phillip, you were just doing what you thought was right."

"Do you think I k—"

He couldn't say it.

"No, Phillip. No. I'm sure he'll be fine."

"And Susan. Oh God, Susan."

The tears flowed freely down his face.

"It's okay, Phillip. It's okay. Come on. Stand up. There will be a time for this, but not just now. We have work to do. Important work. People depend on us. So many people. People we don't even know are in mortal danger and will continue to be until you and I figure out how to stop Ancien. So, come on. Let's go inside. We'll find a quiet corner, and we'll figure this out. Then we can think about everything—"

I couldn't hold it back anymore. Watching Phillip cry reminded me of everything I'd been feeling but couldn't acknowledge. Taye. Heath. Deeper wounds. Older injuries. Wounds I thought had healed ripped right open. I wept with Phillip.

No. Not now. Now was not the time. I couldn't do this now. It had to wait.

"Phillip, come on. I need you right now."

We pulled ourselves together and found a quiet corner in the library with a small table and a couple of chairs.

"So, how do we stop this thing?" I asked.

"I'd go in and just delete everything if I still could."

"Maybe we can call in some favors. We could call Michael or Samantha. Explain everything."

"Alex broke our phones. I don't know about you, but I don't have their phone numbers memorized."

"Shit."

We thought about it some more.

"We could call the press," I said. "You and I have a lot of credibility, after all. They would listen."

"Maybe. But think about it. What's the first thing they're going to ask for?"

"Proof."

Phillip sighed. "We don't have one shred of evidence. It's an entirely circumstantial situation. Alex is probably facing the same problem over there. Maybe we should just wait. Maybe Alex will be able to convince the cops somehow, and they'll take care of it."

"I'm not okay with just sitting on my hands, though. Are you?"

Phillip shook his head.

"Come on," I said. "There's got to be something we can do. Between the two of us, we have twenty years of experience at Ancien. There's got to be something we haven't thought of yet."

"We could stake out the parking lot tomorrow morning and wait for Michael or Samantha to show up."

"Then we're risking being shot at again."

"Fourth time this week," he said. "That's okay, though, because by my count, I've got five more lives left."

I laughed, then, "Wait, what did you just say?"

"Fourth time this week?" he repeated.

"No, you've got five more lives."

"Yeah, nine lives. You know, like a cat."

"That's it. Phillip, you're a genius."

I leaned over and gave him a big kiss on the forehead.

Chapter 77

Chelsea Moore desperately regretted her decision to go directly home from the hospital. She'd arrived at home the night before, and by the afternoon, she'd already run out of prescription pain pills. She shook the bottle just in case there was one hiding. On a scale of one to ten, her pain was a nine. It hurt. A lot. The discharge nurse had told her she should pick up her medication on the way home, but she'd been so tired and only wanted to get home and go to sleep. What a stupid decision. What painful consequences.

It took almost all of her energy just to stay standing. To think about what to do. She could call a cab, but she couldn't afford to pay for a cab and the pills. The fun dilemmas of being poor. Sure, she'd just started her dream job, but she hadn't even gotten her first paycheck yet. And now some substitute was spending time with her children. Build that intimate bond of those first days. She was missing everything.

At this rate, she would be missing even more days. And such formative days too—the students must be so anxious and uneasy about the new year. They needed her warm smile; they needed to know everything would be okay. The kind words needed to be given at just the right time. And the bully—there was always a class bully. And Chelsea needed to be there to undermine that bully's authority from day one. Chelsea needed to be there.

But if she was ever going to get back to her classroom, she needed to survive the next few days. Which was not going to happen without those pills. She had already maxed out the Tylenol she was supposed to take, and then some. It didn't help. She felt like two oversized nails were being driven into her temples. Even the dim lights burned her eyes. She would rather die than keep feeling this pain. She had no choice. She would have to drive.

Chelsea groped at the wall to keep herself steady as she made her way to the front door. She pushed it open and the afternoon sun burst through. Now the pain was a ten out of ten. Maybe an eleven. Why did the sun have to be so damn bright? She considered giving up right then, turning around, covering herself with a sheet, and letting herself die in this miserable agony.

But the kids. They needed her. She tried to think straight. Where was the nearest Walgreens? Was it on El Camino Real? Or the one on Middlefield? Maybe there was a drug store closer. She couldn't remember if Kmart had a drug store.

She made it to her car, but then she couldn't find her keys. Where had she left them? She checked her purse again. She dumped everything out onto the passenger seat and riffled through it all. Some stuff fell to the floor. All this stuff. She needed to keep her purse cleaner. How often did she need any of this anyway?

Now that she thought about it, she wondered how her car had even gotten there. She'd had the heart attack at school. Her car had been parked at the school. How did the car get all the way here? Damn, her head hurt. It was at a solid eleven now.

Someone must have towed it here. Why didn't they tell her that? They should have told her who towed it, so she could get the keys. The keys. Wait. If they'd towed it, they wouldn't have taken the keys. She would still have them in her purse if they had towed the car.

So someone had taken her keys and driven her car back here for her. But who could have done that? Who had her keys? Maybe that person could drive and get the pills for her. It was Sunday afternoon. If it was another teacher or Mr. Carbahol, maybe they could help her.

Or maybe they just left the keys in the car. She pulled down the visors. Nothing. She wished her head was clear. That she could think straight. She opened the—oh God, what was it called?—glove department? There they were. The keys.

She'd been driving this piece of shit green Kia for ten years now. It had recently reached two hundred thousand miles. Both bumpers were hanging on by threads. But the engine turned like clockwork. Those Koreans made good cars.

She put the car into gear, and then paused, muttering, "Fuck."

She put the car back into park again. She shuffled through the crap on the passenger seat. She'd forgotten the prescriptions. Now she had to go all the way back to the house. Maybe she should just give up. This was ridiculous. Then, finally, she caught a break.

There, on the floor, were the prescriptions. She hadn't forgotten them after all. She was good to go. She put the car back into gear and pulled slowly away from the curb.

Chapter 78

"There you are," I cried, as Alex arrived in our nook at the library. "We were just about to leave. What did they say?"

"Come on, we need to go," said Alex. His face was as grim as I'd ever seen it.

"What's wrong? Did they not believe you?"

"We'll talk later."

Alex led us through to the back of the library, following the signs for the emergency exit. I was afraid the door would set off an alarm, but Alex pushed it open without any hesitation. The alarm didn't go off. We found ourselves in a back alley, and I opened my mouth to speak, but Alex shook his head.

"Not here, keep going."

Once again, we walked at random through the city. Alex seemed even more vigilant than before. After about ten blocks we came to a school park. There were half a dozen children playing lava monsters on the slides and a few dads playing basketball on the nearby courts. Alex headed for the soccer field. When we reached the center of the field, he sat down. Phillip and I did, too. Alex looked all around us before speaking.

"This will work. If either of you sees anything suspicious or a police car slowing down, let me know. We can see from all angles here, and there are plenty of places we can run and disappear if we have to."

"Disappear? What's going on, Alex?" I asked.

"Your instincts were right. I shouldn't have gone to the police. They have a warrant for your arrest. It took me the better part of twenty minutes to convince them that I don't know where you are. I don't think they trust me, though. One way or another, we'll know soon enough."

"So did they believe the rest of the story?"

"They wouldn't even listen. As soon as your name came up, that's all they wanted to talk about. I lost control of the conversation."

"Shit," said Phillip. "I guess the cavalry isn't going to ride in and save our asses."

Alex nodded.

"We don't need them," I said.

"Oh?" Alex raised an eyebrow.

"Phillip gave me an idea for how we can take down the whole operation."

"I'm listening," he said.

"You know how a cat has nine lives?"

"Okay."

"At this point, it's pretty clear Gaia is trying to kill the three of us. Damn near succeeded a few times, too."

"Right."

"Taye said Gaia was increasing the death rate completely at random. No one sickness. No one kind of person was being targeted."

"I still don't follow."

"The chances of Gaia targeting all three of us multiple times in a row all at the same time means that they must have figured out how to target individuals."

"I guess," said Alex. "So?"

"We use their own weapon against them."

"I thought you no longer had access to the system. Didn't they lock you out or something?"

"They did. I don't."

"Then how?" asked Alex.

"No," Phillip gasped, cottoning on. "It's a bad idea, Luna. Give it up."

"We need to go back to Ancien," I said.

Chapter 79

Doug drove slowly around the neighborhood, meandering through side streets and back. The matte-black polymer-framed Glock 17 sat fully loaded in the passenger seat. He knew that firing a gun in broad daylight on a Sunday afternoon had its risks. He wished he had gone for the Maxim 9 with a built-in silencer, but that was too gaudy. He wasn't a hit man.

Shooting on sight wasn't the primary plan, though. Ideally, Luna would see the gun and follow him quietly to the car. He would make her drive, and he would sit in the backseat with the Glock pointed at her head. Any funny business and at least the sound might be muffled some by the car. With him in the backseat, it would be impossible for her to do anything but drive. And even if she were stupid enough to try to crash the car, he would be safest back there, too.

Now he just had to find the bitch. If the security guards were right, that she was with Alex Sonne, and it could be a two-for-one deal. He decided he would knock Alex out by hitting him hard on the head with the Glock. No sense in risking anything with an ex-cop.

Doug drove around at fifteen miles an hour. Occasionally, a car would come up behind him. Usually, they would get annoyed and turn off onto a different side street, but a particularly nasty driver had the audacity to honk. Doug slowed down to a crawl. The driver honked again, longer this time. Doug rolled down his window and motioned with his arm for the driver to pass. Doug saw the woman in the beat-up green Kia cursing profanities as she rolled by. But her lips stopped moving when she spotted the pistol in his hand. The woman slammed on the gas and drove away, screeching her tires. Doug wished he could just type the woman's license plate into Gaia. New feature request.

He just had to keep things status quo for a few more days. A few more days and it wouldn't be his problem anymore. It would all be in the hands of the Chinese government. He had made the sword that would strike down his enemies, but he wouldn't use it himself. He wasn't going to make that mistake again.

Driving slowly, watching closely, a predator stalking his prey. Then he hit something. It cracked under his tire like a toothpick. He slammed on the brakes and got out. A small boy was standing on the sidewalk, crying. Doug saw parents rushing toward him from a nearby school. Doug bent down and looked under the car.

There was a small skateboard under one wheel, broken in half. He tried to pull it out, but it wouldn't budge under the weight of the car. He pulled himself back up and got back in the car—more crunching as it drifted forward a few inches. Then he got out again and retrieved the broken pieces of wood with his good hand. He handed it to the crying kid. By then, the kid's dad had caught up. He was tall—six four or six five, at least. His head started where Doug's ended.

"What the hell, dude?"

He crouched near his howling son.

"Your son should watch where he's playing. You're lucky it was just his skateboard."

"Are you fucking kidding me?"

The dad stood up and stepped forward. Doug ignored him and instead surveyed the area.

"Hey, asswad, I'm talking to you."

The dad shoved Doug hard, but Doug didn't care. Another day, he would have taken the man down. A quick knee to the groin would have been more than sufficient. But there were more important things he needed to focus on at that moment. Doug went back to his car.

"We're not done here," the guy yelled.

"Yes, I think we are," Doug said, stepping out again, gun in hand. The dad instinctively stepped in front of his son.

"Calm down," the man said to Doug. "We're cool, we're cool. It's just a skateboard."

But Doug wasn't paying him any mind. He was running toward the soccer field.

Chapter 80

It was then I made my big mistake. There was some sort of scuffle on the street, and my eyes were drawn to a dark Mercedes sedan. I saw some people running toward the scene. But I had an argument to win.

"We need to go back to Ancien," I said. "The only way I can get into Gaia is by having physical access."

A man near the road started running, but I didn't give him much thought. I figured he was headed toward the basketball court.

"The place is teeming with people trying to kill us," said Alex. "We can't risk it."

"I built the place. You know there's a series of hidden passages. We can sneak around, and nobody would ever realize."

Except, then I realized, the man wasn't running to the basketball court—he was running toward us. That was weird. The guy was close enough now that I could sort of make him out. He wasn't a dad.

"It's Doug," I yelled. Alex leaped to his feet, but Phillip sat paralyzed in abject terror. Alex reached over and pulled him up, but by the time he was standing, it was too late.

"Stop or I'll shoot all of you," Doug yelled, as he slowed his approach. He didn't even try to hide the gun. I raised my hands above my head.

"There's no need to do that—put your hands down," Doug snapped. "You'll draw attention to us, and then I'll have to shoot you."

Out of the corner of my eye, I saw Alex looking around. From where I was standing, I could still see the dark Mercedes and the people standing around it. Someone was on a cell phone. Maybe they had seen Doug's gun. Maybe they were calling the cops.

"You three have caused me enough trouble this week. You're quite the troublemakers indeed. But that's all over now. You're going to come with me, and do not try to make a scene."

Alex and Phillip both looked at me, as if I was supposed to give them some sort of signal. We outnumbered him three to one. He could shoot one of us, maybe two. But not all three. We could take him. Alex and

Phillip were ready to do it, too. I could see it in their eyes. Seemingly unconsciously, Phillip patted his bulging pocket. I'd forgotten he still had one of the Ancien guards' guns. But he wasn't going to make a move without my go ahead. Loyal to the end. Then I made the decision, and that was my big mistake.

I shook my head slightly, calling them off.

"We're leaving," Doug said. "No funny business now. Let's go."

I did as I was told and began to walk toward the Mercedes. Alex and Phillip followed, while Doug herded us from behind. It was a calculated risk. I figured Doug was going to take us to Ancien anyway—exactly where I wanted to be. But as it turned out, my assumption was wrong.

Chapter 81

Doug made me drive. He pointed a gun at my head the whole time. He sat with Phillip in the back, sticking Alex in the passenger seat. He told me to go north on Highway 101. There wasn't much traffic at first, even for a Sunday afternoon. It was overcast and gloomy. Half an hour later, as we approached San Francisco, the fog was in full force. The sun hadn't managed to burn through it yet. The thicker the fog, the slower the traffic.

Once we were in San Francisco, the traffic was stop-and-go. I couldn't see more than two cars in front of me. Alex asked where we were going, and Doug hit him hard on the side of the head with the gun. I yelled, turning to see bright-red blood gushing from Alex's head.

We were getting close to the Bay Bridge, and Doug told me to take the exit for Cesar Chavez Street. I did so, following the street until it hit Pier 80. It looked like a construction zone, but it was also full of shipping containers. Nobody was there working. Or if they were, I couldn't see them through the fog.

"Turn right," said Doug. "Then stop at the last shipping container on the right."

I shouldn't have let it get this far. I should have tried to jump Doug in the park—people were watching. They could have done something. Maybe Phillip could have shot him. Maybe he still could.

I stopped the car, and Doug got out.

"All right, everyone, get out nice and easy. No sudden moves or I'll shoot all of you."

Alex laughed.

"You find something funny, old man?"

The bleeding on his head had stopped.

"You're going to shoot us either way, aren't you? Sudden moves or no?"

I watched Phillip climb out of the backseat. Doug wasn't paying him any attention; he was glaring at Alex. Phillip's eyes were locked on mine. He was patting his pocket again. This time, I nodded.

"That's not true. Despite what you may think, I'm not a monster. Even though you three have caused me incessant headaches of late, I'm not one to do the dirty work myself."

I watched Phillip fumbling with the gun stuck in his pocket.

"Then what are you going to do with us out here?" Alex asked.

"Aren't you the curious one? You know what curiosity did to the cat, right?"

Then Doug looked over at me. I turned my head as quickly as I could, but it was too late. He knew where I was looking. He turned toward Phillip, just as Phillip managed to pull the gun from his pocket. But Doug shot first.

Phillip didn't move. He stood there as still as a redwood. The warning shot had hit just an inch away from his foot, spraying red dust into the foggy air.

"Put that down," said Doug.

Phillip dropped the gun.

"Kick it over here."

Phillip kicked it. Doug picked it up.

"Now walk that way."

It was hard to see what he was pointing at through the fog. The sound of a plane filled the air. It must have been landing at SFO, but I couldn't see it. Then there was a gust of wind, which broke up the fog, and I saw a big orange machine come into view behind Doug. It looked like a rectangular box with all its walls taken off.

We walked over to it. Phillip slipped on the gravel and fell to the ground.

"Get up," yelled Doug.

Phillip didn't move. Doug approached him.

"Are you? Really? Stop crying. You're like a little girl. A little fat girl. Look—even Luna's not crying. Come on, pull it together."

Doug lifted him up off the ground, and forced him to keep walking. Doug pulled a zip tie out of his back pocket and tied Phillip's wrists behind his back.

As I got closer to the machine, I could finally make out what it was. It was a crane. Built to pick up shipping containers and load them onto trucks or trains. It was huge. I glanced over at Alex. His eyes were empty, registering no emotion at all. He just stared straight ahead. He wouldn't even look at me.

"Do you recognize this place, Luna?" asked Doug.

I didn't respond.

"You don't, do you? Were you even paying attention during those board meetings? This was the first client Thor closed all on his own. We overhauled all of their management tools and monitoring software, and installed the Ancien platform. You don't remember that?"

I vaguely recalled what he was talking about but said nothing.

"It was Ancien technology that saved this place from being shut down. Thor's kind of a big deal here. A folk hero. Or he was, I guess." Doug let out a deep laugh. "I want to share with you a little-known fact. It's something you wouldn't have been able to know on your own. This also happens to be one of Gaia's first confirmed kill sites. This very crane, in fact. Thor was so proud when we were finally able to confirm that it worked. In a way, it's rather poetic that you will be dying this way."

"What way is that?" asked Alex.

"You've got balls, old man, I'll give you that. Still asking questions after that beating I gave you in the car. That takes, how would you say it, Luna? Cojones?"

Doug went over to Alex and pulled out another zip tie. Alex held out his arms at a strange angle as Doug tightened the zip tie around his wrists.

Then Doug went to the crane, still pointing the gun vaguely in our direction. Doug lifted a service panel and slowly began typing on a console with one hand. The gun waving around. Back and forth. I looked at Alex again. He still wouldn't look at me. Phillip was still crying, but silently now.

"Well?" said Alex.

Doug turned away from the control panel. His face was flushed red; he looked furious.

"This isn't the movies," he barked. "You don't get to know shit about shit. You just get to know that you're going to be dead soon, so shut up and let me finish."

Doug turned back to the console. The gun was wavering back and forth—not pointed toward any of us. Just pointing at empty space. I turned to Alex. Now he was looking straight at me. The crane started moving with a loud crash of noise. Alex made a motion with his hand. I knew what it meant. I started running.

Chapter 82

Doug couldn't believe they had the audacity to run. They couldn't have gotten far, though. One entrance. One exit. The chances of finding it in this fog were slim. First, the girl and the old man. Then the fat one realized what was going on and scurried off into the mist. Doug let out a long low growl from the bottom of his throat. How could they be so disobedient? Their time was up. It was over.

Fortunately, Doug knew the area well. He had spent weeks here, watching and waiting for Gaia to kill someone. When he got bored, he would watch the trains, the cargo being loaded. The order of the system that on the surface looked like so much chaos felt reassuring.

He remembered watching Gaia kill that man months ago and smiled. He'd been waiting so long that he'd almost given up. He thought maybe it would never happen. And then he saw it. The accident with the crane.

At first, he wasn't sure if it was just an ordinary work accident. After all, that's what they were claiming it was. But he checked with Thor, and his development team said it was a confirmed kill. It was such a rush knowing he had watched Gaia kill that man.

Now he had to finish what he'd started. He had to track down the bitch and her friends. They were all going to die today, one way or another. He preferred Gaia's Wrath—it was the meeker solution, after all—but he wasn't about to let that preference get in the way of what needed to be done.

When lions hunt, they instinctively go for the weakest, most vulnerable animal of the pack. Knowing this, Doug ran after Phillip.

The pier was only a maze the first few times one walked around it. Doug knew that there were well-beaten paths, and like a college lawn, the most heavily frequented places were obvious. Just by the direction Phillip ran, Doug knew where he would find him.

Chapter 83

I was lost. I tried to keep up with Alex, but he ran so much faster than me, and within a few yards, he'd disappeared into the fog. I wanted to shout. To beg him to slow down. But I didn't want to give away our location. I turned around. Phillip must have been having the same problem. I considered standing still for a few moments in the hope that Phillip would catch up, but something in my bones wouldn't let me stay in place. I looked back one more time, took my best guess about where Alex was, and ran.

Then I heard something that turned me to stone. Phillip was screaming. It sounded horrible. A scream of agony. Lord, how I wished Alex hadn't run off so fast. I was all alone, surrounded by rusty old shipping containers and I couldn't see. I wanted to give up right there. Doug could have me. He could kill me. We could get this whole charade over with. After all, once you're dead, all your problems are over. No more responsibility. No more loneliness. No more baggage.

I fell to my knees. Phillip kept wailing his long ugly cry. Whatever Doug was doing to him, it did not sound good. It was over. We had lost. There was nothing I could do now. I was a fugitive in two states. My company was little more than a mass-murdering tool for a psycho killer. And I still had no evidence to prove any of it. I had nothing. Not even a gun. Not even a phone. Nobody.

Then I felt it. A hand on my shoulder. I looked up. It was Alex. He had found me.

"Get up, Luna. This isn't over yet."

He was carrying a heavy lead pipe between his zip-tied hands. He handed me the pipe and made a grand gesture with his arms that split the zip tie apart.

So I wasn't down to nothing just yet. I stood up. Phillip's anguished yelps pierced the air like a foghorn. We approached quickly but cautiously. The screams led us back to the car and the crane.

I made out what looked like one of Phillip's shinbones sticking out of his pant leg. He couldn't stand. Doug must have dragged him back there. Evidently, he was stronger than he looked. Phillip lay near the crane, gasping in pain. Doug was standing at the console again, typing something. The crane began to move.

I ran to Phillip. Doug whirled around and pointed the gun at me. I stopped, just a few yards from Phillip and the crane. From there, I could see a trail of blood that led to a red pool under Phillip's body. His ankles were zip tied now too.

"I'm so glad you could join us," Doug said. "And where's the old man?"

I shrugged.

"This is for Simon, you motherfucker," Alex shouted, running up from behind.

There was a deafening gunshot. Alex and Doug fell to the ground in a skirmish I could barely make out through the fog. Blood showered the ground. Grunts and twists. Then I saw the lead pipe rise up and come down with a brutal crash. The skirmish was over. Doug tied Alex's arms together again, but this time, behind his back.

I ran to Alex and held him in my arms. He was unconscious.

"You son of a bitch," I screamed.

"Sticks and stones," said Doug.

The crane's hook block had positioned itself over one of the shipping containers and was gradually lowering.

"Now we can do this the easy way or the hard way. It's all up to you."

Doug leered at our huddled group.

"Go to hell."

The hook block grabbed onto the shipping container, and it let out a wailing creak as it was slowly hoisted into the air.

"Did you know that I didn't even have to program that crane to do this? It's a bit of a miracle, really. You should be proud. Ancien's doing all the hard work for me. I just had to let Gaia's Wrath know Phillip's physical location. Whatever happens next will be completely determined by just bits and bytes. Isn't that cool? Morality isn't even involved. Just deterministic inevitabilities. Cold, calculating mathematical equations. There's a certain beauty in that, isn't there? Not many people can appreciate it, Luna. But you should. If there's anyone in the world still alive who can appreciate that fact, it's you."

"Phillip," I yelled. "Get away from there. Quick. The crane."

Phillip looked at the shipping container. He looked around. He tried to pull himself away, but he wasn't able to do more than inch forward.

"Don't worry, Luna," said Doug, as he stepped closer to me. "You'll be joining him soon enough."

I broke away from Alex and grabbed the lead pipe. It was cumbersome and cold in my hands. Heavier than it looked. I couldn't lift it over my head, but nevertheless, I rushed at Doug, swinging the pipe hard. Doug stepped to the side, missing my swing by an inch. The momentum of the pipe pulled me with it, and I crashed face first to the ground. Doug laughed and pried the lead pipe from my grip.

I sat there with blood pouring from my forehead. I could barely see. I thought of Taye. Of his dead, bloodied hand. How brave that kid had been. He'd realized what Thor and Doug were doing and risked everything to stop it. And he didn't just risk everything. He paid the ultimate price. I, too, had died. But not like Taye. He had died trying to stop this madness. I died because I was stupid enough to fall into a dumb trap. But this was my second chance. I was on borrowed time. I wasn't going to waste it.

Doug dragged Alex beside Phillip, then kicked Phillip back into position. Phillip let out a sharp cry. The shipping container was now hovering directly over them. The fog was so thick it felt like rain was waiting in the air. I felt in my pockets. I had a plan. Doug turned around and came back to me.

"Now it's your turn. Let's not make this hard on either of us, dear."

Chapter 84

I stood up.

"That's the most sensible decision you've made all day," Doug said.

He was only a yard away from me when I pulled the tube of lipstick from my pocket and raised it to eye level. Doug stopped moving.

"What's that?"

I inched forward and said, "What's it look like?"

"It looks like lipstick."

My hand trembled.

"Put that down, Luna. Come on. Enough with all the drama."

I lowered the lipstick a couple of inches and Doug stepped forward. Just a little closer at first.

"Come on," he said.

I mumbled.

"What?" he said. He took another step closer.

"I said, eat shit."

I pressed down on the lipstick case and a beam of liquid shot straight into Doug's eyes. He dropped the lead pipe and screamed, dropping to his knees. I could smell the capsaicin in the air, like it had been absorbed into the fog. My eyes stung a little. The experience at the stock exchange had been a wake-up call. I realized I needed to be better prepared, so I bought real pepper spray that looked just like a tube of lipstick.

I went over to Doug. He was writhing in pain and couldn't see me. I stuck the pepper spray as close to his nose as I could get it and pressed hard, letting it spray twice as long this time, directly into his face. His screams doubled in volume, and he started convulsing in anguish. I kicked him as hard as I could in the balls, but he didn't even react to the added pain.

I looked over at Alex and Phillip. Alex was still passed out. Phillip was trying to drag himself out from under the shipping container's shadow, but there was no way he would make it in time. The shipping container was already halfway down—its movements slow and jerky. I wondered if Gaia's algorithms were having trouble. I ran to them, and tried to haul Phillip away by the arm, but he was too big for me to move. He didn't budge. Alex was smaller; he budged, but not by much.

When the shipping container brushed against my head, I knew I needed to think of something else.

"Luna," said Phillip. "Please tell my son how much he means to me."

"Don't talk like that."

"And I know this doesn't mean much, but I want you to know. You're the best friend I've had in recent years. Thank you for everything."

A bunch of emotions balled up in my stomach. I had to duck down to shuffle over to him. I kissed him on the forehead and wrapped my arms around him as best I could.

"Same here. But don't give up. This is not over yet."

I ducked out from under the container. I had to find some leverage. Something to stop the machine. *Machine.* That was it. Like Doug said, it was just a machine executing an algorithm. I ran to the control panel and saw what Doug had been typing away at so eagerly. It was Gaia. A slightly modified version of the control input Taye had built. The one I had played around with days ago.

But back then, there'd been nothing about targeting people or killing. It was just code built to improve other code. I entered a question mark in the prompt. The menu options were similar to the Gaia I was already familiar with, but there were a few new options at the bottom of the list.

Phillip shouted, "Hurry, Luna."

"I got this," I shouted back.

I typed the targeting option. It gave me options to enter a new name, but I couldn't find anything about unselecting a target. I looked over at Phillip and Alex, but I couldn't see them anymore. The container was on top of them now. There were no options. There was no undo.

But there might be a cord. And the only way this machine could be instructed to do anything was if it was connected to Ancien. I pulled at the monitor. It wouldn't budge. I dashed back over to Doug. He was still writhing on the ground, but I wasn't there for him. I snatched up the forgotten piece of pipe, then tore back to the control panel and swung the pipe into the machine as hard as I could. Sparks flew everywhere. The crane's engine made a loud, high-pitched noise. Then everything went quiet. I heard a crow cawing angrily.

The container had stopped moving. Breathlessly, I ran back to it and threw myself on the ground, peering under the metal. The container was just touching Phillip's belly, but he gave me a big thumbs up.

"We're okay. You did it."

"That's what friends are for," I laughed. "Now let's get you out of there."

"Not so fast." It was Doug.

Chapter 85

Doug was blinking rapidly, but once again he was pointing the gun at me. I didn't have the pepper spray anymore, but even if I did, I couldn't have moved without him shooting me first.

"It's too bad. You can't always get what you want. I thought you would have a poetic death—killed by your own machine. But as they say, man plans and God laughs. The world works in mysterious ways, and all that other bullshit losers tell themselves."

I sat up but didn't respond.

"Go ahead, stand up. If I'm going to have to shoot you, let's at least make it dignified. But I don't want to see any funny business with your hands this time."

I stood up. At least this time I could say that I went out trying. Like Taye. This borrowed time hadn't been for nothing. This time, it would be a good death.

That's when I saw the plane landing through the fog. It was a small private jet. At a vicious speed, it leaped over the threshold of smooth pavement to wet dirt road.

"Any last words?" Doug asked.

The plane was coming in fast, but Doug didn't see it.

"Yeah. When you built the targeting feature, why didn't you build an un-targeting feature?"

"Why would I have wanted to do that?"

Now I could see the pilot's face through the fog. He looked as scared as I felt.

"See for yourself."

I pointed toward the plane. When Doug turned around, gun raised, the jet was just a few yards away. He tried to aim for the pilot, but he wasn't quick enough. It wouldn't have mattered anyway.

I dove. The jet's front wheel turned sharply following my trajectory, but the thick mud under those five tons of steel moving sixty feet per second wasn't going to let the plane change direction. The plane smashed into Doug, crashing full speed into the slightly raised shipping container. Doug Kensington popped like a cordial cherry.

Chapter 86

I was so relieved when they brought us to a hospital where Ancien had not yet been installed. After all that, the only thing I needed was a few stitches on my forehead. The police were chomping at the bit to talk to me, but doctors wanted to keep me overnight for observation. Amazingly, the plane's pilot survived with just a few scratches. Alex had multiple severe concussions, but the doctors were hopeful about his recovery. Phillip needed reconstructive leg surgery. They hadn't put the cast on yet, and when I saw him in the morning, he was pretty groggy from the drugs.

"I told them I was your wife," I said.

Phillip chuckled and said, "You could be my daughter."

"How you feeling?"

"Better than Doug. But not by much. What happened there, anyway? It all happened so fast."

"Apparently, Ancien took over a private jet's autopilot function. There was too much fog for the pilot to override the autopilot, and by the time he realized what was happening, it was too late. When Doug told his program where to find us, the jet was on its descent."

"So the plane was after us, then? Not Doug?"

"Yeah. Doug was collateral damage. If you hadn't been protected by that shipping container, who knows how it would have turned out."

"Holy shit. I bet Cessna's pissed."

"They're even more desperate to keep this whole thing quiet than the board is."

"The board?"

"Oh yeah, they called me this morning. They're freaking out. They asked if I would accept my old position as CEO again."

"And?"

"It was a long discussion."

"Wish I could have been there."

"Me too."

"And after everything that happened, they still want you as CEO?"

"Apparently."

"Good for them."

"Maybe."

Phillip laughed. Then he paused for a moment and asked, "So what are you going to do?"

"I don't know yet. Catch my breath, I guess."

But I did know. I knew exactly what I needed to do. I just wasn't sure I could manage it.

Chapter 87

Chelsea Moore had been nervous and fidgety all day. She wrote her name in big curvy letters on the chalkboard. Her late start to the semester, which had seemed so dire at the time, was now only a distant memory. She'd begun exercising too and had already lost twenty pounds. She would do anything for her students, and to that end, she was working on taking better care of herself.

On her doctor's recommendation, she'd recently gone vegetarian. It was harder than she'd imagined. She spent the first week craving meat like a heroin addict wanted another hit. She had nightmares about Red Robin's Burnin' Love Burger. When she shared that embarrassing fact with her neighbor, he told her Red Robin could make any burger into a veggie burger. She went yesterday, but it wasn't the same. Still, it was close enough.

The burger had given her heartburn, which only made her more nervous. She checked the school clock. Four minutes. Her first guests were about to show up. She wondered if she had time to run to the little girls' room, but decided to hold it. She went back to the chalkboard and wrote in big capital letters under her name: *WELCOME PARENTS.*

Just as she completed the S, there was a knock at the door.

"Come on in," she hollered in her friendliest voice.

The door opened.

"Ms. Moore, it's good to see you."

"Mr. Jones, I'm so glad to see you, too. Will Mrs. Jones be joining us today?"

"You mean Mrs. Kotulski now? No, she's moved down South."

"I'm sorry to hear that," Chelsea said. Then, to change the subject, "Can I get you a coffee?"

Chelsea indicated the box of fresh coffee she had brought. Phillip limped slightly over to the desk with tiny chairs that had been prepared for the event.

"That would be great," he said.

Chelsea smiled as she poured him a cup of hot coffee. This was her first parent–teacher conference and she couldn't have been happier about it.

"There's something I have to tell you about Jake."

"That doesn't sound good."

Chelsea handed him the cup and sat down on the other side of the children's table.

"You know, he started out the semester pretty rough. The kids had been picking on him because of his–"

"Eccentricities."

"Yes, exactly. Eccentricities."

"We were going through some rough stuff back then."

"Yes, and I want to apologize again. We have a strict anti-bullying policy here, and I feel terrible that I wasn't here to enforce it."

"No, please. It wasn't your fault."

"That's kind of you to say. Anyhow, I just wanted to tell you that Jake has come out of his shell recently. He's been socializing well and even making friends. It's been amazing to watch him bloom."

Phillip smiled proudly. "He's a great kid," he said.

"Let me put it this way. If he's our hope for the future, I'll have no trouble sleeping at night."

"He couldn't have done it without you, Ms. Moore. He talks about you all the time. You're his favorite teacher."

Chelsea blushed.

"Are you free next weekend?" Phillip asked suddenly.

Chelsea felt like she might be having another heart attack.

"Excuse me?"

"Oh, I'm sorry—I suppose that sounds strange. It's just that Jake's been begging me to ask you. It's his birthday next weekend, and it would mean the world to him if you came."

"Oh."

There was a slight pause.

"No, no, I didn't mean it that way. I mean. It's just."

"No, I understand," said Chelsea. "It's against school policy. I'm not supposed to go to my students' parties."

"Oh, yes, of course." Another pause. "It's just, well, it would also mean a lot to me, too, if you would come."

She didn't respond.

"You probably have other plans. I understand."

"Yes," she said.

"Yes, you have other plans?"

"No," she said.

"No, you don't want to go?"

"No, I don't have other plans. Yes, I'll go."

This time, it was Phillip who blushed.

Chapter 88

By noon, I was lost in the side streets of Brooklyn. I'd given my Uber driver the address, but construction blockades made it impossible for the car to reach the house. So I jumped out two blocks away, figuring I could make it the rest of the way on foot. I was looking for 11210. But the numbers jumped from 11200 to 11300. No 11210.

I swear I spent an entire hour going up and down that street. Then another hour going up and down side streets. I had a pounding headache. I needed coffee.

I'd never been to Brooklyn before. It felt a little like San Francisco's Mission Street. An eclectic mix of row houses and apartments peppered with mom-and-pop shops, nail salons, and delis. At the end of the block, I spotted a coffee shop and headed for it. Then I saw something even better across the street: Dunkin' Donuts. Coffee and sugar.

It was cramped inside. I ordered and sat down at a table near the window. I stared out at the street as I waited for my coffee to cool down.

"Luna Valencia." The man's voice was deep and guttural. "I'm with the police. We need to talk."

I smiled.

"I never realized before. You weren't a cop when you said that the first time. Isn't that a crime?"

"What brings you to this neck of the woods? It's been a while," he said.

"Almost a year."

"No shit. How'd you find me?"

"I've been doing this a long time," I said with a smile. "You left without saying goodbye."

"I'm no good at goodbyes," he said.

Alex sat down with some effort. He was using a cane now and looked a lot older than I remembered. I could make out a purple bruise on his cheek. He asked again how I had found him. I told him about my expedition to the New York City Police Department headquarters. At first, they'd been reluctant to give me his address, but I was persistent.

"I never got the chance to thank you properly," I said. I slid my uneaten donut—strawberry frosted with sprinkles—toward him.

"Isn't that a little cliché?" he said, looking at the donut.

I shrugged. He picked it up.

"Hey, so there was something else, too," I said. He raised an eyebrow, already a bite into the donut. "You remember that day in the shipyard?"

He nodded slowly.

"You yelled something right before rushing Doug. Do you remember that?"

"No."

"You said you were doing it for Simon."

Alex stopped chewing. Then he swallowed.

"I did?"

I nodded.

"I'm thirsty," he said. He began to haul himself up out of the chair, but I motioned for him to stay put.

"I'll get it. What do you want? Coffee?"

He finished getting up.

"No, I'm going to need something stronger than coffee."

He led me to a small bar across the street. There was only one other person in the place, hunched over at the far end of the bar. We took the first stools we found. He ordered a whiskey. I slid some cash across the bar.

"Drink with me," he said.

"Too early in the day for me."

"Then thanks for coming," he said. "And thanks for the donut."

"So," I said. "Who's Simon?"

He shook his head and said nothing.

"I flew across the country to find you. I never understood why you spent so much time helping me. It bothered me. You had no skin in the game. Ancien wasn't your company. You didn't know me. I wasn't your problem. So, why did you risk your life? What was in it for you? Who is Simon?"

"I thought you were here to say thanks. You're welcome. Let's leave it at that. Goodbye."

"I thought you weren't good at goodbyes."

"You're making it easy." He sighed but didn't move to get up. "Another whiskey, please," he said. "And one for my friend."

"I'm good," I said, shaking my head.

The bartender poured two drinks anyway. I hated whiskey.

"To Simon," he said.

I picked up my glass.

"To Simon," I repeated.

We threw our drinks back. Alex asked for another round. I shook my head vigorously, unable to speak yet.

"I'll make you a deal. I'll talk as long as you drink."

I downed the second glass as quickly as I could manage. I rarely drank and I hadn't eaten much that day. One shot was enough to make me tipsy, even on a full stomach. Two made me drunk. And I'd given Alex my snack.

"Another," Alex demanded. The waiter cracked a smile.

The world was spinning. I breathed slowly and deliberately.

"Was," he said.

I wasn't sure I'd heard properly.

"Huh?"

"Who *was* Simon," he said. "Not who *is* Simon."

I nodded gently. And not just because I finally understood his meaning.

He said nothing for quite some time. I didn't know how much longer I could keep my drinks down, so finally I broke down and asked.

"Who was Simon?"

"The sweetest boy that ever lived. He was my son."

Alex sat with his head between his hands. Instinctively, I started rubbing his back.

"I'm sorry, Alex."

He didn't speak. We sat at the bar for a while longer. Finally he said, "It was locked. I always locked it."

I stopped rubbing his back. I was about to say something when he started up again.

"I was a goddamn police officer. Thirty years. I would get home, kiss my wife, hang up my keys, lock my gun, grab a beer. Always in that order. I was like clockwork. I never forgot. Never."

After a respectful moment, as gently as I could, I asked what happened.

"I swear to God, I had just installed a new gun safe. I mean, it wasn't new-new. I got it off a buddy. Supposed to be smart, or something like that. Had a modem. I had to plug it into a phone socket. Had its own phone number. Was supposed to call me if someone tampered with it."

After this, Alex took a long break in the story. I thought he was going to order another round of whiskey, and I prayed that he wouldn't.

"If I told him once, I told him a million times. Simon, don't go near Daddy's gun. I can remember the day perfectly. Hung up my keys. Kissed my wife. Locked my gun."

He gave me a confused look.

"No. I kissed Chelsea, hung up my keys, locked the gun. I swear to God I locked it. I turned the damn dial. It was a new safe. I didn't trust it. I turned it. Well. You can guess the rest. Wife left me. They fired me. Said I hadn't protected my sidearm. It's a big deal to us, you know. But I know I locked the safe."

Alex mumbled for a while and put his head back in his hands. I rubbed his back again.

"So. When Titus Andronicus—"

"Taye?"

"Yeah, whatever. When the kid said there was a computer virus causing deaths, I thought."

Alex trailed off into murmurs. Or I was drunk and couldn't make out what he was saying. Hard to tell the difference.

"You think Gaia opened your safe?"

Alex buried his head deeper into hands.

"Bartender. Another round."

"Alex, it's been great seeing you, but I can't do it."

"Great. More for me," he said.

I leaned up against him and gave him a hug. He smiled.

"You didn't come here just for an old man's story, did you?"

"Yes," I lied.

"To Simon," he said, and he downed another whiskey.

Chapter 89

The next morning, I woke up with the worst headache of my life. But fortunately with none of the nerves that I had felt this time last year. At least not about the act itself. The building? I didn't want to go back there. And technically, I didn't have to. It was, after all, just a silly formality. The memories hadn't lost their edge. Not even after all that whiskey. Just seeing the facade of Corinthian pillars made me squeal.

"I told you so," Henry said, giving me a big old grin. We met at the front of the stock exchange this time. My request.

"Good to see you again, too, but I'm not sure I understand what you mean."

"I told you I'd see you here again," he laughed. "Maybe not this soon, but I had a feeling." He winked.

I couldn't believe I was here again. Resuming my place as the head of Ancien and getting Gaia back under control had been huge undertakings. Three lawsuits. One was even a class action.

The cash we'd spent settling those cases would have shut the company down only the year before, but Gaia's reputation spread quickly. We turned Gaia's malicious functionalities to more productive uses. By the time we had to pay up, we were making more money than we knew what to do with. The bankers wanted to set the stock price at fifteen dollars a share, which would put us at a valuation of three billion dollars, but based on our current revenues, we were expected to be worth double that.

In fact, the board debated for a long time whether or not we should even go public. We didn't need to, financially. But morally, we needed broader oversight. Sure, maybe it was just financial oversight, but that was better than none at all.

"Security's tightened up," said Henry. "You'll need to take off your shoes this time."

I put my purse and shoes through the machine. As I went through, I saw Ancien's logo on the screen. I smiled.

"Can I see the trading floor?"

Henry's eyes sparkled in delight. "Well, of course you can. Did you know the New York Stock Exchange originated in a small café on Wall Street? It was run out of that same café until 1817."

I let Henry give me the grand tour. I still felt like a jerk for not letting him show me around properly the first time. It was more interesting than I'd expected, though admittedly my mind was elsewhere. In particular, it was on the trading floor.

"And this is it," Henry announced, his arms in the air. "Where all the excitement happens."

There were a few groups of traders already gathering and talking. I could smell expensive cologne as one of the men brushed past us. I turned, and that's when I saw it.

"Isn't this where?"

Henry blushed. "Oh, I'm sorry. It was a poor choice of words."

"No, it's okay, I just want to know."

But I already knew. A chill ran down my spine as I looked up at the spot where I'd been standing only a year ago. This was where Taye had tried so desperately to get my attention. Had tried so hard to reach out to me. And I'd been so blind and distracted. Too caught up in my own shit to pay attention to what was going on around me. I'd been letting other people push me in directions that I didn't want to go. But I hadn't spoken up. I didn't think I had a choice. Everyone around me—my closest advisors—kept telling me this was the right thing to do.

The mature thing to do. Even though it didn't feel right in my gut. I just gritted my teeth and let them do it anyway.

Allowing them to take my company away from me wasn't my biggest mistake, though. Not paying attention to Taye was what I regretted most.

Taye had been everything I wasn't. He'd given up his life to fix what was wrong. And what had I done? How many times had I hung back from doing the right thing because I was afraid? Afraid of being embarrassed or of being wrong or of being unprepared. How many others had Doug and Thor manipulated? How many had kept silent, knowing in some capacity that what they were doing was wrong?

Taye was more than a hero. Taye was the person I now wished I could be. He was the standard to which I was holding myself accountable. At least that's what my therapist kept telling me. But what did she know? She didn't see the poor boy's limp hand. His death was not on her conscience, haunting her every day like a goddamn ghost.

"Luna? You okay?"

I snapped out of my daze and found that we were no longer on the trading floor; we were heading upstairs. Henry glanced at his watch.

"Yeah, I'm fine," I said, unconvincingly.

"Need to powder your nose?"

I shook my head.

"Good. We don't have time for that anyway. I'm always running behind with these things. You remember the buttons?"

I nodded, but Henry was looking at his watch and went on anyway, "There are three buttons. At nine thirty—shit. We're really behind. Okay, just press the green button. If the green button doesn't work, push the red button."

With a gentle shove, I found myself back where it all began. This time, though, it felt right. I was alone. Proud. Not giving up anything. Making no compromises.

I looked at the crowd. Another day, another bell. A few looked up at me. Most kept talking.

I looked at the spot where the crowd had parted for Taye. I closed my eyes and remembered him. The life that had saved so many others. The brilliance that had given the world Gaia.

I opened my eyes and looked down at the console. Nine twenty-nine. I wondered what would happen if I didn't press the button. Would the bell still ring? Then another thought came to me: what was that damned third button for? Henry had explained the green and the red ones, but there was an orange button sitting next to the red one. No one had mentioned that.

The clock changed. It was nine thirty. I did nothing.

I wondered if the electronic stock market was active, or if it, too, was waiting for me to press the green button. If it was active, Ancien stock would now be trading. I looked around, trying to find a screen with the ANCN ticker on it. The floor bustled in anticipation, though most of the traders still weren't paying attention to me. I couldn't find my ticker.

I heard a whisper from behind the curtain. "Everything all right?"

I said nothing. I was watching as the clock turned nine thirty-one. No bell. The trading floor was growing still. More people started looking up at me. I smiled.

My finger lifted and came down quickly on the orange button.

"No. Shit. No, no, no, no. Holy shit."

I turned to find Henry standing next to me, shaking his head violently, his hands covering his face.

The bell hadn't rung.

The crowd was silent.

Nine thirty-two.

Henry lowered his hands, revealing a huge grin.

"What?" I said.

He didn't respond. Just pointed. I followed his finger. I hadn't noticed that screen, but it was the one I was looking for. The Ancien stock price. In big bold numbers, I read the number in disbelief. Forty-five. Fifty. It was going up fast.

"You going to put these traders out of their misery?" he asked.

"What does the orange button do?"

"Nothing. Been broken for years. I just like to freak people out about it. Try pressing the green one."

The crowd was restless. Shouts broke out in the silence. I raised my finger and pressed the green button. The bell rang. The crowd descended into madness.

Afterword

Technology builds on technology. Software builds on software. The rate of change has been staggering, and it is only speeding up. We, as human beings, have barely had a moment to catch our collective breath, to take a step back and ask ourselves the big questions.

Questions like: how do we prevent bad people from getting their hands on software that could potentially destroy us?

Atomic bombs are physical things. They need buildings, which can be monitored by satellites. They require highly regulated physical fuel.

The world's next generation of mega-weapons will be software. Code in machines. Machines that drive our cars, fly our planes, control our homes, run our hospitals, and do something new for us every day.

The Matrix was wrong. Computers aren't going to imprison or kill us all on their own. It's not artificial intelligence that we should be afraid of. Machine learning doesn't know or care about what it does. It only does what humans program it to do. Computers lack intention; humans give it to them.

What should frighten us is our own complicity in the thoughtless adoption of new technologies without any set of rules. Culturally, we need to put some serious thought into the roles and responsibilities technology plays in our daily lives. If we leave it completely up to capitalism and the free market, it will often be cheaper to have computers do the work instead of humans. No checks or balances.

This is not a problem for governments to solve. Technology is not bound by physical borders. We can't just hope someone will do the right thing.

It is time that we, as a global human race, invent and adopt systems of technological checks and balances. Software is infinitely easier to infiltrate and steal than atomic bombs. And if we sit back and do nothing—if we just throw our hands up and ignore the problem—we will have to live with the consequences. Or maybe we won't.

The development of the Internet started only fifty short years ago. Not even an average human lifespan. We're still living in the Internet's Wild West. There are no enforced laws. No judges. No police. No independent oversight. Like the American Wild West, the bad guys are getting away with nearly everything. Except this time, the bad guys have bigger guns. And what's at stake is the very survival of the human race.

ABOUT THE AUTHOR

Lucas Carlson is an author and entrepreneur profiled in *The New York Times* bestseller *The Lean Entrepreneur*. He built a startup that raised ten million dollars in venture funding and was acquired by a Fortune 150 Company in 2013. Through that experience, he fell deeply in love with storytelling, and has since shared his experiences in both a memoir and a thriller called *The Term Sheet*. Currently, he is writing more thrillers with startup and tech themes in San Diego, California.